I0581836

THE SEA WITCH FOLLOWS
A MONSTROUS CREATURES NOVEL
BOOK TWO

MARLENA FRANK

Copyright © 2025 by Marlena Frank

All rights reserved.

No part of this book may be reproduced in any form or by any electronic or mechanical means, including information storage and retrieval systems, without written permission from the author, except for the use of brief quotations in a book review.

No generative artificial intelligence (AI) was used in the writing of this work. The author expressly prohibits any entity from using this publication for purposes of training AI technologies to generate text, including without limitation technologies that are capable of generating works in the same style or genre as this publication.

Edited by: Lara Zielinsky
http://lzedits.com

Cover Art by: JV Arts
https://www.justventurearts.com/

Part & Chapter Illustrations by Brina Boyle

Text Divider Illustration by: Kelley M. Frank
http://morbidsmile.com

Note: This is a work of fiction. Names, Characters, Places, and Events are products of the author's imagination, and are used factitiously. These are not to be construed or associated otherwise. Any resemblance to actual locations, incidents, organizations, or people (living or deceased) is entirely coincidental.

EB ISBN: 978-1-955854-39-9
PB ISBN: 978-1-955854-40-5
HB ISBN: 978-1-955854-41-2

CONTENT WARNING

This book contains themes and depictions that may be upsetting for some readers. Please go to my website linked below for a full list of content warnings.

https://marlenafrank.com/content-warnings/the-sea-witch-follows/

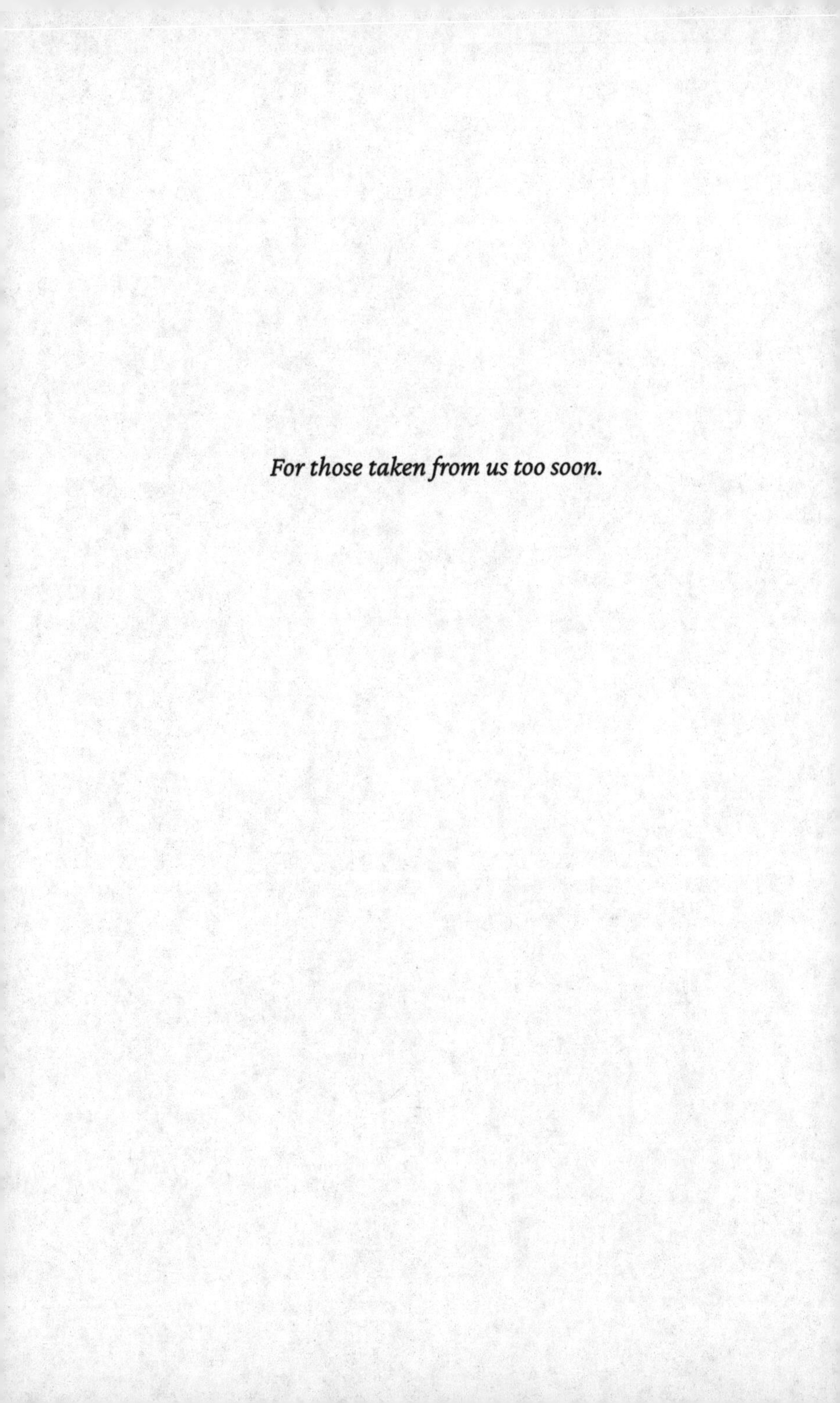

For those taken from us too soon.

Part I:

An Avoidable Disaster

I

THE FATE OF THE WISHFUL

THE SUMMER SUN MELTED INTO ORANGES and pinks on the horizon over the Atlantic Ocean. It was one of the many wonderful gifts Finn enjoyed when he joined his dad on crabbing trips where he couldn't see a speck of land. Despite the hard work, he treasured the rare quiet moments. The boat settled into an easy rhythm on calm waters, the salty air blew through his hair, and the sun beat down on his skin. That's when he felt the most alive. Nothing else matched it. But it never lasted long.

Summer never lasted long enough. The weeks turned over too quickly and the months sped past. By the time he was finally acclimating to life out on the ocean for days at a time, the dreaded return to classes loomed. It was always the dark cloud on the horizon. Now, he was only a couple of weeks away from going back to sitting indoors for hours on end, trying to focus on math and literature, when the beauty of nature called to him. If only his teachers would let him take classes out on the water, he would be so much happier. But Finn wasn't so lucky.

A hand fell on his shoulder. He turned to see Dad with his red, pinched face, narrow eyes and overgrown beard turning gray at the edges. To others, he might look intimidating, but Finn saw the kindness in his face, the smile on his lips, and the mirth in his eyes. He looked out over the water with an appreciative nod.

"You sure you wouldn't have rather spent the summer at home hanging out with your friends?" He gave Finn a wink and a wide grin that wrinkled his cheeks.

"And miss all of this?" Finn gestured to the picturesque beauty all around them. "You've got to be joking."

Dad cocked his head to the side. "I know. It is beautiful. And we're lucky to be fortunate enough to see it. But..." He trailed off, narrowing his eyes.

Finn arched his eyebrows. "But?"

He took a heavy sigh. "You know, it would be better if you went to see them instead of hanging out with your old man every summer."

Finn shook his head. "My friends don't get it, Dad. All they see is the work. They're more interested in chasing girls or playing video games all day. I get bored."

He didn't elaborate more than that. Dad didn't need to know all the details about how his friends detested the idea of netting crabs as a way of life. Even though many of his friends had family who did this, too, they rejected it. They wanted to leave Leekston and forget crabbing completely. Sure, the work made little money, but some things were more important than money.

Usually when the school year started, Finn would lie about what he had done over the summer. He'd research movies he hadn't seen and talk about cities he hadn't visited. It was easier to lie than to tell the truth. He found no shame in crabbing for a living, but it was decidedly not cool to talk about in high school. So he just acted like he spent most of his summer days bored at home, sitting out on the front porch instead of spending time out on the water with his Dad, helping pull in giant nets of crabs on the little schooner from dawn to dusk, day in and day out. Sometimes their trips would last for days on the water. These were his favorites. He got to pretend he lived in a different world where he didn't have to worry about schoolwork or trying to impress his friends. All they had to worry about was the time of day, when to pull in the nets, and what they were fixing to eat.

"I'm going to miss your company next summer," Dad said, turning away from him.

"What?" Finn blinked. "Can't I still come with you next summer? I thought college students only took classes in the fall and spring terms?"

Dad shrugged and started pulling on his gloves. "Your mother always wanted you to go to college. She wanted you to live a better life than what we've got. You're too smart for this kind of work, Finn. But you know that already, don't you? You could get a career in the city, make some real money. Not waste your time here on a boat in the middle of nowhere."

Finn was quiet. He liked being in the middle of nowhere.

"The college fund we scraped together isn't much, but it'll pay for the basics. You get a good scholarship or a part-time job, and you can make ends meet." He let out a rough laugh. "You're lucky there's any money left at all for your college with how little they pay for a load of crabs these days. Don't waste your time out here on the water every summer. Take those summer classes, get through as quick as you can, so it's cheaper. One day you'll be sitting in your fancy office and look around you and be grateful for it."

"I doubt it," Finn said.

Dad didn't respond. Clearly, he was done with this discussion. But Finn wouldn't let him drop it.

"This can't be my last summer, Dad. That's not fair."

"I'm sorry, son." Dad patted him on the shoulder. He wandered off to the bow of the boat, stepping around the cabin. There wasn't any work to be done on that end, but they both knew that. Dad was a master at avoiding a conversation he didn't want to have.

Finn hadn't realized this might be his last time going out on the water with him. Sure, he knew it would happen eventually, but he didn't realize it would be so soon. He thought he had the summers at least before the grind of day jobs and nine-to-fives began, but time was working against him. Just like it always had. As proud as

Finn was of his good grades at school, it seemed to pull him farther away from where his heart wanted him to be.

"You know I still have a year of high school left," he called across the boat. "I'll be back next summer before college starts. I still have time."

Despite his words, a pit formed in his stomach. He already heard stories from seniors about their summers before college. Figuring out class schedules, financial aid, student loans, touring campuses, not to mention finding a dorm, sorting our roommates, and moving. Would he have time to spend with Dad out on the water? The thought made him painfully sad.

Dad glanced back, and gave a small smile and noncommittal shrug. He always did that when he didn't want to actually say no, but meant it. It was always annoying.

Part of Finn wanted to scream at his father. Ask him to say 'No' if that's what he meant. Beg him not to say this was his last summer. Convince him he was wrong. But it would be like talking to a wall. When Dad got an idea into his head and made his final decision, it was almost impossible to make him change his mind. Like the sun dipping near the horizon, he was impervious to change.

Finn groaned and pulled his gloves out of his back pocket. They smelled like briny ocean water and crab. There was no point in trying to argue the point or even counter his dad. Finn had lost those fights countless times. The man would just wander off or pretend not to hear him. He was so against confrontation, it was exhausting. All it did was make Finn angry.

Back when Mom was alive, Finn could remember Dad not being so resolute in his ways. But ever since the car accident, he had become more stubborn. More impervious. When they lost Mom, Dad got a little stonier, less willing to argue or come to an agreement. He made his decisions and then sat in them, regardless of the outcome. Finn had been only eight years old at the time of the accident, but he remembered how much his father changed. It was as if turning off his emotions was better than letting any feelings run free. Yes, he suddenly had an eight-year-old kid to raise alone, so it made sense. Dad did whatever it took to keep from falling apart. He still hated it.

"Those crabs won't reel themselves in," Dad said, giving a forced laugh. "Let's get this haul in, son."

Finn nodded, trying to shake the bittersweet feeling this could be his last summer on the water. His last summer of gorgeous sunsets, ocean breezes... Freedom. Out on the open water, there weren't any loud vehicles, no glaring signs, no giant responsibilities, and no people to please—other than Dad, of course. It was a place where Finn felt like himself, instead of having to hide parts away like he did at school.

The thought of having to act like he was normal, like everyone else for years on end, gripped hold of him. A tightness filled his chest and tears sprang to his eyes, surprising him. He hadn't realized how much this time meant to him, how much being on the ocean meant to him. Foolishly he'd thought he would always have it, but now that might not be the case. And if Finn wanted to buy his own boat or even a schooner one day, there was no telling how much that would cost or how long he would have to save. His next trip out on the ocean grew farther and farther away. It could be years, a decade or more, before he could come back again.

He wiped the tears away with the back of his arm. The mixture of sweat and sea salt on his skin burned his eyes, but that was better than crying. It was better than seeing Dad look at him with that helpless look he always got when Finn cried in front of him. The man never knew what to do or say, so he just did nothing. Somehow, that always made it worse. Finn took a deep breath and turned away from his father toward the stern of the boat, tightening his gloves.

Something in the distance moved, catching his watery gaze. He wiped at his eyes again and squinted up into the sky. The melting colors of the sunset diminished to dark clouds. He licked at his salty lips. Was it just night descending? That had to be it... But the direction was wrong.

A flicker of lightning proved his instincts were correct. His despair turned to action. He called to his father.

"Look at those clouds!" He pointed. As he did, another flash of lightning struck.

Dad turned and narrowed his eyes, deepening the lines on his face. He wandered back across the boat until they were side by side. They watched in silence as the shadows played across the water and lightning ripped across the clouds. Distant thunder followed in its wake like an angry god waking from its slumber.

"Do you think we should head back to shore?" Finn asked urgently.

Dad stroked his beard with his thick gloves. "No, I think we should be okay. They said it's supposed to move inland, away from us." He nodded toward downtown Leekston and chewed on his bottom lip, his brow furrowed with worry. "That's why we're staying out here on the water tonight. It's safer than trying to make our way to land." He sounded calmer than he looked, but Finn knew his father. He could read the fear between the lines.

Finn nodded slow, worried as his gaze locked on those storm clouds.

Dad took hold of his shoulder and gave him a light shake. "Let's pull in these crabs, then we can wait it out inside." He gave a small smile. "At least we're certain to make a big haul when the water gets rough!"

Finn followed his orders, heading over to the port side to pull in the netting. A cool breeze blew in from the storm, carrying the scent of rain. Finn couldn't shake the feeling in his gut that the weather forecast had been wrong.

By the time they pulled the heavy net filled with crabs up to the deck, night had fallen. Darkness had settled in close, shrinking the world around them to the small lanterns hung on the back of the cabin and the few solar lights on the outer rim of the schooner. The water was choppy, bouncing the ship around like a toy. Crabbing was always more dangerous at night. It didn't matter what latest and greatest technology they installed, dark ocean waters were always dangerous.

Finn untangled crabs from the netting using his gloves to keep his fingers from being pinched. It was tedious work. Normally, he found it relaxing, but not tonight. The storm felt like it was breathing down on him and time was against them. He had loosened a crab and tossed it into the ice pit at the bottom of the ship when the storm hit.

Rain fell in solid sheets like a faucet had opened up. Finn had to keep blinking and wiping at his face to see what he was doing. The boat kept rolling on the waves and the lantern light kept swinging beside the cabin. It didn't help that his gloves had salt water all over them from working with the netting. He trembled, but worked cautiously to untangle the crabs. He didn't have to speak to let his dad know he was worried. They had worked enough jobs on the schooner to read each other's body language. Dad was terrified, too, and that didn't help his nerves.

"Keep going!" Dad called, barely visible against the light from the lantern.

All Finn could see was his father's shiny silhouette as

he worked mechanically in his raincoat to roll the spare netting Finn slowly freed down into a storage compartment. He was trying to keep the net from becoming a hazard for them. It was hard to see, and it was difficult to stand with the choppy waters.

Finn's heart raced as he worked. Carefully untangle a crab, avoid its pincers, toss it into the ice, repeat. Again and again. He hoped each one would be his last, but it was like they multiplied at his feet. Every time he reached down to work on the next one, he spotted ten more.

Lightning struck, far too close to the ship for comfort. It lit up the night sky like a flare gun. For a brief few seconds, Finn had a view of all the crabs left writhing in the net, glistening and squirming on top of each other in the darkness. Dozens, maybe even close to a hundred. Dad had said the storm would bring in a haul, but this was too much!

Thunder followed—so loud the schooner rattled from the vibration of it. It reverberated through his body. A powerful wave came in, upsetting his footing. He fell hard to the deck on his rear.

Finn cried out, trying to pull away from the crabs and not get tangled in the netting himself.

"Finn!" Dad called. His footsteps reverberated through the wooden planks.

"I'm okay!" Finn yelled, rain falling into his mouth. He coughed and spat. Pulling further away from the netting and the crabs, he planted a foot and tried to stand, only to have it slip out beneath him again. Too much water was on the deck, the waves were too high, and the netting was becoming hazardous despite his father's best intentions. The downpour was too heavy. They shouldn't be here. They should have turned the boat around and gone home at the first sign of stormy weather, but Dad had insisted. He was always so stubborn.

Finn looked up, trying to find his father, but he couldn't see his silhouette against the light. He looked around for his shiny raincoat to catch the light somewhere, but he couldn't spot him. He thought he had felt him walking toward him earlier, but he never came over to check on him. Where was he?

"Dad?" he called as the icy rain streamed down his face. He thought of his father calling out to him, calling his name. Maybe he hadn't been worried for him, but instead had been calling for help. "Dad!"

Somehow, Finn crawled and scuttled over to where his father had been standing, but there was no sign of him. He reached the door of the cabin and reached up to grab the doorknob, hauling himself up to his feet. He slid inside the cabin, pulling the door closed behind him.

He was breathing hard, his body ached from falling, and he was soaked to the bone. Inside the confines of the small cabin, he realized how bad the weather had become. He had to hold on to the metal side railing as he skidded more than walked to the cockpit. Water fell from his rain slicker down the back of his shirt, making him shiver. He could still get traction on the wet wooden floorboards here with his boots, but the boat was tilting too far to the side, going almost sideways. That definitely wasn't a good sign. He went for the radio, hitting the buttons his father had shown him when he was a boy.

"Mayday, mayday, mayday. This is the boat Wishful, requesting immediate assistance. Ship is taking on water, over."

Static greeted him.

"Come on, damn it!" His voice broke, and a sob caught in his throat. He swallowed down his nerves and took a breath before trying again.

A wave hit. The wooden walls and instruments creaked around him, then the boat went sideways.

Finn cried out and grabbed onto the dash. His instincts kicked in. All he knew was he had to keep his head from hitting anything. His toes barely touched the far wall as he dangled from his fingertips.

"Please, please, just right yourself. You've got this," he whispered to the schooner. "You're a goddamn boat, you can do this!"

But the Wishful did not right herself. Instead, she flipped fully upside-down and the cabin lights went dark.

Finn screamed.

2

THE PLUNGE

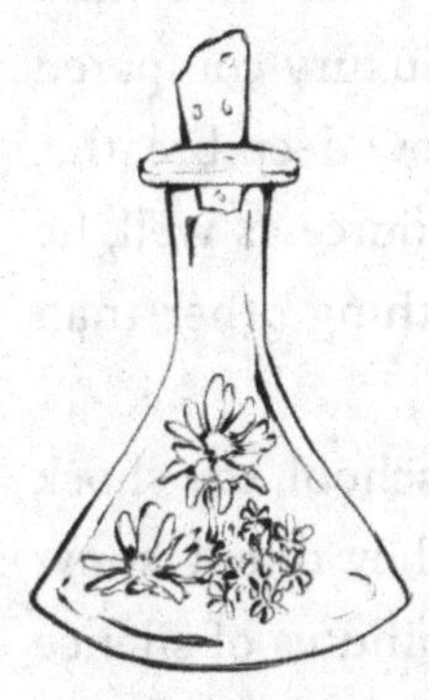

Wood creaked all around him. Somewhere inside the boat, water poured in. It was completely dark and his chest was tight. His body shook from head to toe. Now was not the time to have a panic attack, he told himself, like that ever did any good.

Hanging from his throbbing fingertips, Finn clutched desperately to the dash of the Wishful. The ship was now completely upside-down somewhere in the Atlantic Ocean. Nobody knew where he was or what was going on. Finn was completely alone and if he was going to get out of this alive, he needed to think and not panic.

He dug his fingers into the wooden edge of the dash, trying to ignore the pinprick pain. Dangling beneath him, his feet and toes felt cold and numb. Metal groaned.

Oh, that really wasn't a good sign. The water pressure was building. He was no expert in physics. He couldn't get higher than a C in that class despite how hard he tried. But Finn knew there was no hope of surviving inside this ship.

The edges of the windshield creaked. Water trickled into the cockpit, slowly at first, then faster and faster. It was filling up the room.

Tears streamed down Finn's cheeks, and he had to take deep breaths to calm down. He needed to think and focus. If he didn't escape soon, the boat would fill with water and sink to the bottom of the ocean with him trapped inside. Drowning was a swift luxury compared to the pain of decompression. After a few deep breaths, he felt better. Oxygen was a limited resource as well, he realized. But he had to focus on something other than panic.

He could see the announcement at school, the shock from his friends who maybe realized they didn't know him as well as they thought. The few minutes of silence allowed at school, followed by offers for help from the counseling office. And that would be it. He would be just another dead kid taken by the ocean. Another name on a list. Another sad footnote in history, compiled for annual statistics and sad stories. No, he couldn't let this be the end. He refused to allow that to be the final notes on his life. Somehow that gave him the fire he needed to act. That's what he really needed. A reason to live, no matter how selfish or silly. It didn't matter. As long as he kept going.

Letting go of the dash, he dropped to the ceiling of the cabin, his boots splashing in a couple of feet of water. It came up to his shins. Damn, that was faster than he expected, and it really meant he was running out of time. He needed to move fast and not let fear hold him in place. Delay meant death.

Taking long strides across the cockpit, he had to step slowly over the metal top of the doorway that went to the short hall towards the door. Unlike the glass of the windshield, the door from the cabin was sealed tight. The pressure might make it difficult to open, but he had to try. He didn't have any other choice.

As the water continued to pour in behind him, Finn waded over to the door. It was up past his knees now and freezing. The cold slowed him down, made his limbs slower and heavier. His heart rate increased as his body tried to stay warm despite it. He had to reach farther down the wall to wrap his fingers around the doorknob, but eventually, almost putting his face into the water, he grabbed it. All it took was turning the knob to allow the ocean to enter.

The door slammed open and ocean water surged into the small hall. It slammed him backward despite his attempts to stop. When his boot collided with the top of the metal doorframe that led to the cockpit, he knew that was his only chance. He spread out his legs and lodged his feet against the metal lip of the doorframe. Once his feet were secure, he braced his arms to the lip of the frame to fully resist the torrent of water flowing in. He had to wait for the pressure to ease before he could attempt to leave. But if he waited too long, it would suck him down into the water with the vortex of the ship.

So Finn did the only thing he could think of, the one thing that had helped him through years of panic attacks, grief, and frustrations. He closed his eyes and concentrated on his breathing. He breathed in, counted for a few seconds, and held his breath briefly before breathing out. Then started all over again. All the while, water rushed in against him, and the strength of it made his shoulders hurt. But if he tried to swim out there, it would kill him. All it would take was a strong current to cut his head too deep or slam him against something. So instead, he focused on his breathing, staying as calm as he could, and waited for the opportunity to escape.

The water was up to his waist now and the iciness made his pulse roar in his ears. No, he needed to breathe. He would need to take a final breath before plunging into the dark water, and he wasn't sure when he would get another breath again. So he needed to make sure it was a good one. Even if it was his last.

Now. It was time to go. He had a brief window, and that was it. The room was almost full. His body had adapted to the cold water, which also probably wasn't a good sign. It didn't need to be super cold to be bad for him. It never took much for nature to kill a person. He forced himself to take another deep breath, filling his lungs even though his hands shook. The water was up to his elbows, but the pressure had dropped. He breathed out and let go of the frame with his hands before dislodging his feet.

He was a little lightheaded. His heart pounded in his ears and his hands shook. None of that mattered. It was now or never.

Closing his eyes, he breathed in deep. This was it. The final breath. He had to make it last. There was no other choice. He pictured the boat, his path ahead, remembered where the life preservers were, then took the plunge into the icy darkness.

FINN WAS glad he had given himself time to adjust to the water. It didn't feel freezing now, just cold. One less shock to his system.

He swam as fast as he could through the doorway, letting out a few bubbles of air. The carbon monoxide buildup was the worst part. He knew that from years of being on the ocean with Dad, trying to hold his breath under the water. The bubbles also helped direct him which way was up, because his mind was used to the ship being normal, not flipped upside-down like a pancake.

Instead of heading to the surface, he detoured, filling out the map in his head as he swam. Eyes closed tight, he had to go by memory, by feel alone. It was tough with fear lacing every move he made. Already, the ocean fought against him, trying to pull him down. If he didn't find a life preserver, it would drag him down to the bottom along with the ship. If he wanted a chance at living through this night, he knew he had to find it.

He reached a hand out and felt the rope along the edge of the ship, right where he hoped it would be. He was close! His lungs burned as he let out a little more air, following the rope along the edge of the ship, noting each attached point and counting them in his head. Relief filled him as his finger wrapped around the small inflatable tube. It was a small thing, a nuisance to maintain and a safety precaution to check each time they went out on the water. He never thought he would be in such a desperate situation that he needed it.

Finn wrapped an arm through it, then reached down to unlatch the buckle. His fingers didn't want to work. They resisted him. Everything seemed intent on stopping him: the cold water, the endless darkness, the sea water trying to burn his eyes, and the heaviness of the ocean closing in. But Finn persisted. His lungs burned and his fingers fumbled too much. Maybe he was lightheaded, maybe he wasn't thinking right, and he was unconscious in the cockpit right now instead of here trying to loosen the life raft.

No, he needed to focus! He needed to get this to work. Otherwise, he would drown before he could ever reach the surface.

The buckle released the inflatable, and Finn held on tight. As soon as it was free, the tube sped toward the surface with Finn attached. It was like a ride, but without the fun. He hoped he had gotten out in time before the boat had sunk to such a depth that would give him the bends. But it was getting difficult to think straight, let alone remember his safety lessons from Dad years ago. All he knew was to hold on to that inflatable as hard as he could as it dragged him to the surface. The pressure was intense. The boat wanted to pull him down with it, but it couldn't. Not as long as Finn held on.

Something soft and organic dragged across his arm as the inflatable sped past. His mind imagined a big fish swimming past. Hungry sharks picking over the feast of crabs below, still caught in the net. Many underwater dangers could be just inches away, but Finn would never know, since he couldn't see them. He shuddered. Maybe that was for the best.

The inflatable tube broke through the surface. Rain and wind roared around him. It was like he came up inside of a tornado.

Finn beat his chest with his hand for a moment, forcing himself to exhale the breath he had taken. His lungs didn't want to work right at first. Maybe it was the cold or the lightheadedness. With a cough, he finally let out the breath he had been holding forever before gulping down breath after breath. A wave splashed over his head, threatening to take the inflatable tube, and he coughed again, clutching the nylon ropes with trembling fingers. Shaky and cold, with water pouring into his eyes, Finn pulled the tube over his head so he could rest his body over the side of it and navigate the choppy water a little easier. The waves still crashed against him again and again.

"Dad!" he called out, his voice was small and trembling against the power of the storm. "Dad!" It was hard to be heard over the thunder and the fury of the ocean. But still he hoped to see his dad floating somewhere in the darkness, clutching some part of the ship or to his own inner tube. Finn picked up the whistle attached to the side of the inflatable and put his lips to the cold metal, breathing out a high-pitched squeal. He felt like a tiny finch chirping against a hurricane. A quick flash of lightning lit up the inky sea for just an instant. Finn scanned the waters, what he could see amid the tall waves, but all he saw were bits of the ship, some splintered wood, and a piece of a net. That was it.

His heart dropped. He couldn't see much over the waves, but there was no sign of the boat or Dad. Had it been him he had felt bumping into him beneath the waves mere moments ago? Was he just below the surface, struggling to find a way up to get air?

The insane thought came to him that he should dive under and find him, but he didn't know how he could do that and not lose the inner tube. That thought frightened him. He needed the tube to survive. He was also exhausted. But he should go searching, shouldn't he? Wouldn't his father do that for him?

Hot tears filled Finn's eyes and fell down his cheeks, but the rain and the waves washed his sorrow into the sea.

He was lost, alone, and in the middle of nowhere. He cried to the glowering skies, the thunderous waters, and begged to see his father one last time.

3

THE LIGHTHOUSE ON THE CLIFF

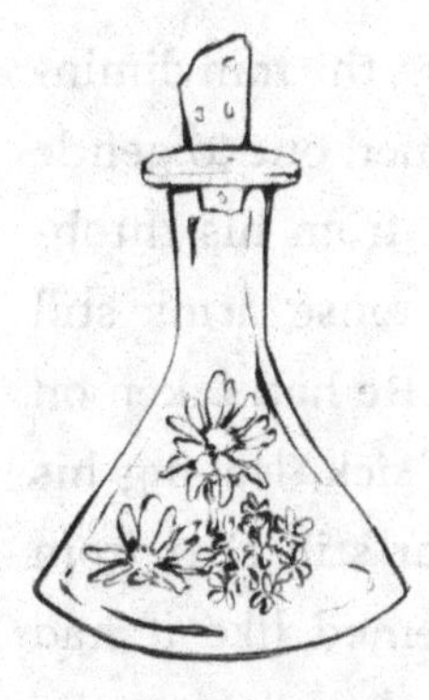

THE OCEAN TOSSED FINN AROUND FOR what felt like forever. Every time the waves came in too high, sea water found its way into his mouth. He swallowed far too much of it, spit up, only to be beaten again and again by the endless waves.

One wave rushed toward him. It was so high he thought it was a shadow at first. It blocked out the clouds, the lightning, and the rain until it towered before him. Finn felt so small beneath it, an insignificant insect before a god. All he could do was gasp before it fell on top of him. He was underwater again, spinning so he couldn't tell which was up. It was like the inner tube was trying to shake him out, but he held onto the nylon rope for his life. When it finally stopped, he closed his eyes and pressed his face against the salty plastic, begging for anything or

23

anyone to help him. Knowing it would be impossible. Knowing he was completely beyond anyone's help.

People died out in the ocean all the time. Entire books were dedicated to them. Shipwrecks were so common people almost expected it to happen at some point. Finn never thought it would happen to him, though. Certainly not in the boat he had considered a second home for over half his life. He never imagined he would float adrift in the ocean during such a horrible storm, his ship somewhere deep beneath the waves. He cried, he screamed, but the relentless power of nature drowned it all out, her fury never sated.

Eventually, the angry sky turned gray, the rain diminished to a dull mist, and the waves evened out to gentle peaks. His entire body was exhausted, from his throbbing head to his achy legs, and his tense arms still grasping the sturdy plastic inner tube. He had taken on too much sea water and kept getting sick, leaving his throat and esophagus burning. His rear still hurt from falling on the deck, too, but that seemed like it had happened in another lifetime, like it hadn't actually happened to him. His body felt like a used up dish rag.

Exhaustion fell over him as heavy and as determined as that giant wave, and Finn wrapped his arms in the nylon rope, so tight he was afraid he might cut off circulation. But that was preferable to falling beneath the waves and losing the inner tube. An uneasy sleep took hold of him, though he still opened his eyes in a panic every few minutes. A wave splashed against his face, forcing water into his nose, and he woke up with a start, coughing and sputtering. The waves were tough enough to deal with, but the salt was drying him out from the inside, from his throat to his sinuses. He was so thirsty he could cry, but he didn't think he had any tears left.

Finn realized sleeping with his arms tangled in the nylon rope wasn't safe enough. The next time, the water might not wake him. The thought of waking up underwater, lost and without the inner tube, was terrifying. Tired and weak, he scrambled on top of the float, lowering his rear into the hole in the middle. He easily could be stuck when he tried to get out later, but at least he wouldn't lose the damn inner tube. He was also more top heavy this way and easier to flip, but the waves were calmer now. And he hoped that meant he could sleep without worrying he would drown.

With caution still tugging at him, he wrapped his arms in the nylon rope. Not his legs, though. If he got turned over, he wanted to be able to kick and swim safely. This also made him feel better about not having half his body dangling in the water like some dinner bell for whatever might want to take a bite of him.

He tried multiple times to see if his head would fall into the water in this position, but only his hair got wet. Good. That meant he could sleep at least a little without his fears dragging him awake. His tests calmed him down. Exhaustion tugged at him again. Only this time, Finn welcomed its embrace, allowing his mind to drift to sleep, knowing it would be difficult to drown in a position like this. Though never impossible.

In his dreams, he floated near the boat. Dad was on

board, keeping an eye on him like he always did. It was a beautiful sunny day and clouds dotted the sky as if painted onto an artist's canvas. Dad called something to him, a smile on his lips, but Finn couldn't hear him. All he could hear were the waves and their endless lapping against his ears. Behind him, he knew there were storm clouds, but as long as he didn't look at them and acknowledge them, they could never overtake the ship. So Finn kept his gaze on the beautiful clouds above his head, the sun setting in the distance, and the sound of his father's shoes thumping around on the deck. For him, this was the closest he could get to peace.

Deep in Finn's heart, he knew this was the only way he would ever have a sliver of that peace again.

FINN SLEPT DEEPLY, his dreams taking him away from the pain and exhaustion that wracked his body. It took away the horrors he had witnessed, and the fears that threatened to overwhelm him. In sleep, he was safe, warm, and dry. Not drifting alone on an endless, ambivalent ocean that had a million ways to kill him.

Hours passed. The clouds parted, revealing a sky filled with stars. A crescent moon glided overhead, but Finn didn't see any of it. He continued to dream beneath its watchful eye. The waves calmed to an easy rhythm that wouldn't wake a child. If Finn had been awake to see it, he would have found it difficult to believe these were the same waters that had taken the Wishful and his father. In the distance, the first streaks of violet illuminated the horizon. Dawn was coming, slowly and steadily pushing away the darkness to a new day.

A beam of light streaked across the darkness, and Finn fell within its reach. The golden beam of light illuminated his face, but he did not rouse, still held tight in the comfort of his dreams. He didn't move as the powerful beam slipped across his face again and again in the brightening morning sky.

Part II:

Unanswered Questions

4

AN UNEXPECTED THIEF

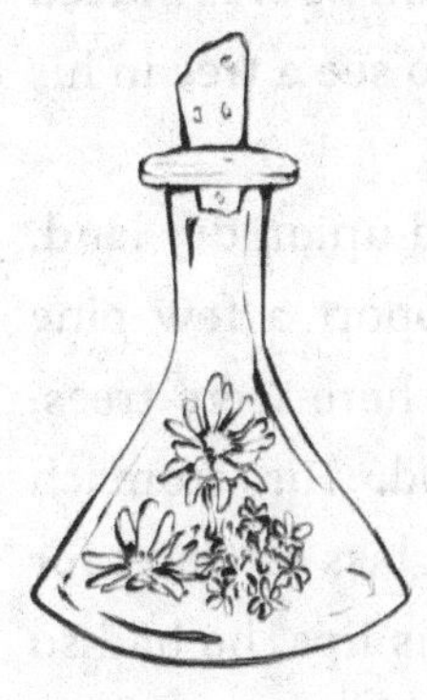

IT WAS TOO HOT.

His skin hurt.

Those were the first thoughts Finn had as he opened his eyes to the blinding sun. He tried to shield his eyes from it, but couldn't move his arm. Oh yeah, he had pinned it down with the nylon rope. He unwound it carefully, working around the rain slicker he was still wearing, which was way too hot now. Then he unraveled his other arm and, finally, held a hand over his eyes so he could look around.

To his surprise, the sky was a beautiful blue with white puffy, cumulus clouds scattered throughout. It was beautiful. He blinked to make sure he wasn't still dreaming, but no, this was as real as the ocean. It was as real as the pain in his arms from the nylon ropes, as real as the discomfort in his rear end. Like he had scraped across something.

Wait... why wasn't he moving?

The constant motion he had grown used to floating on the ocean was gone. He faced the ocean, but clearly he was on some kind of beach. He worked his arms fully free. When he craned his neck back, he spotted the branches of a pine tree further up the beach. The wind swished through its needles and tousled his matted hair. For a brief second, Finn wondered if he was still dreaming, or if he was really awake. The tree swayed overhead, gently stirred by the breeze as if to tell him he was indeed awake. Finn had never been so happy to see a tree in his life.

Dry land! Somehow, he had washed up on dry land. Or at least, it was dry enough to support a few pine trees. That had to be a good sign. If there were trees, maybe there was a way to get food. His stomach rumbled at that thought. Or at least a glass of water for his dry mouth. He couldn't even wet his lips, he had so little spit left.

It took work to climb out of the float. Just lifting his legs up and out was a painful process. They ached horribly from being pinned at such an awkward angle and it took several minutes for the pins and needles sensation to leave his legs and feet. Finally, he swung around his legs to meet the ground, pretty sure they could hold his weight again. His waterlogged boots hit rock and Finn's back complained when he stood up fully. Everything popped and hurt and ached all at the same time. He took a moment to stretch to his left and right, easing his neck around as well.

Despite the pain and discomfort, he was alive and on dry land. That was an incredible start from where he had fallen asleep last night.

Pine trees loomed overhead, casting long shadows across the rocky beach. That must have been why he felt scraped up on his backside. Coming ashore and dragging across all those rocks wouldn't have felt great. He wondered how the heck he slept through it, but then again, everything hurt. Maybe that was just one more random pain. Small rocks and large stones peppered the beach. It certainly wasn't the soft sandy beaches he was used to seeing. He was lucky he hadn't clocked his head coming ashore with how big some of those large rocks were. He felt around his head for any sign of injury, but he seemed mostly unscathed. Another incredible stroke of luck, considering everything.

The pine trees were tall and grew together fairly thick, like they had been here for a long time. Hopefully, this wasn't an undiscovered island. He staggered with stiff legs along the beach, watching his footing around the stones. His boots were too heavy, but he was desperate to find some sign of civilization, some sign of life beyond the island itself. He also wouldn't last long if he couldn't find fresh water.

There—at the end of the beach near the tree line! A dirt path. Grasses grew tall along its edges. He grinned, his smile hurting from sunburn. But he didn't care right now. He could worry about that later, along with all his other aches and pains. People had been here, and possibly still were! He hated to consider himself lucky after last night, but he sure felt like it for once.

Okay, he had a goal in mind. Now he could focus on himself for a moment.

He sat down on a large, fairly flat rock and pulled off his boots. It hurt when he pulled off his socks. Soaking wet, they clung to his skin like spiderwebs. He flexed his feet and toes, swollen and sore from being trapped in the soaked shoes all night. His raincoat had helped on board the ship, but now it was full of holes and actually trapped water against his body. So he pulled that off, too. The wet T-shirt he was wearing also clung to his skin. But that wasn't so bad. His shirt was way more dry than his poor feet. They had been dangling in the water, after all, which was probably worse.

The jeans he wore were soaking wet, too, but he was reluctant to take those off. If he was going to be traveling through the woods, he wanted some protection. He didn't know where that path would lead, or who it might lead to, but he definitely didn't want to greet someone in his underwear. He slid the wet socks into his back pocket, hoping they were usable still once they dried, but salt water had a bad habit of destroying clothes.

Dragging the inner tube to the entrance of the path was more work than he expected. Something like that never used to wear him out, but he had to stop to catch his breath after. But he felt like it was a smart idea. The bright orange and white colors of the inner tube might help him find his way back here if he needed to.

After his feet had a few minutes to dry, he reluctantly pulled back on the wet boots. His swollen feet protested, barely fitting inside, but he laced them up all the same. With a heavy sigh, a dry mouth, and a stomach that kept growling at him, he started down the dirt trail on shaky legs. The walking helped him gain his footing as he followed the trail uphill.

The path was a surprisingly well maintained. It looked as though someone took care of it from time to time, but certainly not regularly. He spotted a clear shoe print at one point. That had to be recent. He crouched down to look at it. Not that he was an expert, but he wanted to see what he could make of it. Dirt washed in from the storm partially obscuring the footprint. So someone hadn't been down here in at least a day or so. Interesting. Assuming that was how long he had been at sea. Honestly, he didn't know how much time had passed since the shipwreck, while he slid in and out of exhaustion.

He got to his feet and continued up the trail. After a couple of miles he found no sign of life other than the plant life, birds, and constant hum of summer insects. There were no sounds of cicadas, though, which was strange for this time of year. He guessed that meant they hadn't found a way out here and it was probably not super close to the mainland.

He heard the ocean waves again. There was already another beach? His heart sank. Was this just a tiny island? One of the hundreds that spotted the ocean where people only visited maybe once a year? Please don't let that be the case. He wasn't sure if he would last another day without help, let alone another year.

But the path hadn't ended yet, so maybe it was simply skirting the coast. The path went around a bend up ahead, so he told himself not to panic yet. He was still lucky to be here, even if it was a deserted island. He followed the bend around, past the tall, thick pines, and spotted it.

Finn stopped in his tracks, gaping.

The lighthouse was taller than any of the giant pines around him. It looked over the hundreds of trees like a giant watchtower. The rocky coast came up to its backyard in a steep cliff, and waves splashed up toward the back of the building. It had once been a brilliant white against the blue sky and rocky cliffs, but time and the ocean had eroded the gleam, leaving blotches of red rust and areas of black decay in places. No light illuminated the windows and for a moment, it looked abandoned.

He would land on an island with an abandoned lighthouse of all places. The ultimate irony was to survive a horrible shipwreck, only to find an empty lighthouse.

At the front was a chipped red door faded from the sun, rain, and sea salt air, turning it almost pink. The windows on either side were dark. He couldn't spot any movement. Perhaps he'd find a kitchen inside. Maybe some drinking water. Possibly even food that wasn't spoiled.

His stomach growled in agreement with that idea.

Mostly, though, he was thirsty, but he would happily

devour a three-course meal if offered. He wasn't sure if he wanted the lighthouse to be occupied or not, now that the idea of sneaking inside to find food came to him. It might be easier to find food if no one was home. If someone was there, what would he do if they refused to help him? No, that was his panic trying to come back. If someone was there, they would help him. Of course, they would. This was what people at lighthouses did, right? They helped people. And shipwrecks had to happen in the area or there wouldn't be a lighthouse.

He pursed his dry lips together, feeling them crack in places. Either way, standing out in the forest didn't ease his thirst or his hunger. He needed to take the risk. He swallowed down his dry throat to prepare to talk to someone and gave himself a small coughing fit. It took him several moments to build up the courage to go inside.

Looking at the myriad of windows up and down the building, Finn realized someone could watch him and he would never know. So he took the main path to the front door to be safe. It was the polite thing to do, even if he looked like a mess and sometimes manners really needed to be thrown out the window. He didn't want someone thinking he came to rob them or something, and maybe pull a gun on him. So maybe being polite was the best option, even if his stomach disagreed.

The dirt path turned to gravel as it got closer to the lighthouse. It clearly hadn't been refreshed in years, judging from the tall weeds that sprung up through it. Thin dirt paths wound around that path, looking more like walking paths than official paths through the woods. Some had lines where grass didn't grow, which had to mean someone was walking there often enough to keep plant life from growing, right? Dang, he wished he knew more about this kind of thing.

The lighthouse loomed high overhead, filling the sky as he drew near. It was hard to tell from the forest just how tall it was, but now he was close to it, it was absolutely massive. It was a giant round building that went all the way to the top. No additional living quarters attached, no little cabin or house nearby, just the lighthouse. Glancing to the side, he spotted a small garden with a few well-tended plants. Definitely a sign someone probably lived here. Not someone who came in once a year, but was currently living here. He couldn't deny the frustration that came over him. It meant negotiating for food and water, instead of just looking for anything to eat or drink. Any other time, he would have scoffed at that thought, but he had been through a lot. Surely he could convince them he needed help. They couldn't really turn him away, could they?

He cleared his throat again, realizing he would struggle to speak if there was someone inside. He wasn't even sure if he could talk properly yet with no water, but he had little choice. The lighthouse was the only option. He was so thirsty all he could imagine were those ridiculous ads on television with drinks filled with ice with condensation dripping down the side of the glass. That had always seemed so gimmicky before, but now he totally dreamed of that.

Lifting his hand to knock, Finn realized the door was open a crack. Maybe the person had stepped out?

The hinges creaked when he pushed open the faded red door. As he stepped inside, the sound echoed up into the massive spiral staircase that sprawled up above his head. Finn craned his neck back, staring up at the black metallic stairs that coiled up against white concrete to the very top. Just looking at it made him a little dizzy.

"Wow." His whispered hoarse voice that didn't even sound like him.

Only rarely had he seen the flash of lighthouses when crabbing with Dad. They usually stayed far out at sea, away from them. Never had he expected to see one up close. They were a background feature, a never-ending spinning flashlight warning of danger. Usually he thought about them as homages to a different time, a slice of a world that didn't really exist anymore, something to put on a greeting card when on vacation. He didn't even think these things were manned anymore, but clearly he was wrong.

"Hello?" His croaky voice echoed up the tower. He coughed some more. "Is anyone here?"

The echo faded. Silence greeted him. Then he caught the smell of freshly baked bread and all fear and caution fled his mind. To the right was a kitchen and a loaf of bread lay on a wooden board topped with fresh rosemary. His stomach kicked his logic aside and took over. He hurried over to it, not caring what anyone thought of him.

With shaky hands, he tore off a sizable chunk that

barely fit in his hand. He must have put too much into his mouth at once because he didn't have enough saliva to swallow it.

Opening the cabinet drawers left and right, he finally found the glassware. He grabbed one, coughing through the dry rosemary bread in his mouth, and filled it with tap water at the sink. Tap water, his mind thought dimly, which meant they had running water here. With a few desperate gulps, he emptied the entire glass in one motion, using it to ease the bread down his throat. He tilted his head back and sighed with relief. The lukewarm water felt amazing on his parched lips. He could even feel it going down. Never in his life had he been so grateful for water. He reached to fill another glass when a voice stopped him.

"Why are you stealing my bread?"

5

AN INTERRUPTION

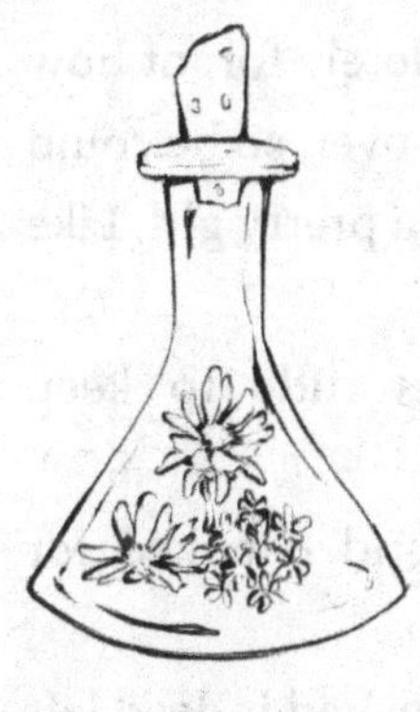

IN AN INSTANT, FINN HAD AN IMAGE OF what he looked like. He wore a soaking wet T-shirt that clung to his skin, wet jeans. His hair was a mess, face and hands sunburned, and he was drinking down water with someone else's glassware at their kitchen sink. He had torn a chunk of bread off the loaf and had stuffed it into his mouth like an animal. Dad would have been ashamed of him. He had intended to make a good impression if he ran into anybody, but now he realized it was a little too late for that. He turned around with water dribbling from his lips.

A girl in a pale purple dress who looked to be about his age stood in the kitchen's doorway. She had pale skin, messy black curls, dark eyes, and an annoyed, languid expression that implied she regularly had people storming into her kitchen and stealing big handfuls of bread right off the loaf. Something in her gaze made him feel even more embarrassed. Perhaps it was how bored she looked with him already, though he hadn't even spoken to her yet.

The empty glass shook in Finn's hand.

"I tried calling out to see if anybody was here, but didn't hear anybody, so I came inside and smelled the bread. It just smelled so good and I was so hungry, I couldn't help myself! I'm so sorry, I really don't do this normally."

The words tumbled from his mouth before he could stop himself. It was like his brain completely forgot how to socialize with people. His nerves took over, so he could make a proper fool of himself in front of a pretty girl. Like that always helped.

He ought to stop talking. It was rude to keep yammering on, but he couldn't stop.

"And then I saw you had water, and I looked for glasses, and finally found one."

He glanced around to see that, yes, he had indeed left every cabinet open in the kitchen, too. He winced.

The girl arched an eyebrow. Something about her had turned him into an absolute fool. Despite telling himself he should stop, there was absolutely nothing he could do. The train of embarrassing himself had revved up. All he could do was watch it tumble forward. Or maybe, he was delirious from the shipwreck and the sun and swallowing so much ocean water. Yeah, that was probably it. Normally he had a much better head on his shoulders. How he wished he could express that in a way that didn't rely on his mouth working properly.

"See, I was in that terrible storm last night. We were out catching crabs together." He pointed toward the ocean, as if the girl didn't know where the ocean was. "My dad and I got caught in it. The weather said it was supposed to go to the mainland, but it didn't. It came right for us. The waves were enormous, they were so big it blocked out the sky. By the time we realized we were in trouble, it was too late. Then the—"

"It was awful last night," the girl said. Her brows furrowed and her mouth tugged into a frown. "The waves came up almost to the top of the lighthouse last night." She put a hand to her chest, rubbing at the base of her neck like a nervous habit. Her gaze was distant, like she was far away from the tiny kitchen. "For a little while there, I thought it was finally going to do it. I thought it was going to drag this whole building down into the water with me in it. You know?"

Her neck was turning a little pink from rubbing at it. She blinked quickly, as though forcing herself back into the present. Finn understood what she meant in a strange, macabre way. He, too, thought the storm was going to take him last night, drag him down into its dark waters like it had his father. Trapped in the upside-down ship, waiting for the ocean water to fill up the cabin so he could make his escape, part of him had wondered if he should have just let the boat take him down with it. Join his father's fate. But he didn't dare give voice to such dark thoughts and impulses. It felt wrong to allow them into the light.

This girl clearly had those kinds of thoughts, too, and his heart went out to her for it. That was a scary path to tread, and he knew it.

"But the ocean didn't win," he said carefully, finally feeling like he had control over his mouth again, even if his voice was hoarse.

She met his gaze as though really seeing him for the first time. She gave a quick nod and took a deep breath. "No, not yet, anyway." She crossed her arms, as if to keep him from seeing her too clearly. "Where is your dad? Back on the damaged boat?"

"Damaged? No, it sank. There was no rescue, nothing. Nobody knew anything about where we were. The radio didn't work. It was all just static. It was like the world forgot we existed for a little while." He gave a nervous laugh. "There was just an inner tube and me floating on the waves." His voice shook, and he took a moment to swallow down the emotion, fearing it would explode out of him.

"In that storm?" She narrowed her eyes, gaping at him. "How did you survive it?"

Words failed him for a moment. His mouth opened then again, and he shook his head, not sure at first what to even say. He did survive it. He had survived. That was hard to even really wrap his head around, but it was true.

"I don't know. Dumb luck and a clear head when I panic, I guess. Dad... he always said I had a good head in dangerous situations. I usually keep my cool in an emergency. I didn't used to though. When I was little, I was terrible at freezing up, but I worked on myself. Now I think quick on my feet."

He remembered his dad's laugh when Finn had bandaged an injury on his arm. The compliments and awe in his voice, and the pride and love in his eyes. Love and loss mixed in his heart, making his eyes burn. Finn cleared his throat, trying to keep himself in check. He had to keep himself together, at least for a little longer. The last thing he wanted to do was chase this girl off with the terrors he had seen last night, but she seemed to see right through him.

She cocked her head to the side, her messy curls falling into her eyes. "And your dad?"

"He, uh..." Finn's throat closed up. His hands shook so badly he had to put the glass down for fear of dropping it. He placed his hands on the edge of the cold counter, taking deep breaths. He had to say it, had to put it into words, even though his mind railed against the idea. Even though his heart thundered in his chest, refusing to fully believe it still. He had thought about it several times, sure, but it would be different when he said it out loud. Words would make it real. It was like his entire body was in revolt against speaking it, making it hard to wrap the truth around his tongue.

"My dad..." he started to say, in an octave higher because of his throat clamping up. Tears sprang to his eyes. A hand pressed on his shoulder, warm and comforting, just like his father had done before the storm. She meant it in kindness and in support, he was sure, but it broke him all the same.

"He's dead," he whispered through awful sobs that wracked his body. His chest already hurt from fighting ocean waves all night. He had kept his cool head for so long, focused on survival, always getting to the next step, and putting off the emotions until it was a better time for them. He hadn't had the luxury or time to process it all, hadn't allowed the truth of it to sink in. Even in his dreams, his father was still alive, still calling out to him, still watching over him. But it wasn't real. He was gone and there was nothing Finn could do about it.

He cried, his tears rolling down his sunburned cheeks and onto sunburned hands. It hurt. Everything hurt. And he couldn't stop the sobs that tore through him or the words that sorrow pulled from his lips.

"I think I bumped into him under water. When I found the inner tube and it was taking me to the surface?" He looked at her and attempted a smile, like they were having a normal conversation, then the sobs took hold of him again. "I think he was right there with me, maybe even drowning beside me. I could have reached out to him, I could have grabbed him, and maybe even saved him. He was right there. And I did nothing to help him. I just saved myself. Only me."

"Shh." She rubbed between his shoulders. Her dark eyes glanced from his face to his sunburned hands, his body proof of all the things he had lived through that night and morning. She furrowed her brow with worry. "Come, follow me."

He did as she asked. He would have done anything she asked of him in that moment because of the horrible state he was in. She could have led him to a dungeon to lock him up and he would have helped her closed the door. Instead, she led him to another small room opposite the kitchen and to a long, flowery couch.

She lay a thin blanket on the couch, and a thick, fluffy blanket to the side. But when he went to lie down, she held up a hand to stop him.

He froze, still too shattered to even question her.

With a stern expression, she approached him and took his elbows in her hands. The kind touch and her beautiful face pushed aside his broken heart, though briefly.

"I need to figure out what to do with your burns. In the meantime, I want you to leave your clothes on the floor here. Then lie down and cover up for me, okay?"

He nodded, his voice broken up by hitching breaths. "I'm so sorry. I don't want to be a burden to you. You have a whole lighthouse to run. I can lie down on the floor if that's easier. I don't want to ruin your pretty couch." He sniffled.

The girl shook her head and gave a soft smile that lit up her face and made Finn almost cry again at how lovely she was. "You are not a burden. This isn't my light-house, anyway."

Finn blinked, his mind slow to turn that over. "But then, whose is it?"

She squeezed his elbows and headed for the stairs.

"Please, go ahead and get undressed. I'll see if I can find something for you to wear."

Her quick footsteps echoed on the circular metal staircase as she climbed up the stairs. He watched her go, mesmerized by her in a way he couldn't explain. She was like the lighthouse, overwhelming everything beneath it, including himself.

Finn did as she asked and took off his boots. His feet were so grateful to be free of those shoes he gasped from the relief. He stripped off his clothes, piling everything near the couch. He hadn't realized how soggy his legs were until he peeled off the jeans he had been wearing. It took more work than he expected, and he was winded afterwards. Everything was so difficult, far more than it needed to be. Getting undressed shouldn't be this tiring.

The underpants were more complicated. He didn't even know this girl's name, and he wasn't sure if he trusted her enough to be completely nude. But she was trying to help him. He had been the one to steal her food, after all. And his body really needed to air out. He didn't want to think about how his skin would feel if he left the ocean soaked underwear on for much longer. So with a sigh, he added them to the pile as well.

He climbed beneath the blanket, fixing the pillows to support his head. The blankets were soft against his skin and he was so grateful for it. It was like he hadn't ever appreciated the softness of a fluffy blanket before. After the pain and struggle he had been through, it was like laying beneath a cloud. Stillness fell over him for the first time since he had stepped onto the Wishful with his father. No tasks, no work, no plans, just rest. He felt like he had been living in survival mode for so long. His face and hands throbbed from the sunburn and he found he couldn't keep his hands beneath the blanket because his skin was too sensitive to the texture of the fabric. So he kept them on top, folding them carefully over his chest.

Beside him was a thick glass window as tall as the high ceiling of the room and almost as wide as the couch. From here, he could look out over the giant rocks that lined the cliff where the lighthouse stood. Even in calm waters, he could see the occasional white foam fly up from the ocean spray below, just visible over the grass and bushes. He could only imagine how high they had gotten last night when the girl thought the waves would tear the lighthouse down into the ocean.

He looked out toward the horizon where the steady, dark blue waters bobbed beneath a serene sky. It was surreal to think those waters had nearly killed him. That they had taken his father's life. Waters he had considered himself an expert on just a day ago, and a boat he had grown up on. Not to mention his father, who had spent almost his entire adult life making a living on the water.

When tears threatened again, Finn closed his eyes and allowed them to fall. The salt streaked pain down his cheeks. Upstairs, the girl's footsteps creaked on the old floorboards. This place felt more like a haunted house than a lighthouse.

A hard breeze swept off the ocean, thundering against the concrete tower like a low drum. It might be unsettling for someone else, but Finn found it relaxing. It reminded him of the wind howling at night while sleeping on the Wishful, gentle waves rocking him to sleep at sea.

He looked out at the waves in the distance with blurry vision and thought of his father. Not of his death for once, but how he had been before the storm. He probably would have loved to visit this lighthouse. All it would have taken would be one trip, and his old man would have dug up all the information he could about the history of the lighthouse, including the shipwrecks it prevented, the ones it couldn't, and when it had been established. Dad loved history, but he loved boats more. He would have seen this place as the perfect spot to have a miniature vacation if he could have wrangled it with the lighthouse owner.

The thought brought a smile to Finn's lips.

This wasn't the girl's lighthouse, he thought as sleep tugged at his eyelids. The girl. He kept thinking of her like that. He didn't even know her name. Yet here he was, about to fall asleep naked on her couch. He sure as hell hoped he didn't wake up with a knife to his throat or something. The thought made him antsy, but then he remembered her smile and the concern in her eyes when she had looked at his sunburn.

She was worried about him. Oddly enough, that made him feel better about this whole bizarre situation. Dad always said people were innately good, and for the first time in his life Finn hoped his father had been right, because he was about to test that theory.

He leaned his head back on the stiff pillows, taking a

moment to get comfortable. His neck still hurt like so much of his body, but sleep would help and he knew that. His belly wasn't full, but sated. That's all he needed for now.

The wind swept through the pines outside, a soothing, low humming sound that reverberated against the lighthouse. Ocean spray pattered against the window beside him, and slowly Finn allowed sleep to pull him in. This time without fearing for his life.

FINN STARED out at the endless ocean at night. The waves hid so much beneath them. A full moon hung high overhead, but it only illuminated the surface of the water. Sand sank between his toes as he paced back and forth on the beach, curling his arms around his waist to fend off the chill of the powerful wind at his back.

Fear and worry filled his heart. Something was wrong, but he couldn't put into words what it was. He wasn't alone. He knew that. As he looked out at the ocean, something stared back at him from those dark waters. Try as he might though, he couldn't spot what it was. There were no boats he could see, no rocky islands where something could hide, but he knew it was there. It made the hair stand up on the back of his neck.

Part of him wanted to see it, to know what it was so he could understand it. Another part of him was afraid to, knowing if he saw it, he could never forget it.

"Show yourself!" he cried at the sea, but it did not answer.

He picked up a rock, like sandpaper in his hand, and tossed it into the ocean. As soon as it landed, he knew he had angered the thing that watched him. This was its waters, after all. He was an interloper here.

The sound of wet, bare feet slapping on the sand drew a shiver down his spine. He froze, his feet sinking into the sand like quicksand. Finn couldn't move.

He had thought it was in the water watching him, but it hadn't been there at all. It was behind him, waiting for him to turn around, waiting for him to acknowledge its existence.

"See me." A high-pitched voice hissed in his ear, hot breath against his skin.

Finn whimpered. It wanted him to turn around, to look at it, but he couldn't. The sand had covered his feet, trapping him in place. Keeping his gaze on the water ahead, he tried to ignore the shadowy movement in his peripheral vision. It circled him, moving side to side like a predator, never coming out to stand in front of him. But Finn knew better than to turn his head to see it. If he did that, it would only have more power over him.

"See me!" it demanded again.

"No." Finn shook his head, trembling from head to toe.

He didn't know what it was, but he knew this was its island. He was interrupting something, and the creature was not pleased he was here. Finn had stumbled onto something he shouldn't have, and despite his best efforts to understand it, all he could do was stare at the ocean and wish this creature would turn its gaze away from him.

"Please, leave me alone." His voice was small to his ears, barely audible above the roar of the ocean.

"Do not cross me, child, and I might let you live through this."

His knees wobbled beneath him and his ankles sank deeper into the muck. "I won't, I promise," he said.

When icy fingers wrapped around his shoulder, Finn ducked his head down, knowing he couldn't escape now. This creature had taken hold of him as soon as he stepped on the island, but he didn't know what it was—or even what it wanted from him.

Even though he couldn't look at it, it saw him clearly.

6

ARE WE ALONE?

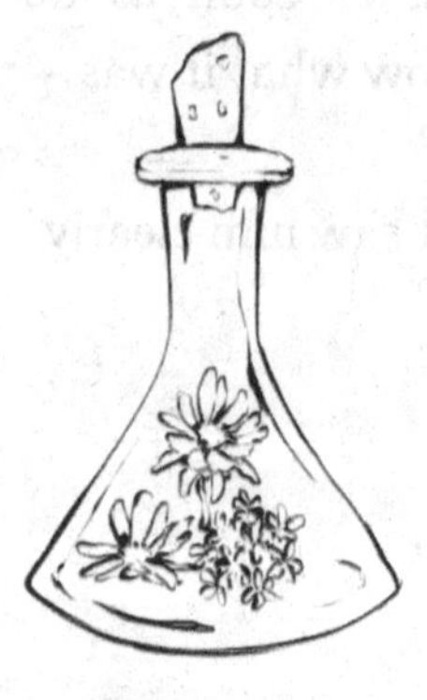

THE SCENT OF LANTERN OIL DRAGGED Finn back to consciousness. A beach with secrets to hide, a dread he couldn't name, and a high-pitched voice that sent a shiver down his spine. His heart was racing. The memory of the dream faded quickly, but he couldn't deny the lingering discomfort it left behind. Night-mares weren't surprising, considering everything he had gone through, but he much preferred his dreams while he had drifted on the ocean. It was wild his dreams turned darker when he was safe and warm, and kinder when his life was in danger.

A throbbing headache pounded in his ears, and his stomach growled. Clearly, the handful of rosemary bread he had scarfed down earlier had not been enough to sate him. His tongue was dry and swollen, and the aftertaste of saltwater lingered in the back of his throat. He was groggy, like he still needed to sleep for a long time. Apparently, sleeping out on the ocean, followed by a quick nap, wasn't very restful.

The sun had sunk beyond the horizon and outside the dark sea loomed. Just like it had in his dream, which he could only remember glimpses of now. The waters were calm tonight, but seeing those nighttime waters ran a chill up his spine. Not from the dream, but because he knew how deceiving they were. How quickly they could turn tempestuous and deadly. He would never look at the ocean at night the same way again. Not after barely surviving that night. Despite its beauty, he had seen its true colors when that storm rolled in.

Finn shuddered off the memories and sat up, letting the blanket fall from his chest. The cool breeze across his skin made him grab up the blanket though, and pull it to his neck to get warm again. That's right, he was naked. A flush came to his cheeks as he remembered everything. The pile of his wet clothes was gone, including his underpants, which made him blush even harder. At the end of the couch sat a folded set of clothes, dry but certainly not his style. He reached out and sorted through them: a pair of underwear, an oversize undershirt, a blue flannel button up, a belt that had seen better days, and a pair of cotton pants.

He looked around the room into the kitchen. The girl was nowhere to be seen. Three large hurricane oil lamps were lit, their flames low. That must have been where the scent of lantern oil came from. He glanced up the stairwell, but without getting off the couch, he could only see a few steps up, not even to the first landing he had spotted earlier. Nothing moved, but that certainly didn't mean anything. He was still naked in a giant lighthouse on an abandoned island with a girl he didn't know. But he had slept for several hours on her couch. If she had wanted to hurt him, she could have.

Other than the distance sound of waves and the occasional crash of spray against the rocks, the lighthouse was silent. It was eerie at night inside this giant building with just a few flickering flames to ward off the darkness. The lighthouse was kind of cute and nostalgic during the day, but at night it looked like a giant forgotten beast, and he was in its belly.

Finn took a deep breath, clearing his throat from the salty brine that lingered. He needed food and water, but that meant getting dressed. He looked around one last time to make sure the girl wasn't hiding somewhere watching him. Despite her kindness, he wasn't quite ready to trust her completely. Not yet, anyway. She was still a stranger, and he was still relying on her help. Though she had been kind to him so far, he couldn't expect that to last.

With a hefty sigh, Finn pulled on the clothes. Standing up was more difficult than he expected. Everything hurt, his arms, his legs, his back, even his sides hurt. His head pounded harder once he was on his feet. The ocean had done a number on him.

All the clothes were too big for him, even the underwear. So he rolled up the pant legs and the long sleeves of the checkered flannel shirt. He used to the belt to hold his pants and underpants up on him. His skin still felt like it had a sheen of salt all over, like a crusty second skin, but at least he was dry. Taking a few cautious steps around the room eased some of the pain throughout his body, though he was still very stiff and sore. For the first time in ages, he actually felt human instead of a bobble toy tossed around on the ocean. He even had dry clothes to wear. It felt almost luxurious.

Finn padded out to the entryway and looked up the staircase. It was quiet up there. He thought about calling out, but then hesitated. Best not to make a nuisance of himself. He should probably look for something to drink before trying to talk, let alone calling out to anyone. Clearly, he was dehydrated because he wasn't thinking right.

In the kitchen, he found a bowl and a glass left on the counter for him. He gave a small smile as he picked up the glass. That's when he saw the small note the girl left behind.

"No need to steal this time."

He smiled. The girl had a dry sense of humor, which he had not expected. It was strange how her offering a glass and a bowl made him feel more like a house guest and not so much like a complete stranger.

A throbbing headache came again, and he put a hand to his temple. That was probably dehydration kicking his butt. He grabbed the glass and filled it at the tap before drinking about half of it, remembering it was a good idea to slow down despite what his body wanted him to do. On the stove sat a pot. Inside, he found what smelled like corn chowder. Finn yelped with joy, a sound that would definitely embarrass him if any of his friends at school had heard it. But here he didn't care. It smelled and looked incredible!

After getting a bowl and taking another sip of water, he dug in. He didn't even sit down at the little table and chairs off to the side. He just ate while standing at the counter, eating and drinking as quickly as he thought safe. After polishing off a second bowl and finishing the pot of chowder, he glanced up the metallic staircase, looking for any kind of movement. But all was silent. It was like the giant metal building was abandoned, but he knew that wasn't true.

Finn had grown up in a house that always had motion. Dad enjoyed listening to podcasts and audio-books all the time, or watched the news or the weather. There was always talking in the house. Always something going on. Finn listened to music a lot. Genres and bands of all kinds. He wasn't used to being in a place so quiet, so silent he only heard his slurps. It wasn't bad, but it was very different for him. Even out on the ocean, it was never completely silent. The lapping of the waves against the boat, the creaking of the boat and ropes and the wind always blowing.

Outside, the wind swept by and he could hear it reverberate up the staircase. He paused, listening to the haunting sound. Yeah, he much preferred listening to podcasts to that creepiness.

He cut a proper slice of the rosemary bread. The girl had left him the section that he had pulled a chunk off before. That was only fair. It was only polishing that off along with another glass of water did realization click into place.

It was nighttime. This was a lighthouse. She was probably upstairs working to keep the light on. Dang, his brain really was waterlogged.

He found some dish soap and cleaned the dishes he'd used, setting them aside to dry. She had mentioned him stealing food earlier, and that made him eager to prove himself a better house guest. He was already borrowing some poor person's clothes and the girl already took his old ones, presumably to wash them or trash them. If his dad were alive, he would be glad to see him remembering his manners.

The thought hurt, but he pushed it away and dried his hands.

Finn started up the menacing, black, metallic spiral stairs. He hadn't reached the first landing before it became quite dark. No lights hung in the stairwell. Soon, he wouldn't be able to see the stairs beneath his feet. The tiny flames of the hurricane lamps on the bottom floor didn't penetrate the darkness up here. It didn't help that the higher up he went, the more the wind echoed from outside. The roar from the ocean was constant as waves splashed up against the rocks, spraying up the side of the lighthouse. It was more intense than he liked. It reminded him of the shipwreck and his hands shook at his sides.

He hurried back down the stairs. Getting near the flames of the oil lanterns and stepping back into the light pushed back the edges of his slight panic. He took the handle of one of the hurricane lamps and examined it. The glass flute looked light enough, but the base was large and intricate, making the lantern quite weighty. It was tough to carry one-handed, even though he'd worked reeling in crabs all summer. But the lantern would be worth it to see where he was going up the dark staircase. The flute made it harder for breezes to affect it, but as he headed up the stairs, it still flickered. As if it, too, was trying to fend off a panic attack.

Outside, the wind roared against the walls of the lighthouse. It wasn't even stormy outside. As he climbed into the darkness, holding the lantern ahead of him, occasional bursts of air seeped in through the cracks in the walls. It was a cool breeze, and he was grateful the hurricane lamp was built specifically for high winds. He wished he could look outside from here and see the beacon fending off the darkness of the night, but there were no windows up the stairwell. Wooden floorboards above creaked with every blast of wind outside, and the few cracks of wind made a whistling sound within the stairwell. Finn switched hands with the lantern, so he could hold on to the railing to keep from getting dizzy.

Every closed door he passed was dark. No light shone from beneath them. One room was labeled storage, another tools. Hooks on one wall held rain boots, rain slickers, rope, and other maintenance materials. The entire building was set up as a workspace. When he got to the upper floors, he spotted a room with the door cracked open and light flickering underneath.

He knocked, then nudged it open when there was no response. "Hello?"

It was a bedroom. A hurricane lantern sat beside the bed on a squat dresser. The bed was simple enough, with a floral quilt laid over it. The walls were whitewashed concrete. It looked like it had been built a while back. The style suited an early 1900s bed-and-breakfast instead of a modern day lighthouse. It was odd and a little unsettling. This whole place felt like a small time capsule.

"Are you in here?" he asked, feeling foolish that he didn't know the girl's name. He licked at his sore lips. When he turned his back to the bedroom, to return to the steps, he saw another room on the opposite wall of the stairwell. This one was dark, but the door was cracked open.

Curious and a little nervous, he pushed the door open and held the lantern forward to illuminate the room. It was an old storage closet with a cubby near a tiny window. A rolled up bedspread lay on a thin mattress with a few pillows tossed alongside. Had she been setting up a place for him to sleep? Finn couldn't help but smile.

She barely knew him. He had broken into her home, stolen some of her food, but still she showed him kindness. Not only did she allow him to sleep all day on the couch downstairs, but she was also fixing up a space for him, too.

Finn looked up toward the top of the spiral staircase. A brilliant light illuminated beneath the door at the top of the staircase, then disappeared at regular intervals. That had to be where she was. He just had to keep climbing. Finn sighed. The stairs weren't steep, there were just a lot of them.

He swapped the lantern to the other hand and started up again. His thighs burned as he climbed the last flight of stairs. Once he got to the top, he had to stop and catch his breath. He was even a little shaky. Considering how much work he did pulling in nets and catching crabs all day on the boat, Finn was surprised he was so tired. This was a tough climb, but not nearly as strenuous as what he normally did. But he had survived a lot. He guessed his body still needed to recover.

A powerful wind rose outside, howling and whipping around the building. The spray of the ocean hit next, splattering against the walls of the lighthouse. Down below came a heavy clattering like something striking against metal.

Finn paused. What was that? He looked down the center of the spiral stairs, but everything was still. Maybe it was a trick of the wind? Or maybe he had simply not stacked the dishes right when he cleaned them.

But Finn knew that wasn't it. It was too heavy of a sound. Too metallic. But nothing was metal down there… except maybe the front door.

An eerie feeling overcame him. Some deep, dreamlike

memory surfaced briefly, floating past just out of reach, like grasping at smoke. A harsh voice, a dark ocean, and that sinking feeling of dread. The memory of that dread formed a pit in his stomach.

He pushed away those strange thoughts, shaking off the spiderwebs of the memory with a shred of horror. Where had that come from? This wasn't a dream, not a nightmare. This was real life. It was probably just his dehydration making him jump at shadows.

The heavy clattering sound, if it had happened at all, was probably something outside that had been dislodged by the wind. It struck the side of the lighthouse somewhere, like an old shutter that finally gave up. That wind was pretty powerful coming off the ocean, and this was an older lighthouse. He had seen the spots of rust and worn paint from the outside. The place was in dire need of maintenance.. He needed to stop freaking out over every little noise. It was a creaky, windy place. He would get used to those strange sounds eventually.

He turned his back to the stairwell. The clattering sound came again.

The hairs stood up on the back of his neck. He turned, his gaze shifting around the bottom of the staircase, searching for what could have possibly caused it. That wasn't his imagination. Or a trick of the wind. He knew it now. Something was very real and very physical. Then he spotted it.

Someone was rattling the front door. Not just the handle, but the entire damn door.

The red door shook back and forth, as though

someone was trying to yank it out. He could tell now it was indeed a metal door, too. The hinges shook, and the metal ground together, squeaking in agitation. Whatever pulled at it wasn't strong enough to break it down, but it was strong enough to test those hinges. It was strong enough to shake that heavy metal door.

Wind didn't do that. Hell, Finn wasn't strong enough to do that, even when he was well-rested.

He swallowed down his own panic, his hands shaking again at his sides. Maybe it was the girl. His rational mind tried to explain it, but it wasn't coming up with any good options, and he knew it. There was no logical reason for it.

The girl wouldn't have to shake the door like that. She could just walk inside. That was ridiculous. If she needed help, she could just call for him. She would know he was right there beside the door.

A burst of light filled the space around him. The door to the light chamber lit up behind him. He turned toward it, only to be blinded. Out of instinct, he held up a hand. When the light faded, the girl stood in the doorway, gesturing for him to come toward her. Only her silhouette at first emerged out of the light burn on his irises. At first, all he could see was the outline of her dark curls and the urgency in her gesture. When his eyes adjusted again, her eyes were wide. She was terrified.

Finn let out a nervous breath, glancing back down behind him as the metal door on the ground floor rattled again.

"I've been looking for y—"

She hurried forward and pressed a finger hard to his lips, fear in her eyes. Finn went silent as the noise came again from the front door. Was it more intense this time, or was that his imagination?

He didn't ask questions and instead followed her into the room. His hands were shaky, making the flame on the hurricane lantern dance. His legs felt wobbly, and he was breathing too fast.

The girl closed the door behind him so quietly he wouldn't have known it was closed if he hadn't seen it. She looped an arm around his and dragged him to the opposite side of the room. He pursed his lips and kept quiet, still feeling the lingering sensation of her finger against his lips. He thought about speaking again so she would have to silence him, but that was not a good idea right now.

The giant light spun in a slow, steady rhythm. Every time the light landed on him, his eyes were forced to close against it because it was so damn bright. There had to be more than a single bulb to make it so bright, but he couldn't keep his eyes open long enough to see it.

The girl put her hands on his waist and spun him around. Her hands deftly pressed against the flannel on his sides. A warmth rose to his cheeks. He could get used to this, too.

"Keep your back to it," she said. Her lips were so close he could feel the heat of her breath on his ear. "It makes it much easier, trust me."

"Trust you?" He chuckled, blinking to clear the light burn from his eyes. "How do I do that?"

She came around to his side, arched her eyebrows and smirking. "I gave you clothes. I fed you. And I let you sleep on my couch. That sounds like trust to me."

The brilliant light gleamed off the plates of glass that surrounded them and disoriented him. He rubbed at his eyes, trying to adjust. "How can I trust you when I don't even know your name?"

"I'm Ash," she whispered and took his hand. She led him behind a large cabinet with a good amount of room for the two of them. It also blocked off the intense glare of the light enough, so they could sit down without being blinded.

They sat down on the floor together, though it took Finn a few minutes since his body was so achy. She gave him a hand and helped him down with her. He gave a huff when he finally got down and stretched out his legs.

Ash's dark gaze bore into him. Spread out behind her were the deep blue waters of the ocean, and the rocky cliffs that dropped right behind the lighthouse, and even a few patches of beach that looked close to where he had washed ashore. They were so high up and the world so small beneath them. He felt godlike.

Ash wrapped one arm around her knee. She wore high rise jeans and a blouse with lace that looked too old-fashioned for her age. She seemed completely calm up here in a place that would terrify anyone afraid of heights. He felt he'd been pulled into her secret hiding place at the top of the world.

A gust of wind hit again, making the lighthouse creak

beneath them. Finn tensed. It didn't appear to bother Ash at all. Her calm demeanor eased his anxieties.

She leaned forward and took his hand. Her skin was soft against his. Her messy black curls framed her pale, rounded face. Freckles stippled her cheeks. She arched her eyebrows and gave a warm smile. "So, what do you think?"

No one had ever looked at him like Ash did. No one asked his opinion or worried about him like that. Everyone expected Finn to be self-reliant, independent. Ever since Mom died. For most of his life, he'd felt separate from the rest of the world, like he had a mark on him everyone else could see. He had always been an outsider, not fitting in at school for his love of the ocean. And not fitting in with the crabbers because he was too young. Even Dad had wanted him to move on from the life he loved so much. Everyone had expectations of him. Everyone made demands of him. But Ash didn't treat him like that.

She saw him and she accepted him into her world like it was only natural to do so. Finn's insides melted for the first time in his life. Was this what it was like to fall in love? Or was he being ridiculous?

"Beautiful..." he said through a slow exhale, his gaze entirely focused on her.

"It is, isn't it?" She grinned, looking out over the ocean.

Finn's heart beat harder in his chest, like it had never really needed to pay attention before.

"I like it up here. It's peaceful," she said.

Finn pursed his lips, afraid he might say something he would regret. Be a polite house guest, he thought. Don't mess this up! He barely knew this girl, but his heart didn't care. Even though he reminded himself to be patient and cautious, it was a losing battle. It was like trying to keep the ocean out of the Wishful. Once it had flipped over, there was simply no way to reverse it. His emotions soared whether or not he wanted them to. He had most definitely flipped upside-down for the strange girl who lived in the lighthouse, and he was perfectly fine with that. He only hoped she felt the same way about him.

She folded out an old padded quilt for them to sit on and leaned back against the dresser, taking his hand again seemingly without thought. He tried not to think about how nice it felt to hold her hand, but he had no interest in letting go.

Ash focused on the sea. Her small glance toward him made his heart flutter. "You never told me your name."

"Oh!" His mind scrambled. It took a moment for him to remember his own name. "I'm sorry. I guess that helps for you to trust me, too, doesn't it? My name is Finn."

She grinned and his stomach did a little flip-flop. "Finn? Like a fish's fin?"

He laughed. "Yeah... like a fish's fin."

Ash trailed a finger on the back of his hand. Finn thought he could die right there and be happy.

"The water was so high last night I remember being glad I couldn't see any ships. You could have drowned out there last night, Finn. That's just awful. I've read about that happening before."

He blinked and gave a laugh. "You've read... about drowning?"

She nodded with enthusiasm. "I've read about many terrible things. There's a whole handbook for the lighthouse workers who live here. It warns about the dangers of drowning, especially during a storm. It's why I never set foot in the water. I don't dare. It's too dangerous. Bad things happen to people if they set foot in the water."

"You realize we're on an island, don't you?"

She sighed.

Finn scooted closer to her. "I promise the ocean can be wonderful, too. It doesn't have to be frightening. Not everybody who goes out on the water drowns. If you stay near the shore where there are calmer waters, you'll probably be fine."

It was her turn to laugh. "Probably. I like that." Ash dragged a worn pillow over to put behind them. "You can share with me if you want." She grabbed a nearby blanket and pulled it up over them.

Finn looked between the pillow and the blanket, and realization dawned. "You sleep up here?"

"Every night."

He furrowed his brows and pursed his lips. "Aren't the beds downstairs more comfortable? I saw you have them all made up for us."

She didn't respond. Instead, she pulled the fluffy blanket up to her chin, her gaze fixed on the waters outside and the endlessly rotating light that illuminated the dark island and the waters.

Finn sighed and bit his lips with worry. It felt wrong to curl up under the blanket with this girl, whom he barely knew, whom he had only met hours ago. He looked at the door that led downstairs. A heavy metal latch secured the door, not to lock him in, but to keep something out.

Ash was clearly afraid of something coming through. That made him nervous. He thought back to the red door below.

"Ash... are we alone on the island?"

She didn't answer, but looked up at him with dark eyes and a stern expression. Like she could convey the seriousness of the situation going on downstairs without saying a word. It was uncanny.

"Get comfortable already." It wasn't a request, but a demand.

He gave a resigned sigh. So much for him trying to figure out anything. He pulled the blanket up, feeling anxious about laying beside her like this, beside a girl he didn't know very well. She pushed the blanket up to his chin like she had done for herself. Then she snuggled down under the blanket and returned her gaze to the sea.

"This is the best way to watch, and the best spot to sleep," she said.

Another heavy burst of wind came, vibrating the windows of the lighthouse. Down below, the whistling of it seeped into the cracks and crannies of the building. There were holes all through the place, just like trying to understand Ash. No matter what he said, she refused to give him answers. And the more he pushed, the more ridiculous he felt about even asking.

He wasn't sure what was going on here or why they were hiding at the top of the lighthouse. But he knew he didn't like whatever was going on with the red door downstairs. He had to trust Ash. He had no other choice. He also knew he was falling for her.

He got comfortable beneath the blanket, and pulled off the blue flannel and the belt to toss them aside. At least the oversized pants and undershirt were comfortable to sleep in.

"Ash?" he asked.

"Mmm?" she grunted as though being pulled from a deep sleep, but her eyes were wide open.

"Why did you bolt the door? Not the front door downstairs, but this one?" It was a roundabout question that addressed both doors. But maybe it would be easier for her to answer.

She glanced at him, annoyance in her eyes. "You ask a lot of questions."

"Sorry, I'm just curious."

"Just go to sleep. Stop being curious about everything already. Can't you just relax?"

If only it was that easy. He gave a small smile as the ocean crashed against the rocks, tossing spray high against the stone walls of the lighthouse and even landing a few drops on the glass windows. Any time he was told to stop being curious, it only made him more curious.

"Hey, Ash?"

"What?" she groaned.

"Thank you for helping me today. You saved my life."

She was silent a moment before answering. "You're welcome. I wouldn't have done it if I had known how many questions you would ask."

He chuckled at that. She was definitely strange, but at least she had a sense of humor.

Ash turned over, putting her back to him. "Go to sleep, you nosy boy."

The wind picked up again, howling as it drove against the lighthouse. When he closed his eyes, he could feel the entire building vibrate with nature's fury.

His headache returned with a pounding insistence in his temples. He furrowed his brows against it as sleep beckoned to him. His belly was full and his body ached.

He dreamed of dusty libraries inhabited by a beautiful girl with dark eyes and a beguiling smile. She kept trying to talk to him. He could see her mouth moving. But he couldn't make out what she was saying.

All he heard was the roar of the monster outside, demanding to be let in.

Part III:

No Past and No Future

7

LOST WANDERERS

WHEN FINN AWOKE, HE WAS WRAPPED IN a blanket. His face was covered against the glaringly bright sun shining through the giant glass windows. It was like he was living in a giant aquarium. Too warm, he struggled to kick off the blanket. He peeked around the bright room, his gaze drawn to the calm waters of the sea. What a beautiful sight. He could get used to waking up like this, seeing the ocean without being in the middle of it. Rubbing at his eyes and dragging a hand through his salt-encrusted hair, Finn felt comforted looking out over the ocean.

Steady blue waves stretched out to the horizon. The sky was a brilliant blue that perfectly complemented the deep ocean waters below. This would be a perfect day to go out on the water if he had a boat.

It was hard to imagine days ago he was fighting for his life on those same waters. Nothing about it felt real. It was a terrible nightmare that had happened to someone else, not him. But his lingering aches and sunburns reminded him it hadn't been all in his head. He tested out his arms, his neck, and lightly investigated the burns on his face. It wasn't nearly as painful as it had been the day before. He had slept a long time, but clearly he had needed it to recover. He hadn't felt like he was fully himself or even fully awake, until he got a full night's sleep and a full meal in his stomach. It was like he had to cocoon for a while until he could finally emerge as his proper self again.

Finn yawned and stretched, his shoulders and back popping from spending the night on a wooden floor with only a thin mattress for support. How did Ash manage it every night?

Because she was afraid of something. The thought came to him unbidden. He thought of the latched door and how she had gestured for him to come into this glass room without speaking a single word.

Last night might as well have been a dream. Waking up surrounded by oil lanterns, climbing those metal steps, peeking into empty bedrooms, and the howling wind outside. Not to mention how something shook the front door on its hinges. A knot of worry formed in his throat and he swallowed it down. Ash had silenced him when he spoke to her. She had wanted them to keep quiet until they came in here with the lantern.

Something was going on here, though he wasn't sure

what. Ash knew more than she was letting on, but clearly insisted on keeping him in the dark. Any time he had asked questions, she deflected. What did she know? What was the secret of the lighthouse on the shore and the tiny, rocky island it inhabited? He had to find out, if for no other reason than to ease his worries.

He pulled his gaze away from the sea and spotted a plate of rosemary bread, a glass of water, and a pile of fresh clothes Ash had left for him. A bucket sat beside it with a slab of soap and a washcloth.

He chuckled. One minute, Ash was keeping secrets from him, the next, she was leaving him clothes and food. Of all the enigmas about this place, Ash confused him the most. She lived here alone, but said it wasn't her lighthouse. Drowning in the ocean was something she had read about, though she lived on an island surrounded by the sea. She slept on the floor when there were beds downstairs for both of them, and pressed a finger to his lips to keep him from asking more questions.

The memory of her touch came back to him. How gentle it was. The softness of it. He pursed his lips to push away the memory, and swallowed down the confusion in his heart. He didn't know much about her, but she was kind. Kindness was more valuable than gold after the hell he had survived. But he couldn't deny the feeling in his stomach at the thought of her, the way he held his breath when she touched his lips, or the nervousness he felt laying down beside her. He was falling for her, that much was certain. But was it smart to fall for a girl like Ash?

He turned to the enormous beacon in the center of the room. Its light had been snuffed out and its rotation stopped after its long vigil overnight. He walked around the room in a full circle, but Ash was nowhere to be found. But nobody was here, just the two of them and the lighthouse.

He locked the door first, even though he still felt like he was on display surrounded by all the windows. He didn't think he could handle it though, if Ash walked in on him half naked. The water was still warm in the bucket, so he stripped off the clothes he had worn overnight and sponged down. He hadn't realized how much grime was on his skin from the storm and the ocean. And the bruises. He could only see a few of them, but they were dark blue and tender to the touch. He washed those gingerly, trying not to put any pressure on them. The entire ordeal had beaten him up more than he liked to admit. No wonder he had slept so long. He washed out his hair in the bucket, feeling like he could actually separate the pieces of his hair again. The water was dark by the time he was done, but he felt so much better being clean. Using a dry part of the cloth to dry his body, he then wiped down any places where he spilled, mindful to be as tidy as he could.

The clothes were once again too big for him, but Finn used the same belt to tie up his pants. The underpants at least fit better this time. He rolled up his sleeves and his pant legs so they wouldn't trip him, especially with that enormous staircase to climb down. A fierce hunger took him and he downed the bread and water in a few bites. He didn't used to have a hunger like that before the ship-wreck, but now he was starving whenever hunger came. He picked up the bucket and dishware, and headed for the stairs, careful to balance everything.

The stairwell seemed even longer when he was carrying something breakable. And balancing the bucket of water in his opposite hand was a challenge on the metal steps. Ash must have superpowers to have brought them upstairs. Somehow, he brought everything down without dropping a thing. He wanted to brag about it, but the kitchen was empty. All he found was a pot of something that smelled like delicious corn simmering on the stove. That was strange. No doors had been open upstairs, and he didn't hear any sounds from the rooms. Had Ash gone out? He had walked most of the island coming here. Where had she gone?

"Ash?" he called, but heard no answer.

That wasn't good. He thought of the metal door rattling on its hinges the night before, as if someone had wanted inside, wanted to reach them. His heart pounded in his chest, but he told himself to calm down. He had just gotten here. There was no need to panic... yet. He put the dirty dishes into the sink and put the bucket near the door before calling out again.

"Ash?"

Still no response. Could she be in trouble? That was his actual fear. What if it wasn't just the two of them on the island? She hadn't exactly said they were the only people last night. She had been cagey about it, didn't want to answer the question straight out. So were they alone or not?

No. He shook his head. He was jumping to conclusions. He needed to keep a cool head. His pulse still raced as he turned the handle of the front door.

It was unlocked.

THE EARLY AFTERNOON sun glared in his eyes, assaulting his senses for a few seconds. He held up a hand to shield his face from it and blinked to clear his vision.

No monster stood at the door, no threat or danger. It was a normal, beautiful day. A warm breeze came off the ocean, swaying the tall pine trees, creating the high-pitched white noise of the wind moving through the thousands of pine needles. The scent of sea foam wafted by, but Finn didn't let it distract him. Beautiful days could unfurl to stormy skies.

He cupped his hands around his mouth and called out. "Ash?"

His voice echoed into the forest, lost against the splash of ocean spray on the rocky cliffs. The pine trees continued to sway unperturbed. He scanned the forest for movement, looking for her to come out, but there was nothing. The world stood still as Finn's heart thundered in his chest. This was surely the time to panic.

His mind cycled through all the potential possibilities. Ash could have gone out to the beach and fallen into the water. Or maybe she'd been taken by whatever tried to get into the lighthouse last night. Or she was hurt somewhere and he would never know.

No... he couldn't lose her. He couldn't lose someone like that. Not again. Even just considering it made his hands shake at his sides and his chest tighten up. Even if she was a strange girl he barely knew, he couldn't handle losing someone again without completely falling apart.

"Are all boys so noisy?" Her curt voice came from his side.

Ash came around from the side of the lighthouse, stepping around overgrown bushes. She was wearing a plain old-fashioned blue dress with a white apron around her waist. There was no mirth in her eyes, just annoyance.

The relief that washed over him made Finn put a hand to his chest. He couldn't speak for a moment as he pulled himself together, feeling silly and embarrassed for panicking at all. He licked his lips and let out a shaky sigh, with one hand gripping the concrete wall of the building. It was the only thing keeping his knees from giving out beneath him.

"Don't do that, please! You scared me."

"I scared *you*?" she arched an eyebrow at him. "You're the one screaming into the forest."

He gave a small smile at that. Her strange sense of humor was like a calming balm to his nerves. He had been thinking some monster had taken her. He had gone from looking for her one second, to immediately assuming she was dead somewhere. What was wrong with him? He needed to calm down. There was no need to panic every time something didn't work out the way he expected.

She walked away from him and he watched her weed her garden, tossing the weeds into a pile closer to the forest. She tended to a large rosemary bush, pinching off some sprigs that she placed into her apron, holding it up in front of her as a sort of cloth bowl. It was a very normal thing to do. Watching her work was oddly calming.

"Where were you?" he asked, finally getting proper hold of his nerves and his voice.

"I just went around the side, not far. Cat needed attention. After you screamed, I had to calm him down again."

"Cat?" He blinked. At her feet, partially hidden by the rosemary bush and her dress was a fluffy white cat.

Ash squatted down to pet him and the cat furiously marked her fingers with his fluffy cheeks. He was big, maybe large enough to be related to a Maine Coon. He wound around Ash's legs as she worked, shaking his tail with excitement.

All the worries in Finn's heart melted as he watched the cat show such complete adoration for her. He crouched down and put out a hand for the cat as an introduction.

"You have a cat?" he asked. It was an obvious question, but he couldn't think of what else to say.

The cat hurried over to him, bouncing his fluffy tail

behind him, eager for pets. The cat marked his face so hard against Finn's fingers he could feel the cat's teeth. Finn couldn't help but smile.

"He's not my cat," Ash said. "He lives here. You and I are his guests, so you had best be polite."

The cat continued to rub his face all over Finn's hands, purring so hard his sides fluffed out with the intensity. It was hard to be anxious when a purring cat demanded so much love.

"What's his name?" he asked.

She narrowed her eyes at him. "I told you. It's Cat."

He climbed to his feet, wiping his hands on the back of his pants. "You can't call a cat Cat. That's just wrong."

"Why not? That's what he is. He's a cat, so why can't I call him that?"

Finn shook his head and strolled over beside her. She had moved on to a basil plant, plucking some of its large leaves for her basket, but the stems were a little long. She didn't look at him, but a flush filled her cheeks like she was embarrassed. Maybe she couldn't come up with a good name, or maybe she had nobody around to share the name with, so hadn't given the cat a real name yet. That was weird, though. Finn didn't know anybody who would call a cat just Cat. Half the fun of having pets around was getting to come up with funky names for them. Why didn't Ash jump at the chance to name him too?

"Most people just think it's a mean thing to do to a pet," Finn said.

She paused, readjusting her apron before meeting his

gaze. "I'm not trying to be mean to him. He's my friend. I've just always called him Cat. I don't know why that's so bad."

He shook his head and shoved his hands into his pockets. "No, it's not bad exactly. It just sounds like you don't like him much. He needs a better name, but he's your kitty. You ought to name him."

She let out a long sigh and leaned back down to her plant. Finn arched his eyebrows. "Or... maybe you don't want to give him a different name?"

"I'm terrible at picking out names. Just come up with one yourself, if he needs it so badly."

"Okay, I can do that." He rubbed a hand on the back of his neck. "A name for a big white, fluffy cat. I'm sure I can come up with something."

The cat, as if knowing Finn was talking about him, came over and wound figure-eights around his legs like he had done to Ash earlier. It was incredibly cute. The cat had very long hair around his face. Some of his whiskers were so long they were almost double the width of his body. It was as if someone had made a cat and then drawn on ridiculously large whiskers on the poor guy.

"Why don't we call him Whiskers?" Finn suggested.

She shrugged. "Is that a better name?"

He grinned. "Not by much, I know. But it's better than Cat. Anything is better than that."

"Okay, Whiskers it is then." She gave him a little smile, and it warmed him more than the sunlight did.

Finn leaned down to pet Whiskers again and the cat gave a little high-pitched trill. "He's probably hungry. I doubt there's a ton to eat on this island. Hardly any bugs. Maybe the birds are too smart for you, huh, buddy? Maybe there's some canned meat we could give him. Where is all the food stored?"

"Inside. I can show you." She led the way back into the lighthouse. Whiskers followed close beside Finn's heel as if he knew where they were going. Ash dropped the herbs in a basket by the sink before heading up the stairs.

"You have a whole system down to keep this place running, don't you?" Finn asked.

"I have to. The only way to eat is to have a system for cooking. I enjoy having the herbs outside because they add some flavor. Though the basil won't last for much longer, I'm afraid. I use it too often."

Finn followed her up the stairs. As kind as Ash had been to him, sometimes she seemed a little off. She acted like she had never been around cats before, or even knew what to name one. In his experience, kids loved getting to name animals as soon as they could talk. So why was it such a burden for her? Then again, she had befriended Whiskers and visited him often. So much that Whiskers clearly loved her. The more Finn found out about Ash, the less she made any sense.

They went up a few flights of stairs before Ash stopped at a lonely squat door hidden in shadows. Finn hadn't even seen it the last two times he had passed by. She stepped inside, lit an oil lantern by the door with some matches she picked up nearby, then turned the flame up high. Light spilled across the windowless room, illuminating a large pantry filled with crates and boxes.

Finn stepped inside and his jaw dropped. He had never seen so many cans and bottles—all stacked to the ceiling. He grabbed a giant can of corn and flipped it over. Its expiration date still had two years left.

"These are almost new," he said, replacing the can back on the stack. "Someone bought a ton of food to stay here. And recently, too. That's so weird."

"The ones in the front are newer, but the ones behind them seem older. I've tossed out a few that I've found already." She reached up for a stack against the wall. "We have canned chicken and canned tuna. Which one would Whiskers prefer, do you think?"

He smirked. "The tuna, definitely. I wouldn't give it to him every day, but once a week maybe. But today's a special day. He just got a new name. I think that's a good reason to party it up some."

She nodded, though her brow furrowed a little like she was confused. But she didn't elaborate on it. "We have a bunch of tuna and chicken in here, so that's good. We need to feed him every day, you said?"

He almost laughed, but noticed the confused look she gave him. "Yes, every day. Mostly chicken with some tuna sprinkled in, too."

She nodded. "We can do that. They don't expire for a long time, too, so we have plenty of food for him to last as long as possible."

Finn pursed his lips and shoved his hands into his pockets. Ash spoke like she was going to live here forever, as if she would never leave, or ever want to leave. But clearly she feared something. The island had a limited food supply and clearly never had visitors. Why was she so invested in staying? Why wasn't she trying to leave? There was nothing for her here.

Of course, if he asked her directly, she would probably sidestep the question like she had so many of his questions the night before. He had to dance around it to see what he could figure out about her, and about the island itself.

"Ash, did your father stock all of this food here? Was he a lighthouse worker?"

"No," she said in a flat tone, then stepped toward the doorway.

"Huh. Was your mother? Surely one of them brought you here."

She paused in the doorway, looking rattled by the question. "No," she stated firmly before quickly heading down the stairs again.

Finn cursed under his breath. He blew out the oil lantern and made sure Whiskers was following Ash down the stairs before he closed the door to the storage room. It was impossible to gather any kind of information without upsetting her. He really was trying not to, though, and it was frustrating. Every question he came up with made her almost angry.

"Ash, wait. It had to be something like that. Someone had to have brought you here. There's no way to make it to the island otherwise. Unless you took like a helicopter ride to the lighthouse or something." He gave a nervous laugh.

She was already in the kitchen, spilling a can of tuna into a bowl while Whiskers whined at her feet. She didn't even smile. "You didn't take a helicopter. You floated ashore."

He stood by the counters, breathless from hurrying down the stairs. Ash wasn't even winded.

"Yeah, after surviving a horrible shipwreck. Surely that didn't happen to you too, did it?"

Ash didn't respond, instead she dropped the empty can in the trash bin, still averting her gaze. She didn't like him asking so many questions, but he had to know something. He hated being kept in the dark like this. He wanted to understand this place. He wanted to better understand her, but she put up barricades every time he tried.

"How did you get here then?" he asked.

She scrunched up her brow. Either she was focusing really hard on feeding Whiskers or she was angry again. He dragged a hand through his damp hair. Clearly, this wasn't going to work. If he kept pushing her, she would shut down completely. And who knew when he would find anything out. He decided on a different approach.

"Look, I'm not trying to be a jerk. I just want to know more about you, that's all. We're stuck here together, at least for a little while, until someone comes to find us or we find a way back to the mainland. What's the harm in getting to know you better?"

She put the bowl down on the floor, and Whiskers

immediately buried his face in the tuna. She washed her hands and dried them on a thin, worn tea cloth before turning to him. "What if there is nothing more to tell? What if there is no satisfactory answer to your endless questions?"

He gazed at her, not quite understanding. "What do you mean?"

She held out her hands, gesturing around the small kitchen and opposite sitting room. "What if this is it, Finn? I have no secrets to share, no wisdom to give, and no terrible stories to unfurl. What you see is all I can share with you. I can't even tell you where I came from because I don't know. I have always been here. Cat and I... er, Whiskers and I have that in common. We're both lost wanderers with no past and no future. We live in the present, in the day to day. Our lives are the island and the lighthouse. They're part of us and we're part of them. That's it."

Her eyes shone with unshed tears and Finn felt bad for bringing any of this up. Maybe she was right. Maybe he did ask too many questions.

"I've always been the girl who lived in the light-house, and I will probably haunt these grounds until I'm gray." Tears streaked down her pale, freckled cheeks. "This is simply who I am. And if you're not happy about that, I'm sorry, I can't help you. This place is all I know and I do my best to take care of it, to keep going, because there is nothing else. There is nothing other than this place. I have no home other than the lighthouse."

Finn bit his lip. "Don't talk like that. You had to come

from somewhere. You didn't just appear on this island one day. Everyone has a past."

Ash gave a bitter laugh and wiped at her eyes. "It's easy for you to say that. You know who your mother and father are. You know where you come from, where you're going, and what you want to do with your life. It's not so easy for me. I don't have an identity to call my own, Finn. I don't know who I am. For all I know, I could have sprung out of the sea foam like Aphrodite." She laughed and slipped her hands into her black curls, gripping the sides of her head in an alarming manner. "Or maybe I died a long time ago, flung myself off the rocky cliff, and now haunt this island for the rest of my days." Her dark eyes bore into him as she put a hand to her chest. "Maybe I'm a ghost, Finn. Did you ever think of that?"

He stood there in shock, not knowing what to do or say. This wasn't at all how he had expected this to go, and he certainly had never meant to hurt the person who saved his life.

"I'm sorry," he whispered.

"No, you're not! You just want answers. And you'll do whatever it takes to get them!" Tears poured down Ash's cheeks and sobs took hold as she buried her face in her hands.

Finn hurried over to her, wrapping her in his arms and pulling her into a desperate hug. Part of him was worried she would be angry at him for this, for holding her without asking first, but she leaned against him and cried hard into his shoulder.

"I'm sorry," he said again. "I shouldn't have brought this up."

His shirt grew wet from her tears as he rubbed her back. He felt bad. This wasn't what he had intended, but he had pushed and pushed, ignoring the signs she was in distress. He had answers now, but that wasn't how he had wanted to go about getting them. He had messed up big time and it would take work to regain her trust, if he ever did.

After several minutes of sobs and sniffling, Ash pulled away. Her eyes were red and puffy. An abyss of sadness spread across her face. Finn wanted to help her. He wanted to take away the pain, so she never had to feel it again. But he wasn't even sure where to start. How could he help the girl at the lighthouse find her past again? How could he help her live a life in the future and the past, not stuck in an endless loop of the present?

"I'm really am sorry," he whispered. "I didn't mean to hurt you."

"It's not your fault. You're lost, just like Whiskers and me. You have a right to know where you are, and who you're living with. I wish I could tell you more to ease your worries." She reached down to pet along Whiskers' back. The white fluffy cat was still so engrossed in his food, he didn't even pause. "And I'm sorry, Whiskers, for calling you Cat for so long. I didn't know it was mean. I just didn't know I was supposed to give you a name."

Finn leaned back against the edge of the countertop and watched her.

There was no way he would ever see his father again.

It was a terrible truth, but one he eventually had to accept. He couldn't live in the past forever. He'd had time to think about it while he was being tossed around like a balloon in the storm. He'd had more time to think last night as he lay beside Ash. His father was gone. He couldn't change what happened that day, even if his mind wanted to go down all the thousands of roads of alternatives and potential possibilities. There was no point. He couldn't have done anything different to save his father, without putting his own life at risk. All it would have done was put two bodies in the water instead of one.

Now, there was Ash. She was different. Maybe he could help her. There might not be any chance of her recovering her old memories, sure, but maybe he could help her build a better future. Something more than thinking she was a ghost haunting a lighthouse. He decided he was going to get them off the island together, and maybe even bring Whiskers with them. Finn considered himself a fairly decent sailor and crabber. If they could get off the island somehow, they might just have a chance. This wasn't a deserted island in the middle of nowhere, it had a massive lighthouse. Somebody had put a lot of money into this place and stocked it with food fairly recently. That meant there had to be a way to escape. He just had to find it.

Finn glanced down to Whiskers. "You know, Whiskers can't tell us where he came from, but we know we're going to help him from here on out. He's going to be taken care of because he's with us." He looked at Ash, who met his gaze. "And now that you're with me, I'll make sure you're okay, too."

She stared at him for a long moment. Then she leaned over to put a hand on his shoulder and planted a kiss on his cheek. "Thank you," she said. "Of all the shores you could have washed up on, I'm grateful it was mine."

She got to her feet and climbed up the stairs, clearly off to tackle another task on her endless list.

Finn stayed rooted to the spot, unable to will his legs to move. His cheek burned where she had kissed him and his stomach flip-flopped. He reached a hand up to feel the spot, and felt a dorky grin on his face.

"I'm glad, too."

8
THE OLD PATH

FINN FOUND A FAUCET OUTSIDE, ONE where he had to crank it to get water to come out. He made sure Ash was upstairs first before fetching the towel and soap from the bucket. Then he took off his clothes, using the clean water and bar of soap to properly take away the rest of the grime. The sponge bath earlier had helped, but he had needed fresh water to truly feel clean. He had grime and sand in places he preferred not to mention.

His mind lingered on the kiss Ash had given him and his cheek still burned where she had touched him. She had bewitched him in a wonderful way. It was one of the reasons he wanted to make sure he was properly clean. He wanted to make sure he didn't smell anywhere if she decided to kiss him again. He gave a dorky grin at the very thought of it, then shook it away, trying to focus on the real problem.

If they hoped to get off the island, they would need a boat. Or at least something that would float well enough on the mercurial ocean waters of Leekston. If they had a sturdy enough boat, he was pretty sure he could navigate back to the mainland. It wasn't a perfect plan, but it was a start. And if he wanted to find a good boat, he needed to scour the island. If someone had built a lighthouse here, then there had to be ships around of some kind. Especially if no one had come searching for the real lighthouse worker who was supposed to be here.

Finn used the small towel from earlier to dry off. It was slow, but the warm ocean breeze helped. When he pulled his clothes back on, he felt much more comfortable in his skin. The fabric on his shoulder was still a little damp from Ash's tears, and the feeling pulled him back to his task. Back to his promise to help her. He had a job to do, even if he wasn't entirely sure how he was going to do it.

He washed the towel with soap, then hung it to dry on a branch next to the faucet. Then he poured out the old water from the bucket and left the soap inside by the door. Satisfied he had properly cleaned up, he headed toward the thick pines at the front of the lighthouse. It wasn't really clear where he should start looking, since he had to examine the entire coastline of the island for anything he could use. He paused for a moment, trying to figure out where to look first, when a familiar meow caught his attention.

Whiskers bounded up to him, his purrs so loud he almost sounded like a miniature vehicle. Finn grinned at his enthusiasm.

"Hey buddy, care to join me on an adventure?" Finn bent down to pet his soft head. The kitty pranced in place. "Though I bet you know this island better than I do. I bet you could show me all the highlights, huh? Maybe you should be the one to lead."

Whiskers gave his tail a little tremble of excitement then headed in the opposite direction Finn had been facing. He was headed down the path opposite the one that Finn had taken from the beach after coming ashore. Finn laughed and shook his head.

"Are you sure, buddy?"

But Whiskers wasn't waiting for him. He trotted down the path with the confidence of a cat who had done it many times before.

Finn was a little torn. To his right was the path that led down to where he had washed ashore, and where he could get the inner tube he came in on. Some parts of it might even be salvageable. He was thinking of that tiny whistle, for example. To the left was the path Whiskers chose, and he was already several yards ahead.

"I know what's down there," he said, nodding to the right. The memories of bobbing in the ocean, wave after wave trying to drown him, it all came back to him in an instant and he put a hand to his chest to ease the rising panic. The sun baking his skin under the enormous sky and his tears mixing with the salt water. At the time, he hadn't been sure if he would live to see another day. And he was almost certain he would never set foot on dry land again. He could picture that bright orange inner tube sitting on the beach like a slain animal, representing the death he had almost met.

An urgent meow pulled him from his thoughts. He looked down. It was Whiskers. He had come back for him. The little cat stood up on his back legs, his front paws propped up on Finn's leg. He was pushing his whole fuzzy face into the palm of Finn's hand, whining. Finn swallowed down the dryness in his throat and properly petted Whisker's face, letting the cat drag his cheeks and tiny teeth against his fingers. His hand was shaking. When had that started?

He gave Whiskers an appreciative rub behind the ears. "Thank you, pal. You're right, I don't need to go down that path again, do I?" His voice was cracked and small, as if a part of him was still on that ocean out there. He took a deep breath. Whiskers dropped to all fours again and turned down his path, glancing back at him as if making sure he would follow him this time.

Finn gave a shaky laugh. "Yeah, that's fair. You're right, buddy. Let's take your way instead. I'm not sure—" His throat closed up, and it took a moment for him to talk again, though his voice was more shaky. "I'm not sure if I'm ready to take that old path yet."

With more energy in his step than Finn certainly had, Whiskers hurried down the left path. His long white tail looked more like a feather duster as it bounced along behind him. Finn couldn't help but crack a smile as he followed on wobbly legs.

The island wasn't that big. He could easily find his way back if Whiskers got him lost. He glanced back to the lighthouse quickly getting hidden by the thick pine trees. At least, he hoped he could.

THEY WALKED for what felt like a solid half hour. Finn's legs were sore, muscles still healing from the ocean's beating were trying to keep up with being on land. Some of his bruises pulsed with pain, too, which wasn't fun. Whiskers kept turning around to make sure Finn was still there, as if he expected him to wander off into the woods like an easily distracted kitten. It was pretty cute, honestly.

The farther they walked, the more the tremors in his hands calmed until he felt like himself again. He had never understood that kind of panicked reaction he had heard about until he faced it. It first hit him when he couldn't find Ash. An irrational panic took hold. Then again, he had experienced the panic at the fork in the paths. The mere thought of going down to see the inner tube again had set his whole body shaking, terrified. Like seeing the inner tube meant all the baggage that came with it. Sure, there might be pieces he could salvage, but was it worth the mental turmoil it would do to him? Ash needed him to keep a cool head, to focus on the big picture here. So here he was, following a cat instead. That was way more logical.

The island was larger than he expected. Even from the top of the lighthouse, he'd noticed places hidden from sight behind the thick pine trees. Abruptly, the path narrowed. The trees grew thicker here and crowded the path. Sunlight passed only dimly through branches heavy with pine needles. It was like the forest had dipped to twilight. Weeds grew up at odd intervals in the middle of the path. It wasn't taken very often, unlike the other path he'd taken from the beach when he washed up. He wondered if Ash ever came down this way or if she avoided it. He could understand that. The darkness here was intense, even in the middle of the day.

Whiskers kept leading the way, the bounce in his tail not diminished by the thinning path or looming pine trees. The cat seemed to be in his element here and it was probably a good hunting ground for him. Finn imagined lots of birds and mice would make excellent prey here to a cat that could easily see with this limited light. Finn didn't have that benefit. He was getting concerned.

"Whiskers? I sure hope you know where we're going, buddy."

Sure, he could have turned around and gone back. The path back to the lighthouse would be easy enough to follow, but then he would have to face the other path and that damn inner tube again. He knew he couldn't do it. He wasn't ready for that. Maybe someday. A small voice in the back of his mind wondered if he would ever truly be ready for that again.

He shivered. It was colder here, though it shouldn't be. It was midday, probably around noon, if not a little later. But the sun didn't penetrate far here. Finn folded his arms to keep warmer as he continued following Whiskers down the overgrown path.

Down a short hill, Finn caught the scent of the ocean. Relief washed over him and a smile tugged at his lips. It was an unsettling path, sure, but Whiskers hadn't led him astray. He knew where he was going after all. The pines turned to thick grasses and sunlight glinted off ocean waves. He squinted at the brightness of it, adjusting from the dim forest light. Over the ocean waves, he heard an odd sound, like something hitting a hard surface over and over again. It reminded him of the door from last night. Finn jogged ahead to catch up with Whiskers, who kept a much faster pace for such a tiny little cat.

The grasses broke away to soft sand, the kind people turned into hotel fronts and public beaches. His feet sank into it and the feeling brought calm to his soul. The ocean spread out before him, inviting and calm. He didn't feel anxiety here. No tightness in his chest or horrible images filling his thoughts. He was afraid he would after everything he had been through. But no, not even the damn shipwreck could take his joy of the ocean away from him.

Finn took a deep breath of the warm, salty air and let it fill his lungs before huffing it out again. He felt like a kid, going out to the ocean with Dad, taking in all that the ocean offered. He pulled off his shoes and left them near the grass line. Digging his toes into the sun-warmed sand brought so much joy, he laughed. Tears came to his eyes, but not out of sorrow. They were tears of joy.

The beach was still beautiful. The ocean was still majestic. His hands didn't shake at his sides. A deep fear was down in his heart of the ocean ahead of him, but it didn't hold a candle to the beauty of it all. He was so grateful as he wiped tears from his cheeks.

"I wasn't sure if I would ever enjoy the beach again, Whiskers. I wasn't sure..." He nodded in confirmation, sniffing and shoving his hands in his pockets. "Thank you, buddy. You knew what I needed more than I did."

He looked around for the white cat and eventually spotted him sitting farther up the beach. White fur fluttered from the ocean breeze and the cat looked back at him, eyes narrowed from the wind and the sand. His tail twitched impatiently. Finn laughed and trotted over to him, his feet sinking into the soft sand as he went.

"We've got further to go, huh?"

Whiskers twitched his ears. He wasn't nearly as relaxed as Finn was, which was strange. He had been so confident on the way over here, so calm and collected. A cat used to hunting for prey was surely used to scavenging for fish that washed up on shore or hunting sea birds overhead. Perhaps the cat knew something he didn't, and that wasn't a comfortable thought.

Finn went to the water and let the waves wash over his feet and seep between his toes. He had to test himself, but that also didn't panic him. It was relaxing. Good. The storm had taken his father, but it hadn't taken his love for the ocean. That was a small gift, but it meant a lot to him. After everything he had been through, he hadn't been sure if he could enjoy anything about the ocean again. At least he could take in all this beauty without falling to pieces. That helped more than he could say.

He turned back to his friend. "Alright, Whiskers. What do you want to show me?"

Whiskers gave a little trill before heading down the beach.

Finn squinted up ahead. Farther along the beach on the shoreline stood some kind of wooden structure. It extended out to the dry land, covered the beach, and extended over the water. He held a hand up to shield his eyes from the sun. What was it?

His eyes went wide as Finn gasped.

With a speed he hadn't known he possessed, he grabbed his shoes from the grass line, tossing sand all around him in his haste. Hopping on one foot, he pulled the shoes on one at a time. He ran for the wooden structure, his heart pounding in his chest. In the excitement, Whiskers ran alongside him as if it were a game.

But this was so much more than that. This was a way off the island. A way to get home. Finn knew exactly what it was: a dock with a little boat house attached. That meant he might find a boat inside.

9
SOMETHING SO BEAUTIFUL

As Finn and Whiskers drew closer, the sound of something smacking a hard object grew louder. The ocean still overwhelmed the sound, but it was clearer and clearer as they drew closer. Something was off about it, something he couldn't quite put his finger on. Something wooden and muffled. The building didn't seem entirely made of wood now that he could see it better. That made him confused. Finn had been around docks, boats, skiffs, and anglers all his life. He knew the normal sounds of an older wooden structure, the sounds boats could make when they were anchored. This was not a normal sound. Something was definitely wrong.

The boathouse was attached close to the water, and it was bigger than he had expected it to be. It could easily house two boats. Maybe he could find a seaworthy vessel here. Some kind of escape ship they could use to get home.

Whiskers found a crack in the wall and darted inside, his fluffy tail disappearing around the jagged edges.

Finn huffed. "Okay, show-off. Some of us can't get in quite that easy."

He climbed up on the dock warily, worried it might not be in the best condition, but it held his weight just fine. It was an old dock, but the ocean hadn't taken it apart yet. Some areas showed newer pieces of wood. Someone had made repairs on it, though he had no idea who had done it, or when.

The banging sound was loud here, almost as loud as the waves hitting the shoreline. It was so strange. He pushed back his nerves and turned to the front of the boathouse.

The door wasn't in the best shape. Too many storms had made it loose on its hinges. The thought of the noise from the front door of the lighthouse came to him again, the rattling of the metal against the hinges. Could someone have done that to this door? Either way, it was fortunate. Breaking and entering wasn't exactly Finn's forte. When he tried the handle, one of the hinges fell off and landed with a smack on the wooden deck.

He smirked. "Okay, fine I guess." He worked at the remaining hinge and lifted the door off the threshold, leaning it against the outer wall of the boathouse. Looking closer at the building, several places looked like someone had put in new boards, replacing old ones. More signs that someone had fixed up the place.

Someone cared enough about the structure to put in the sweat and work to maintain it, but who? Ash never came down here, so it couldn't have been her.

Darkness met him as he stepped inside. Again, his eyes had to adjust. Light streamed in between the wall boards of the boathouse, illuminating thick sand dust on everything. There was a boat, but part of the building had fallen and damaged the hull.

"Aw, come on!" he cried. He walked to the edge of the deck, crouching down to get a better look at the damaged boat. Sea water had gotten inside for who knew how long, making the boat partially sunk. The boards would all be warped by now, making it practically unusable with his limited skills. He kicked the side of the boat hull in frustration and it dipped up and down in the water.

A confused meow came from the boat as Whiskers poked his head out from behind one of the half-open windows of the boat.

"Oh my gosh, buddy, I'm so sorry!" He hurried over to the edge again. "I didn't know you were in there. Why are you in there?"

Whiskers shook water off and climbed back onto the deck of the boathouse. Finn braced the boat and stuck his head through the window Whiskers had emerged from. Inside were crates of canned supplies, now lost to the corrosive power of the sea. Up on a shelf, he spotted something actually useful.

A hard plastic pet carrier stood high above the ocean water. He had to work to pull it off the shelf at a weird angle and yank it out of the window, but eventually he got it out. A bell jingled inside and he spotted a cat collar.

"You belonged to someone, didn't you, Whiskers?"

The cat was too busy cleaning his wet fur to give him attention.

"Someone brought you all the way out here as a companion. Did something happen to them?"

Whiskers met his gaze with bright green eyes before turning to exit out his preferred hole in the wall. Finn sighed. "If only you could talk, pal, it would make this mystery a lot easier to solve."

He looked at the collar first, but it didn't have a tag. There was no name, no contact information, or anything. He sighed in frustration.

Then there was the cat carrier itself. If he was going to find a way off this island, he wasn't about to leave Ash or Whiskers behind. That meant they needed the carrier. Tipping it forward and shaking it dislodged a lot of the sand and grime out into a gross little pile on the deck. Then he spotted something between the cracks of the boards at his feet. Something was beneath the dock, floating separate from the boat.

"No way!" He put aside the carrier and grabbed an oar on the wall. Using it to leverage the floating piece out from under the dock, he worked it to the side and eventually he could pull it out. It was a yellow canoe with two seats and plenty of room to store a pet carrier.

"Yes! Oh my gosh, yes!" He pulled it out onto the deck. The ends had taken damage, and would probably need some patching, but that would be nowhere near the work to make the boat ocean-worthy. He propped it with the cat carrier against a wall of the boathouse. That ought to keep it from getting any more damaged by the intense storms.

A low, moaning meow caught his attention as he was about to leave. It wasn't the high-pitched trill Finn was used to hearing from Whiskers, or the whining sound when he was hungry. The deep, upsetting sound hit him right in the chest.

"Whiskers?" Finn hurried out the front door, but the cat's moaning cries continued. "Whiskers, what's wrong?"

He stepped out into the sunlight again, blinking in the garish afternoon light. He hurried to the side of the boathouse opposite from the one with the hole Whiskers used as an entrance. The cat stood on the short deck that wrapped around the boathouse, meowing down at the waves. He didn't even turn to look at him when Finn came around the corner.

The pounding noise was so loud here it put Finn even more on edge. Something struck at the legs of the boathouse under the water. The strike reverberated up his legs. Something seemed loose, or had fallen in from the roof of the boathouse.

The pit in his stomach told him otherwise.

Whiskers was staring at something, something that made him very upset. That wasn't normal for a cat. And Finn's gut feeling agreed.

He climbed over to the side of the boathouse to where Whiskers stood. He reached out for the cat, worried how he wasn't even looking up at him. "Buddy, come over h—"

He barely got the words out of his mouth when his foot slipped. It was bad enough the shoes were too big for him but the boards were dangerous. He lost all traction in an instant. Years of growing up on a boat meant he had developed fast reflexes, and they kicked in all at once.

He reached out away from his body toward the boathouse, grabbing hold of anything he could. His fingers wrapped around one of the poles that made up the legs of the boathouse, digging his fingernails into the weather-beaten wood as he grit his teeth. For a moment, he hung there, legs wrapped around the pole as something beneath him in the water repeatedly slammed against it. Each reverberation moved up his body. Finally, he pulled up onto all fours, cautious of the very perilous wood. He looked over his shoulder at a cluster of sharp rocks right where he had been about to fall. If his reflexes hadn't kicked in, he could be dead right now.

He climbed to his feet on dry boards, breathing hard and shaking from head to toe. His gaze repeatedly went to those rocks and the churning water that had almost taken him.

That's when he saw it.

Something pale and swollen bobbed into view beneath the waves, crashing up against the rocks. Finn gripped the pole with both hands and his breath caught in the back of his throat.

Bam!

Was it a fish? Maybe it was a canvas bag of supplies or something that had fallen and gotten caught in the rocks?

Bam!

No, that wasn't it. But his mind didn't want to admit what it really was. Finn held on tight as he leaned over the water, gripping the pole so hard his fingers blanched. The water here was murky, and it was hard to see anything through it. But something kept banging again and again. Beside him, Whiskers sat staring down into the water, not leaving his spot. Then a soggy, misshapen limb flopped up onto the rocks and Finn jumped back.

He counted two swollen sausage fingers and a thumb, along with two severed digits. It flopped back into the churning waters like a dead fish.

Bam!

Whiskers moaned sadly at his side.

It was a person. Someone who probably fell right where Finn almost had. Someone who wasn't lucky enough to catch themselves in time. They clocked their skull on the rocks and bled out, dying beneath the waves. Finn looked out at the ocean. This was a very rocky spot to have a dock, but also maybe too shallow for scavengers.

He put a hand to his mouth, mesmerized by the body moving like a ghost beneath the waves. A weight hit his gut as his stomach turned. This was probably the person who had stocked all the newer supplies at the lighthouse. This was the owner of Whiskers who had brought the cat to the island. They were the lighthouse worker.

Finn backed away on shaky legs. Then he turned and ran away from the boathouse, legs pumping fast as he stepped out onto the sand. He put his hands on his thighs and gulped down the salty air. He felt too warm and too cold all at once, and he couldn't get enough air in his lungs. This was too much. This wasn't fair.

First his father. Now this person. The nameless lighthouse worker and his poor cat standing vigil for the person he loved. Finn barked out a sad cry. He couldn't take any more death.

Light glinted off the ocean in the distance as the waves crashed against the shore. Finn shook his head against it. He loved the simple beauty of the ocean, but not like this. Not when it kept taking and taking, again and again.

How could something so beautiful steal so many lives?

Part IV:

A Promise

10

NOT THIS TIME

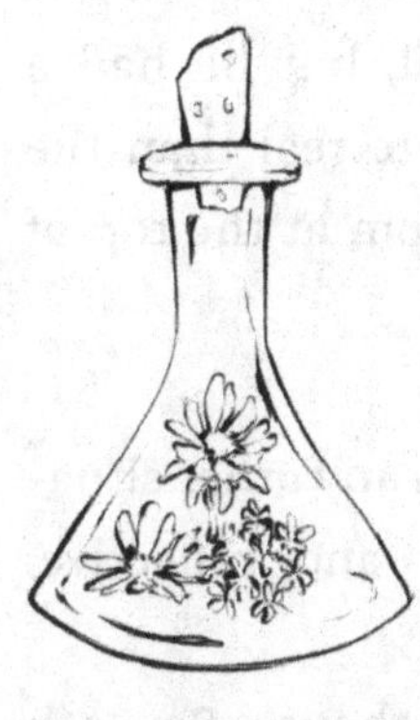

IT TOOK TOO LONG TO GET CONTROL again. Finn's hands wouldn't stop shaking and his stomach was in complete revolt. He paced back and forth on the beach, creating an oblong rivet in the sand. The sea came in and filled the hole he had created. Only when the water touched his feet did he finally stop, realizing the body was still slamming into the boathouse. And poor, sad Whiskers still paced near them, giving his sad calls.

The body. No, it was a person. Someone who had visited the island or came to manage the lighthouse. A person who had never expected their last few minutes to be slipping into the ocean, or for their body to be left to the whims of the sea for who knew how long. The

113

thought made him shiver and shake his head at the injustice of it all.

He turned back to the building, realizing with some alarm that he had been pacing for a long time. His feet hurt in the oversized shoes. The oversized shoes that could have belonged to the person underwater. Just like the pants, the shirt, and even the underwear he was wearing. Heat rose to his chest. For a moment, he felt nauseous, but pacing helped it to pass.

Across the sky, red and pink clouds were picturesque against the ocean beneath. The sun was setting he realized with numb alarm. But then he pushed down the worry. Ash was frightened of nightfall, but he had a corpse to deal with. That felt way more real than the nameless fears Ash had them hiding from at the top of the lighthouse.

No, not a corpse. *A person.*

The view was beautiful. The scene in any other situation would have made him relaxed and reflective. But now...

Whiskers sat on the edge of the boathouse. Beneath him, the body continued its endless beating against the wooden frame of the structure, insistent and angry. Like the person wanted him to notice it. Whiskers clearly had known where he was going when he came here. He intentionally had led Finn here. The cat gave another deep meow as he peered over the edge of the boathouse into the water. It gave Finn chills. This was probably Whisker's owner, someone who had brought the cat to the island in a cat carrier. Someone Whiskers loved enough to bring Finn all the way out here to the edge of the ocean to see. No... not just to see. *To help.*

Whiskers paced in front of the boathouse, letting out a sad whine. Not just sad at losing his previous owner, but let down by the boy who now took care of him, too. Finn's heart broke at the thought. He had to do something. It might not be what the person deserved—a proper burial surrounded by people who had loved them in life—but at least he could give them some closure. Anything besides being buffeted against the boathouse again and again like a rag doll. What a horrible end to a horrible death.

With renewed purpose, Finn went back to the boathouse and stepped inside the shadowy building. As the sun set in the distance, there were far more shadows than he liked. He had the dim thought he might come across whatever it was that had shaken the door to the lighthouse the night before. But no, he couldn't think about that now. He had a job to do. For Whiskers and for the lighthouse worker.

After his eyes grew accustomed to the gloom, he located the oars attached to the wall and pulled one of them down. It was tough. The handle had been jammed into the clasps that hung on the wall. A cloud of dust was his reward when it finally came loose. The oar was heavier than he expected and he struggled to regain his balance.

Back outside again, he carried it with both hands and headed toward the edge of the boathouse deck. Whiskers meowed non-stop. He was a smart cat and clearly had some idea what Finn was going to do. The cat hurried over, his white fluffy tail bouncing behind him and rubbed on Finn's legs, making figure eights around his feet. Then he hurried over to the edge where his previous owner had fallen.

"Stay back, buddy. I don't want either of us falling in, okay?" Finn nudged Whiskers gently with his leg. Finn had barely survived the fall himself. He couldn't imagine trying to get the cat out, too. Knowing his luck, he would probably get pulled down and Whiskers would climb his way out just fine.

With a final excited meow, Whiskers headed to the beach, swishing his tail back and forth expectantly in the sand.

This time Finn knew where the slippery boards were, so he straddled them carefully. From this angle, the sheen of mildew was clear on the wood, almost invisible from the splashing of ocean spray. That small microscopic mildew had meant death for the poor person. What a sad way to go.

Finn plunged the oar deep into the water. He could feel the hard rock and then the unnatural softness of the body stuck between the cracks. It was spongy, like a piece of bread left to soak for too long. His stomach turned, and a shudder tore through him, but he stayed focused. He hadn't been able to help his father, but he could help this person have a more honorable resting place. He started twisting and turning the body with the oar, trying to find leverage somewhere, searching blindly for some way to get it free from the rocks.

Sweat broke out on his forehead as he clenched his teeth. Between the heavy oar, the odd angle, and the worry he was only making things worse, this was more difficult than he expected.

The tide coming in shot big sprays of water up, soaking his clothes and spraying his face. He spat out salt water even as his eyes burned. The plastic smell of the life preserver came back to him in a flash, the memory trying to take over, to take him back to that horrible place out on the ocean. He felt helpless. There was no way he could do this. How could he hope to free this body stuck in these rocks for who knew how long? How could he expect to do this on his own?

The oar slipped in his hands a little and he almost lost his balance. But Finn planted his feet, bent his knees, and kept trying. This was no time to give in to doubt. He had to do this.

"Not this time," he said. "This time, I'm going to help!" He looked at the ocean waters that splashed up on his face again. "You can't keep him!"

With a cry, he shoved down the oar again, this time finding what felt like a weak point. He shifted the oar beneath the soft parts and felt it start to give. With one last roar, he pushed with all his might.

The oar snapped. His center of gravity tipped dangerously forward, but he shot out a hand and gripped the wooden pole that came up the side of the dock. Those reflexes from crabbing with his father really didn't disappear. A swollen, white blob bobbed closer from beneath the dark ocean waves. He squinted to see, but he couldn't make out any features, nothing that told him anything. Then the body sank down into the depths.

The furious beating against the wooden boathouse was gone. The silence left behind was like a breath of calm after a storm.

Finn shook as ocean water sprayed up against him, the sea frothing just beneath him as if angry at him taking the body away from it. But he didn't care. Whisker's lost owner would finally be at peace, given some meager amount of dignity in death. Relief washed over him, but Finn couldn't bring himself to smile.

The body might have escaped the island, but it would take a lot more work for him and Ash to do the same. It was a disturbing thought he immediately dismissed. He was upset, that was all. It was an intense experience. That had nothing to do with them being trapped on the island. But still, his hands were chilly as he walked toward the front of the dock again.

He looked at the broken oar in his hand and wished he could have had the same closure for Dad. Even just a short goodbye, a glimpse of him going overboard, anything would have made him feel better. At least then he would know what happened to him.

He would never know the truth, and that fact made his insides tremble.

LONG SHADOWS STRETCHED out across the beach as Finn dropped the broken oar off at the boathouse. He kind of tossed it inside, not really caring to put it back in its proper place on the wall. Outside, the last rays of sunlight reached out from the horizon, dying the sky in reds and purples. If Finn had been still out on the water with Dad and there was no work to be done, he would lie out on the deck and stare up at the sky, watching the stars slowly glint into existence overhead. It was one of his favorite things to do when he spent the night out on the water. It made him feel alive and part of something bigger than himself.

That seemed like such a simpler time now.

Whiskers was wrapping himself around his feet, purring so loud he could be heard over the crashing waves. Finn bent down to pet him and the cat climbed up his arms, claws and all. The sharp little pinpricks of pain made Finn cry out, but he couldn't complain. The cat had been through a lot. So had he.

"Okay." He laughed. "I'll carry you. You're so needy."

Whiskers snuggled down in his arms, purring harder than ever. He wrapped his long fluffy tail around his body, looking more like a plush toy than an actual cat.

"You feel better now, buddy? You sure seem like you do."

Whiskers licked his hand.

"I don't blame you. That would have been upsetting if that had happened to me. I'm just glad you found us." He paused for a moment as he swallowed the lump in his throat. "And I'm glad you showed me what happened. You're a smart little kitty."

Whiskers purred harder, soaking up the praise.

In the distance, crickets chirped. It was indeed getting darker. Minute by minute, it was getting a little harder to see out here. It wasn't as noticeable when he looked out over the ocean, but it was definitely obvious when he looked back toward the brush and trees to the path that led inland.

Finn thought back to the creature that shook the metal door last night. He couldn't think about it earlier. His mind simply had been too overwhelmed by everything he had to do. But now, it was different. Now night descended far faster than he liked. His chest tightened as he held Whiskers a little closer to his chest.

"Maybe we should get back to the lighthouse," he said, turning back the way they came.

The waves were coming in way faster than when they came out. Even as he hugged the line of scruff, his shoes still got splashed and soaked by encroaching waves. It was strange. The surf had brought in a bunch of black seaweed, but it didn't settle in a line at the edge of the waves. That was what he was used to seeing when it washed up onto shore. This seaweed was scattered all over the place like someone had come in and thrown it around like confetti. It was scattered up the full length of the beach, even up past the treeline. It was only in this section of the beach, too, not on the other side of the boathouse like it ought to for it to be a natural phenomenon. Why was this island so strange?

Finn had been on beaches his entire life, but he had seen nothing like that before. He paused and considered picking some up to show Ash, but his hands were full with a content cat. There was no need to bother Whiskers for that. So he headed down along the beach and turned up the path back to the lighthouse.

He had only taken a few steps when there came an odd scraping sound, like something coarse being dragged through the sand. He had an image of someone throwing the seaweed around like confetti. Were they really alone on this island?

Finn turned as Whiskers leaped from his arms. The cat darted up the path toward the lighthouse, his tail bushed out twice its size. Licking his salty lips, Finn stepped off the path and into the bushes. Despite his fear, he had to see. He had to know what scared Whiskers so much that seemed to scare Ash, too. Slowly, he crept back toward the beach while the strange scraping sound continued.

A woman's whispered mutterings came from the beach and made the hairs on the back of his neck stand up. Carefully, he pulled back a pair of branches, looking out at the violet sky and black ocean.

Something was standing on the beach. A shadow against the twilight sky, she resembled a person. A woman whose body was wrapped from head to toe in something skintight. But she had so many things hanging off her body. He couldn't make out any resemblance of a face.

She leaned down to the ground and picked up some

of the leafy black seaweed and plastered some against her arm. She wrapped her body in the seaweed from the shore. Or maybe she had brought the seaweed to the shore to use as wrappings. The thought of her lurking around on the beach while he was struggling with the lighthouse worker's body in the water made a sweat break out on his forehead.

The strange human-like creature turned her head, illuminated only briefly in the dim moonlight. She had no face, only a mesh of seaweed and shadow emulating a face.

Finn gasped and clamped a hand over his mouth as soon as the sound came out.

The creature turned her face toward him, streams of seaweed flinging out around her head with the speed of the movement. The eyes flashed yellow like a wild animal.

"Finn?" the creature asked. The high-pitched voice sent shivers down his spine.

Ice took hold of his chest and he took a shaky step backward.

"How do you know my name?" His voice came out thin and shaky. Like he couldn't properly breathe and talk.

"Won't you help me, child?" the creature said, taking a posture like a spider about to pounce instead of a woman truly needing help.

She knew his name. Somehow, she knew who he was. He thought of washing ashore and this creature watching him. Him talking to Ash in the lighthouse and this creature near the window listening in. What all had she heard? What all did she know?

Finn stood motionless, his body suddenly disconnected from his control. He froze up.

The creature lumbered toward him, legs a little too unsteady on the sand and scruff, and her eyes flashing yellow again as she stared at him. It was like she was looking through him. She knew where he was now. Worse yet, she knew who he was.

With a whimper, Finn forced his body to spin around. He needed to get away. Far away. He needed to run, but it took a moment for his own legs to carry him. He was too shaky, too uncertain. If only he had the confidence and the determination Whiskers had when he took off up the path. All Finn knew was he had to get back to the lighthouse.

Slowly he gained speed, avoiding the roots and rocks in his path, moving his legs faster and faster. He had to tell Ash what he had seen, to get some answer for this thing that stalked the beach at night. He needed to know what it was, even though, at the same time, he was horrified to know.

Behind him, it scraped along the sand. It was struggling, as if walking was something it took time to orient itself to. But Finn refused to look back or slow down. His legs ached, especially after fighting with the oar earlier. But he kept going as fast as he could, even as his lungs burned and a stitch formed in his side. When the lighthouse came into view, he gave a shaky, breathless laugh of joy.

Whiskers had beaten him to it. The white fluffy cat was up on his back legs, scratching at the metal door, begging to be let inside. Even he knew where it was safe. Finn should have listened to him.

He grabbed the front door and yanked it open. Whiskers jumped aside, probably afraid of getting trampled. In a quick, fluid motion, from years of working the crabbing boat with his father, Finn scooped up Whiskers with one arm, ignoring the pain of his claws digging into his skin. Then he hurried inside and slammed the door closed behind him. Standing inside, he pulled in deep, shaky breaths.

Footsteps hurried down the spiral staircase. Finn looked up. Ash stopped at the last step, an oil lantern gripped in her hand. It was the only light visible on that level, and Finn couldn't help but note the flickering light gave Ash an angelic appearance as it glinted in her eyes.

He shook his head, and guilt reverberated in his voice. "You said not to stay out till nightfall. I should have listened, but I didn't. Never should have stayed. Never should have gone back to look. I'm so sorry—"

She hurried forward and pressed a finger to his lips. He went quiet, panic filling his chest as he continued gasping for air. She pushed past him and dropped the wooden bolt into place, barring the front door.

For a long moment, they both stood still, and Finn strained to hear beyond the gusts of wind off the ocean. Time slowed down to a crawl as bits of dust floated in the still air and the flame of the oil lantern flickered shadows along the walls. Ash put a hand to her chest, clearly relieved.

Finn gave a nervous grin. He had made it, and maybe the creature on the beach couldn't make it back up here. Maybe it was still struggling on the sand, still trying to figure out how to walk properly.

Then something heavy slammed against the door.

II

NOT A BAD DEATH

WHISKERS JUMPED TO THE GROUND, flattening out so small he was almost unrecognizable as a big fluffy cat. A millisecond later, he took off up the stairs, his tail bushed out behind him, clearly terrified.

Finn turned back to the door. It served as the only barrier between them and that creature he had seen on the beach. He couldn't get the vision of its golden eyes out of his head. The creature slammed into the door again, and the hinges groaned in protest.

Even though the door was metal, the hinges were too old. It wouldn't keep the creature out. In the flickering candlelight, he could see the indentations of the metal from how many times it had been attacked. It was her, Finn realized with horror. She was what had been shaking the door so much the night before, loosening hinges, wearing down the metal, finding a way to get inside. How many nights had the creature from the sea thrown herself at the door? How could he possibly sleep here again, knowing she would eventually get in? The persistence to warp a metal door, even an old one, was terrifying.

In a panic, he looked around the room. Maybe he could barricade the door somehow. He spotted the couch and took only a few steps toward it when Ash grabbed at his arm. Her eyes were wide and terrified. But she held the lantern high in one hand and pointed urgently up the stairs. Finn glanced toward the door again, not sure of Ash's plan. But he trusted her, so he followed her lead.

They climbed flight after flight of the stairs, listening to the creature slam again and again against the door. The noise reverberated up the long metal staircase and echoed against the concrete walls of the lighthouse.

When they still had a good quarter of the staircase left to climb, the door gave way completely. Finn's stomach dropped and his legs almost gave out beneath him. The sound had been like a gunshot against wood and creaking metal. Finn couldn't help himself. He looked down the center of the staircase. Splinters were scattered around the kitchen and across the living room. Ash was right, there was no way the couch would have survived that assault.

He swallowed down the lump in his throat and searched the shadows for the terrifying creature that had followed him here. His pulse pounded in his ears. It was madness, but he had to lay eyes on it, to prove to his mind that it really existed and wasn't just a figment of his imagination.

The creature lumbered into the lighthouse. She was so tall she had to crouch to step across the threshold. Had she been so tall out on the beach? He honestly couldn't remember. But she had been plastering seaweed all over her body like she was made of it.

The creature turned its gaze up the center of the stairwell, golden eyes glinting in the lantern light like a fish. It locked eyes with him and Finn gasped, unable to move, unable to breathe.

Ash grabbed his arm, yanking him, urging him up the rest of the stairs. Down on the bottom floor, the creature turned its gaze to Ash. Her entire demeanor changed. Her golden eyes went wide, she raised her arms into the air, and opened her mouth, unleashing a horrible squeal of fury.

He jumped when the creature launched up the stairs on all fours, climbing several steps at a time in a flurry of limbs. She looked like a cross between a ravenous canine and a spider.

This time, Finn didn't need Ash's motivation to sprint up the stairs. The creature's shriek split the air and echoed up the metal staircase. She scrambled up each metal step, the bolts of the staircase clanging as they creaked with her fury.

Ash was ahead of him, somehow always a step ahead. She wasn't leading him to a safe room or even a closet. She was leading him to the very top of the tower.

What the hell kind of protection would that give? They would be sitting ducks up there!

But there was no time to argue. Even if he tried, she probably wouldn't hear him over the sound of the monster clamoring up the stairs behind them.

As soon as they reached the top of the tower, Ash grabbed his arm and pulled him around to the opposite side of the beacon, behind the shelter of the shelves so they wouldn't be blinded. He tried his best to close his eyes against the brilliant spinning light, but didn't succeed. It made him partially blind, which didn't help his panic. But he followed Ash regardless. The beacon turned its endless path, shining a light into the darkness, filling the room with an endless spinning light.

Ash wrapped her arms around his waist and held him tight.

"We can't stop here," he said, trying to catch his breath. "We need to keep running. Ash, she'll find us up here!"

She pressed her lips to his, soft and gentle. For several long moments, his mind was dazed into silence. When she pulled away, he could still taste her on his lips. It was chamomile. He pursed his lips together, wanting her to linger on his lips.

"No more questions." She gently tugged his arms around her waist. "Just hold me. Please?"

So he did. He held her tight against his chest. Her warm breath brushed on his neck and the rapid pace of her heartbeat matched with his. The creature clawed to the very top of the lighthouse until she was just a few feet away.

When the door cracked open, the creature loomed just beyond the doorway. The shadowy form was intent on reaching them, intent on reaching Ash. Here in the garishly bright room, the creature didn't look like it belonged here. Like she didn't belong in this world. Seaweed stuck up from her body, her silhouette looking like her skin was flaking. He swallowed down the dry patch in his chest and tried to calm his racing heart. Instead of giving into his instincts to run or look for a weapon, he stood with Ash and held her tight against him. He focused on her, not the monster at the door.

"The sea witch will leave us alone. Trust me," Ash whispered. Her voice was breathless and panicked, very different from the calm of her words.

The sea witch. That was an apt name.

Standing here holding Ash, waiting for the sea witch to make her move, Finn's trust in Ash wavered. He wanted to trust her. Hell, he wanted to at least believe her. But his mind said differently as he stared at the looming creature just beyond the flimsy door. He wanted to fight the sea witch, not stand here and wait for her.

Bits of dust fell from the top of the doorframe when one hand emerged first from the seaweed-shape and scraped against the wooden door. Then one seaweed-wrapped foot pushed through before the whole of the sea witch entered the beacon room.

Long strands of black seaweed hung down like hair behind her, swaying and long enough to touch the floor.

The sea witch was so close it would only take her a few steps to reach them. Her golden eyes gleamed so brightly in her strangely shaped face.

"You should not have run," she said in a hoarse, high-pitched voice.

"Leave me alone!" Ash cried and buried her face in Finn's chest. She was shaking from head to toe.

Finn shook his head in frustration. He ought to protect her. But just like he had on that inner tube when the ocean tossed him around like a doll, he felt power-less. What could he do? There were no weapons here, and considering how she had taken out that metal door, weapons wouldn't do much good.

The sea witch lurched forward, reaching an arm toward Ash. Like something out of a nasty fairy tale, a nightmare come to life, all Finn could do was hold Ash to his chest. All he could do was comfort her. He had to trust Ash knew what she was doing, even if everything in his body told him to run. He had to follow her lead. So he swallowed down his fear and prepared for the worst.

It was ironic he was about to be killed by a horrid sea witch after surviving everything else the ocean had thrown at him. At least he had Ash, a beautiful, myste-rious girl who only wanted his arms around her as she waited for the inevitable. In a dark, gruesome sort of way, it wasn't a terrible way to go. It was better than his dad's death, and certainly better than Whiskers' past owner.

Finn breathed in Ash's sweet, flowery scent that mixed so perfectly with the brine of the sea.

Not a bad death at all.

The beacon spun toward the door and lit up the sea witch in all her wicked glory. He wished he had looked at Ash instead though, because he was horrified to see her in full light. She had gray skin beneath the seaweed. She even had her mouth exposed revealing all her sharp teeth. Her body, covered in black and deep green seaweed, looked like a corpse washed ashore. Only her eyes and gray mouth were visible. Like a zombie. Her arms were finely wrapped bundles, and her torso a basket-woven mess of crossing leaves. Those golden eyes were the worst. If wrapping her body up in seaweed hadn't been horrifying enough, those eyes really pushed it over the edge.

He couldn't handle it. He looked away. A high-pitched shriek filled the room. Only this wasn't a sound filled with determination, but one of pain. The sea witch staggered back, shaking her head as though dazed.

"Oh, you wretched child!" She snarled.

The light was slow to come back around on its endless, predictable path. But it came back all the same. The sea witch was shaken on her feet, putting one hand to her eyes.

"It's the only thing you hate. The light!" Glee filled Ash's voice that he hadn't heard before. She clearly enjoyed seeing the sea witch suffer, something Finn hadn't expected. But he also couldn't blame her.

He realized Ash had faced this sea witch before. They had some kind of history together, and he wasn't sure what to make of that. She had known the sea witch lived on this island, but hadn't said a word about it to him. If she had told him a crazy strong sea witch came out at night and lived on the beach, he would have definitely heeded her warnings.

The light struck the sea witch again, and she screamed, hurrying back to the safety of the stairs, pulling the door closed to a crack again. Her rattled breaths and scuttling footsteps moved onto the metal staircase.

"Get out of here. You're not wanted here!" Ash screamed, reaching a painfully high pitch in her rage.

Finn winced. "Ash, it's okay. She left."

Ash pulled away from him, and hurried over to the door. She yanked it open, and the sounds of the sea witch scuttling farther down the metal stairs were clearer. Ash leaned over the banister and shouted down, "And never come back!"

Finn blinked. The sea witch's footsteps retreated until he couldn't hear her anymore. Ash came back into the room and fell to her knees, tears rolling down her cheeks. "Just leave us alone!" she cried through sobs.

Honestly, he didn't know what was going on. He needed answers, but this clearly wasn't the time to ask. He helped Ash to her feet, and she turned, bawling against his shoulder again. He led her toward their little nest in the back of the room before returning to pull the wooden door closed, latching it. Not that it would do much good against the sea witch.

He cuddled down into their sleeping nest. Ash clung

to him and cried, but he couldn't do much to comfort her. He barely understood what was going on.

The beacon continued to spin, casting light out over the black ocean and illuminating the rocky crags below the lighthouse. Finn searched the water for any sign of a ship, though he had never seen any ships out here. But he still had to look. Right now, more than ever, he yearned to be home, to be away from this nightmare, but no rescue was coming. There were no fairy tales with happy endings in real life. If they wanted to escape the island, they were on their own.

Eventually Ash's sobs stilled, and she fell asleep against him, her salty tears dampening his cotton shirt.

The more he tried to unravel this mystery, the more he gave himself a headache. Whiskers appeared beside him with a hop that almost took his breath away. The fluffy white cat looked ghostly in the darkness. He purred hard and sniffed both of them completely before curling up against Finn's leg and falling asleep. Finn gave him some good pats, marveling he hadn't run out of the room when the sea witch came up here. He was a brave cat, braver than he was, for certain.

Finn smiled. Maybe those two had a good idea, or maybe the universe was telling him to go to sleep.

But sleep wasn't easy. His mind struggled to relax, and his body was slow to come out of the panic. He would almost slip off to sleep when the sea witch kept appearing in his dreams. Her golden eyes stared through him. He had the feeling there was an odd piece to this puzzle he was missing. He had no clue what it was or how to even find it.

Eventually, his eyes were too heavy to keep open. He was worn out after freeing the body at the boathouse, the run back to the lighthouse, and the encounter with the sea witch. He watched the stars flicker in the sky, the waves bobbing across the ocean, and the ever steady spinning of the beacon. Even though the sea witch still haunted him, he refused to let her win. After a few hours, sleep finally found him and he dreamed of blue waters, clear skies, Ash smiling, the warm sun on his face, and a playful Whiskers at his feet.

12

FEAR THE OCEAN

FINN WOKE TO THE SMELL OF BAKING flour and sugar. It traveled down his throat and his stomach growled in hunger. He grumbled in his sleep, wanting to stay with the warm sun and playful Whiskers. But something incessantly nudged his arm.

"Finn, wake up. I made us breakfast."

He groggily opened his eyes to the gray skies of an overcast day. Beside him Ash held up a steaming plate of pancakes alongside some apple jam. His mouth watered. Damn, he hadn't realized he was so hungry. Then again, he had spent the entire day yesterday out on the beach with Whiskers and...

The memories from the day before overcame him, whisking away the dreamlike haze that had insulated him while he slept. He dragged a hand over his face, remembering it all as crisp and clear as if he were there again. The body at the boathouse, the sea witch coming through the door, and the chase up to the top of the lighthouse. He saw again the sea witch lunging for Ash, stretching her fingers toward her like some sort of monster movie. Now, here Ash came with a pile of steaming hot pancakes, as though everything was fine and normal. As if they hadn't nearly been killed by the sea witch the night before.

She set down the plate on his legs as he sat up straight, rubbing sleep out of his eyes. The plate was warm through the blankets and the freshly made pancakes created a little trail of steam. Ash sat cross-legged beside him, wearing baggy tan pants and a navy blue lace top square at the neckline. Her outfit looked nothing like the sort of things girls wore at school. It was way too old-fashioned to be anything the popular kids wore, but it was cute on Ash. It suited her somehow and fit her unusual personality. If she were ever to wear more modern clothes, it wouldn't be right somehow.

Ash plopped down her own plate on her legs and dove into her pancakes, barely looking up at him. Finn turned the narrow fork over in his fingers, unable to bring the first bite to his lips. His stomach growled in protest, but he pursed his lips. They had to talk, and Ash wasn't going to like what he had to say. He felt like a heel, preparing to bring up what happened last night when she was clearly trying to make it all out like the world was fine. But he couldn't live like that.

"Thank you for the pancakes. They look delicious," he said.

She mumbled a thanks through bites of food, not looking up at him.

He swallowed down the regret in his throat, then he said what he knew needed to be said. "She'll be back."

Ash slowed her chewing, swallowed, then placed her fork down on her half empty plate. "Why do you have to bring her up? I thought you would be happy to see a plate of food first thing in the morning. I made an entire stack of pancakes for us."

Her dark eyes burned into him, her brows furrowed. She was always so quick to anger, but something didn't sit right with him. The anger felt too fragile on her, as if it was a deflection rather than actual anger. Her lip trembled ever so slightly and she kneaded the blanket in her hand as she spoke. Her gaze bore into him, but the quickness to her breath made it seem like she might run down the stairs like a frightened animal if he kept pushing.

"Because I can't play pretend any longer, even though it's tempting. These look delicious and I'm starving, but I have to know what's going on. You know more than you want to tell me. Please, help me understand all of this."

She put her plate aside and huffed in annoyance. "I already told you. I don't know anything."

He shook his head. "You say that, but you knew the sea witch was at the shoreline. That she comes out at night. You even knew how to chase her off with the light." He gestured to the giant beacon over their heads, sitting dark and motionless now during the day. Then he put a hand to his own chest. "She chased me back to the lighthouse, but she howled when she saw you. Just the very sight of you enraged her. It made my skin crawl. It was like she only had eyes for you once she saw you."

Ash averted her gaze.

"And you know why, don't you?" he asked.

She rubbed at her bare arm. "Well, sort of. I only know a little."

"Just tell me, please?" He took her hand in his, remembering the kiss they had shared last night and the desperation of their embrace. "Regardless of what you're afraid of, we have to face it together. We're stuck here on this island together. And the sea witch will come back. She was so angry last night I can't see her not." He rubbed the back of her hand with his thumb, making lazy circles along her cool, soft skin. "It's not a matter of if, but when she returns."

Ash let out a shaky breath and her gaze softened. "I'll tell you. But only if you eat the pancakes first."

He smiled. "Deal."

She rubbed at her arm. "And... we can cuddle under the blankets. That's the only way I can get through telling it."

His heart fluttered at the chance to cuddle with her again, but this was also clearly a tough topic for her. Ash had already been through a lot after last night. He needed to be here for her and support her, not pushing his own urges forward. She needed his support, not his affection right now. So he pushed that feeling aside and nodded.

"I can do that."

As usual, Ash's cooking was delicious. The apple jam tasted off, like it should have been tossed out a while ago. So he ate only a tiny taste. It looked like Whiskers had already had his breakfast. He was licking at his mouth and lay out now in the sun bathing himself.

It was kind of nice having a cat around. Finn had one when he was very young, a gray tabby kitten he had lured off the streets and taken to the vet. He remembered playing outside, climbing trees, the kitten always at his side. Then one day, she just disappeared. He put out food night after night, but the kitten never returned. His father told him she had probably been taken in by another home, but Finn had always feared the worst.

Whiskers wasn't nearly as adventurous as that little kitten. He preferred warm blankets, soft cuddles, and a nice deep scratch under the chin. He was a good little buddy and after their frightening encounter last night, he seemed especially close to Finn now, curling up at his side and purring deeply.

Finn lifted the quilted blanket and Ash moved back to their cozy little corner. She laid down beside him and curled up to his chest. She pressed a palm to his cheek, her skin slightly chilled against his.

Finn's pulse quickened when she took him by surprise, leaning in to kiss him. His body wanted to lean in, too, to kiss her and see where this went. But as much as he would love to kiss her sweet lips again, he wouldn't let her get out of telling him the truth.

He placed a finger on her chin when she was so close he could feel her breath on his face. Her eyes blinked open in surprise and her lips parted. "But—"

If Ash had her way, they would spend every day up here cuddled together and kissing, and while that did sound amazing, that wasn't an option with the sea witch lurking in the shadows at night.

Finn shook his head and gave a light chuckle. "No, not yet. No more kisses for you until I hear the story first. Remember?"

Her gaze slid away from him and out through the glass walls toward the sea. Several moments passed and for a moment, Finn wondered if this was a new method of stalling. When she finally spoke, her voice was soft and fragile.

"I'll tell."

His heart broke at the tremor in her voice. "You don't have to if you don't want to. I don't want you to do something that might be painful to experience again."

He thought of his own trials on the ocean, tossed about by the storm and the waves. He cupped her cheek and gradually drew her attention back to him, pulling her away from the endless water.

"It's... difficult. You want answers, but I'm not sure that I have any to give. I don't remember coming to this island. There was no violent storm, no plane crash, nothing like the books say. Many people find themselves on islands like you did as survivors. Shipwrecks, mutinies, pirates, crashes, all the violent ways. But not like me. I've always lived here."

Finn pushed a stray strand of her curly black hair out of her face and tucked it behind her ear. In the gray light, her hair shone a deep bluish black, as if even the sky couldn't take the ocean out of her. As if she was made of the sea itself. He loved it.

"You've lived here since you were a child?" he asked.

She shook her head. "No, I've always been like this. Trapped and hunted. It's been a long time, but not years, I don't think. Not yet, anyway." She gave a small smile. "I wasn't climbing the stairs of the lighthouse in diapers, if that's what you're asking."

He gave a light chuckle. It was easy to relax with her. They got along so well together, as if he was always meant to be here with her. He knew what he had to ask, and he really didn't want to. But he knew her story would find its way to it, eventually.

"And the sea witch?"

Ash coiled in against his chest, her body forming a ball against his with such a fluid motion, as if it was a pose she had taken her entire life. It was like the very thought of the sea witch took the air out of her lungs.

"I've always had an instinct to stay away from the ocean. Something about it was dangerous, maybe even deadly." She paused as her breath came faster. "One day I went down to the beach. I thought I shouldn't be afraid of the water, especially when I'm on solid ground. But Finn... I couldn't do it. I couldn't put a single toe in the water. Doesn't that sound crazy? We're here on an island together, and I couldn't even step foot in."

"Was it because of the sea witch?" he asked, wrapping an arm around her waist. She was trembling.

"It has to be her. Why else would I have that fear? Who else could have possibly caused it? That night, she found me. I don't know if she was waiting for me out on the beach, or how she knew where I was." She dragged a hand through her curls, her eyes wide as she tried to form the words. "I was in the lighthouse reading a book downstairs, on the couch where you napped the other day."

Finn nodded.

"She saw me through the window. She let out that horrible screech like a banshee and I screamed! It made my blood turn to ice. I've never heard anything like it before. You heard it!"

"I did. It was awful." He swallowed down his own fear just from hearing her story. Having the sea witch walk by the window downstairs, he couldn't imagine the fear that would give him.

"She clawed at the window trying to get inside. But I noticed she retreated with the oil lanterns. That's why I keep them lit all the time at night. The sea witch was furious. She ran around the lighthouse, scratching at the walls like her anger alone led her. I don't know why she hates me so much. So I ran upstairs as fast as I could and hid with the beacon. I figured if she hated the oil lanterns she would hate that light. She never made it inside until last night."

"You've kept her at bay for a long time."

She nodded. "One time when I met Whiskers, I lost track of time. He had run off when I went inside to get food for him and he didn't come back until dusk. The sea witch found me outside. It was terrifying."

Finn shuddered at the thought. "I can imagine." He said with a dry throat.

"She had just grabbed hold of me—"

An icy tendril lanced through Finn's heart. "She grabbed you?"

Ash nodded, wiping away tears that spilled down her cheeks with her palm. "I had just barely made it inside when she grabbed me by the wrist."

She held up her right hand.

Finn could imagine the sea witch's hand grasped around that thin wrist, clasping it with those seaweed wrapped fingers. He couldn't help but shiver.

"When she did, my skin hurt and changed color in places. I don't know what she was trying to do to me, but Finn, I've never been so scared in my life. I got away because I was holding onto that oil lantern in my other hand and I shoved it into her face. She screamed and let me go, so I closed the door behind me and bolted it. I was so scared!"

Tears overwhelmed her and Ash wept into Finn's chest. He held her tight, stroking the back of her head while she cried. Finn couldn't blame her either. He would have been a mess if the sea witch had grabbed him like that.

But she didn't want Finn, she wanted Ash. She wanted to *hurt* Ash.

He pursed his lips. He couldn't let the sea witch have her. He refused.

"I won't let her get you," he said and kissed the top of her head.

Ash looked up at him and gave a sad laugh. "How, Finn? How in the world can you keep her from me? She can tear through doors now and tried to claw up the windows before. What chance do we have?"

"There has to be a way. I'm going to get us both out of here. We'll go someplace the sea witch can't reach us."

Her voice broke. "Really?"

"I promise."

Slowly, she unfurled her body from the protective pose she had taken when talking about the sea witch and leaned up, wrapping her arms around him and hugging him tight. When her lips met his, this time he gave into her charms. They kissed deeply, and Finn held her tight against him.

Outside, the waves crashed upon the rocky crags of the lonely island. The spray came so high, it left water droplets on the windows of the top of the tower. Finn and Ash ignored it though as the quilt twisted around them and the sea continued to churn.

Part V:

Impossible Dreams

13

TO THE ENDS OF THE EARTH

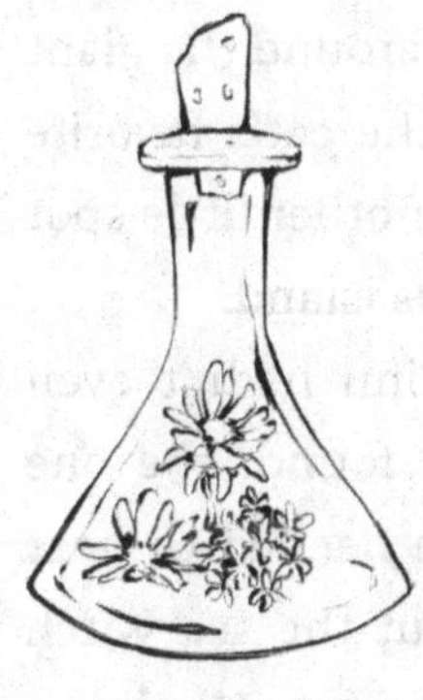

WITHOUT THE BRIGHT SUN COMING IN through the windows, the stairwell of the lighthouse was much darker and more ominous. Finn had to stand at the top of the stairs and let his vision adjust to the darkness before he trusted himself to go down them. He carefully held the railing as he descended the steps, balancing a small stack of dishes in the other hand.

After their time together, Ash had fallen asleep in his arms. Outside, the rain had turned to a light misting, overcast and cloudy. Finn had watched the clouds for a while before Ash was fast enough asleep she wouldn't wake when he untangled from her. Her breathing got lighter when he stood up, but she looked like she was still asleep. It didn't help that Whiskers had curled up on his other side, fluffy belly aimed up and paws curled inward. He wished he had a camera to snap a photo.

Finn had brought the dishes down to be of some help. Ash had been cooking and even brought plates of food up to him at the top of the lighthouse. The very least he could do was take them downstairs and clean up. He had done little to help since washing ashore days ago, and he aimed to change that.

The metal stairs were cold under his bare feet as he padded down. He was halfway down when Whiskers joined him. Apparently, he hadn't been as asleep as he looked. Finn appreciated having the little furry companion at his side while he padded around the giant building. Somehow Finn had become the cat's favorite person, though he didn't mind. It was another little spot of brightness on this dark and mysterious island.

Everything had been so chaotic, Finn hadn't even gotten to tell Ash about the body he found, the one Whiskers had led him to. Not that she needed to hear about that right now. Just talking about the sea witch had worn her out, and he felt awful for her. He didn't want to drop any more bad news on her until she was ready to hear it. If sleeping for a few hours made her feel better from all of that stress, then he wanted to let her sleep.

One door was cracked open and a dim, flickering light caught his eye. He stepped off the staircase and pushed open the door. Whiskers darted inside first, nearly knocking him over as he tried to balance the plates in his hands.

"Hey, no fair!" He laughed, then pushed open the door completely.

The room was lined with shelves upon shelves of sideways bottles. A grimy porthole window at the far end of the small room didn't let in much light, especially on a cloudy day. Ash must have lit the oil lamp to help with that. After last night, he couldn't begrudge Ash's insistence on having light everywhere.

The oil lamp sat on a small side table with a pile of matches beside it. No, those weren't matches. They were miniature logs for a puzzle. Beside it, what he had assumed was a matchbox was really the hull of a tiny ship, only partly assembled.

This wasn't a room full of dusty bottles. It was a room full of tiny ships, all protected in their various bottles, trapped and corked in their miniature seas. This wasn't a small hobby. This collection had taken years of work, maybe even decades.

"I see you found the shipbuilder's quarters." Ash stepped into the room with a yawn. She was in the same outfit she had been in earlier and still barefoot like him. Her hair was disheveled and her clothes wrinkled, but she actually looked happy for the first time. She crossed the room quickly and planted a swift kiss on his lips.

Oh, how he wished that kiss could last longer. How much he wanted to lead her back up the steps and cuddle under the blankets to continue what they started. But they couldn't spend all day making out, not when the sea witch would surely be watching for them to make a mistake at night.

"That was fun, Finn. We should do that again some-time." Her smile could send a thousand ships to sea.

"Yeah," he said, suddenly unable to think of words. "Yeah, we should." His body still buzzed with their time together. "I, uh, thought you were asleep."

"I felt you leave," she admitted. "Then Whiskers got up and jumped on me in his excitement to follow you."

Finn winced. "Oh. Sorry about that."

She stretched, "It's fine. There's a lot to do, anyway. I need to be up." She leaned down to give Whiskers a good scratch. "I didn't build these, just so you know. I haven't been here that long. The shipbuilder did."

It took some effort to yank his mind out of the haze where it wanted to live and into the present. "Who is the shipbuilder?"

Ash grinned, sitting down in a squeaky old brown office chair. She held up her hands to the room. "This... is the shipbuilder. The person who built all these damn ships. I don't know how long it took them, probably way longer than I would have patience for. They almost filled up the entire room with them. There are a few empty shelves way at the top covered in dust, so I know it was only a matter of time before they had little ships, too."

Finn was only partially listening. While Ash rattled on about the kits she'd found and how tough they were to put together, he had a sudden horrifying realization.

He knew the shipbuilder. He had seen them just yesterday—or at least what was left of them. His stomach did a flip-flop at the same time Whiskers jumped into Ash's lap, pulling his claws on the arm of the worn leather chair with its remnants of all the times he had clawed it up in the past. That was his chair, that was his owner's chair, that was the shipbuilder's chair.

"Oh, God." Finn put a hand to his mouth.

"Finn?"

At first, he couldn't answer. He had to get his body under control first.

Ash got to her feet, dropping Whiskers to the floor with a thump. She was at his side in a moment.

"Finn, what's wrong? Was it about the ship? Did talking about them upset you? I didn't even think about that on the shipwreck. I'm so sorry."

He choked out a hoarse laugh at the realization he had been witness to not one, but two deaths in the past few days. And here he was, thinking about making out some more with a girl. What was wrong with him?

"I think I need to sit down."

She gestured to the brown chair, but he shook his head. The thought of sitting in that seat where the shipbuilder had sat for hours on end, after he had seen what had become of them, made his stomach queasy.

"We can go downstairs. I'll make us some tea." She took the plates out of his hands—he hadn't recalled he still held them. The weight disappeared from his fingers.

Ash took his arm and led him out of the room, somehow balancing dirty dishes and the oil lantern in one hand and holding his arm to steady him down the metal steps with the other. He felt so useless. Here she was, being stalked by a vicious sea witch and somehow keeping the lighthouse running, while he fell apart every other day.

Only once they were on the stairwell again could he bring himself to speak. "Ash, I'm sorry I'm such a burden to you."

She smiled. "You're not a burden. You're my friend." Her cheeks went red. "And probably more than a friend at this point, let's be honest."

He leaned against her as they took their time descending the spiral stairs. If he moved too fast, the spiral would have taken him out completely.

"I think I saw your shipbuilder yesterday." That was all he could say. Those few words made his entire body quake with revulsion.

Her brows furrowed as she blinked at him. "You'll need to tell me. When you're ready, I mean. But first tea."

ASH WAS RIGHT. The chamomile tea helped. It settled his stomach and his nerves until he was ready to talk about everything that had happened to him and Whiskers the day before: Whiskers leading him to the boathouse, the pet carrier he found in the old broken boat, and finally the bloated, disfigured body of the shipbuilder.

She listened to all of it, sipping her tea, and slowly leaning in closer as the details got more gruesome. By the time he finished, they had both finished their cups, and Ash had a hand to her chest like she had been running alongside him on his breathless journey back to the lighthouse.

Whiskers laid in Finn's lap, purring hard while Finns stroke his soft fur and warm pink-lined ears.

"She could have caught you easy, you know. Especially if she was near enough to hear you. She's fast," Ash said.

"I realize that now. She must have hoped I would lead her to you. And I did exactly what she wanted me to do." He sighed. "I'm sorry."

"It's not your fault. You didn't know. I should have explained what we were dealing with." She leaned back in her chair, a frown pulling at her lips. "I had thought she wouldn't try to come back again. I thought with the light and me staying upstairs with the beacon every night, I assumed she would eventually give up her pursuit. But I was wrong."

He licked his lips, tasting remnants of chamomile. It was an excuse to kill time while he built up to asking the question he didn't want to ask.

"Ash... do you think she killed the shipbuilder?"

She winced and looked down at her empty cup. "I don't know. She's always stalked me, pursued me. I never thought about her hurting someone else. Maybe she did. I don't know why she's so angry all the time."

"I think the shipbuilder was the lighthouse keeper." Finn scratched the back of Whiskers' head and the cat purred harder. "I think Whiskers belonged to them. They had to keep the lighthouse, too. Why else would you bring a sweet cat like Whiskers to this island unless you wanted a companion with you? They must have been lonely, so they brought Whiskers here."

"Poor little guy. Stuck on his own on this island."

Finn gave her a small smile. "You two have a lot in common, then. You both were stuck here alone, but not anymore. Now we're a team. All three of us are together. None of us are on our own anymore."

Ash shook her head, a smirk on her lips as she poured herself the rest of the tea. Steam trailed up into her face, mingling with her black curls. She leaned back with a sigh. "Even if we are a team, we're still at the sea witch's mercy. She won't give up. She'll keep pursuing me. I know that now. And one day she'll sink her claws into me for good."

Finn reached forward and put a hand on Ash's forearm. Her skin always felt cool to his touch. "Don't say that. She won't get you. I'll make sure of it."

Her brow furrowed as she met his gaze. "Don't make promises you can't keep, Finn. You can't protect me from her forever. No one can, not really."

"She won't lay a hand on you while I'm around."

Ash stared into her teacup, looking resigned to her fate.

Finn got to his feet and pulled her into a side hug. "I'll do everything I can to keep the sea witch from hurting you. I'll get us off this island. Just you wait. One day, you'll be out of her reach, where she can never frighten you again."

Ash pulled away with a bitter laugh. "Oh? And what magical place is that, Finn? I'm pretty sure you can't call up a helicopter to come pick us up." He could see her sorrow shifting into anger.

"I found a surprise in the boathouse. Did I tell you? Something that will guarantee our escape from the lighthouse, the island, everything."

"Was it a boat?" She blinked.

"No—not exactly," he lied.

"Because getting on a boat in the ocean where the sea witch lives would definitely put both of our lives in danger, Finn. We don't even know where we are. How would you get us to the mainland from here?"

"There have to be maps or something around here. This is a lighthouse that's built to keep people safe. Besides, I practically grew up on the ocean with my dad. I have a general idea where we are, and we're not too far from the mainland. It's maybe a day trip, if that."

She huffed. "It *is* a boat, isn't it?"

Her dark gaze bore into him and Finn realized the futility of trying to keep it from her. "The boat was busted. But the canoe is only a little beat up."

She shook her head. "Aren't those the ones where there's only a little bit of plastic between you and the ocean? That sounds terrifying."

"Listen, it needs some patching up, but there's plenty of room for you, me, and Whiskers. We leave early in the morning, just at sunrise. The sea witch isn't out during the day like you told me. By the time night falls, we'll be halfway to the mainland."

Ash stared at him in silence for a long moment. Finn

couldn't decide if she was still angry at him or if he had finally won her over with his bizarre plan.

"If only I had your confidence. You think you can patch up a canoe you found to take us from here to the mainland with only the knowledge you gleaned from helping your father on a fishing boat for years? Only, you told me before that you mostly helped him in the summers and your job was more hauling the crabs onto the ship rather than actually navigating. Which is it, Finn?"

He let out a heavy sigh. It sure sounded like a bad idea when she said it out loud. "Look, I know it's going to be a challenge. I never said it would be easy."

"No, there's no need to say more. I get it. And I think it's the best chance we have."

The words in defense he had been ready to spout died on his lips. "What? Really?" he whispered.

"It's a crazy plan. I have no idea if it will even work, but it's better than anything I've come up with. I guess we'll be riding a canoe with ocean water all around us and I'll just have to get over my fear of the water. We'll just have to hope it all works out if we keep to the daylight." She reached over, cupped his cheek, and dragged a thumb along his jaw. Her touch was pure electricity.

"It's a damn good thing you're cute, Finn. I think if you gave me that determined look you get when your heart's set on something, I might just follow you to the ends of the earth."

He pulled her close. Their lips met, and it was like a

spark connected between them. Their hands roamed as the kiss grew deeper.

Whiskers scurried off for a safer sleeping spot. The remaining chamomile tea grew cold. And Finn knew he would do anything in his power to keep Ash safe.

Even if it meant going to the ends of the Earth. Even if it meant risking everything.

14

DOOMED FATES

NOW THAT FINN UNDERSTOOD THE importance of keeping the beacon of the lighthouse running, not only for the sailors on the sea, but for their own safety, he was more determined than ever to help. Ash had an entire book with instructions of every step to be taken to maintain the lighthouse. The book looked several decades outdated to Finn, but then again, so did the lighthouse.

Several tasks needed doing every day, and Finn volunteered to tackle some of the harder work that had been neglected. He soon stood on the thin catwalk that circled the glass windows of the beacon, a super long squeegee in his hands, and a bucket full of window cleaner at his feet.

The wind howled past him, sounding like the whistle

of a train. Even though he had his the hood of his rain-coat up, his hair was thrown all over the place. He dunked the old squeegee into the water again and raised it high above his head to wash the glass windows. The window cleaner kept sliding down the handle and collecting on his hands. That, combined with the wind, made his hands freezing cold. He was glad to help, though, and the glass windows definitely needed it. He wasn't sure how long it had been since they were cleaned, but the glass was foggy and hard to see through in places from all the salt water and ocean breezes beating against the surface.

Afterward, he went inside and cleaned the glass lens of the beacon, another task that took way longer than expected. The beacon had metal bars around it to keep it from sliding around. That made it a strange angle to get his elbow in and wipe down the glass. The lens of the beacon was even grimier than the glass on the outside, which didn't make much sense to him since this was enclosed within the lighthouse. Then again, there was no telling how long the lighthouse had sat without a proper keeper. He and Ash did their best to maintain it, but they weren't exactly qualified for this. Still, the brighter they could keep the light at night, the farther the beam went into the darkness, and the better off they would be against the sea witch.

Daylight hours slipped away too quickly. After he had changed clothes, washing off from all the cold, grimy cleaning, the sun dipped against the horizon. It was like daylight loathed bringing safety to their small little world. Downstairs, Ash was cooking dinner and the first fragrant smells of the food wafted up to him. She was kind enough to cook for them, and he was grateful. He didn't have the energy after that work outside, but he was glad he could help some.

It would be dinnertime soon. It was too late to go down to the boathouse to gather supplies or assess the damage to the canoe, so he went throughout the lighthouse instead, finding tools to make the task easier for the next day. Fortunately, plenty of tools were on hand. Some pieces of tarp could help keep out water and prevent the canoe from sinking, keeping it buoyant. Or at least... he guessed it would. Some waterproof glue should help keep the pieces together and let him reassemble some broken parts. He hoped it would work on the canoe, but again, he wasn't exactly an expert. Sailing a ship and pulling in crabs were more his specialty, and he kicked himself for not knowing more about these things.

The tough part would be getting into the water at the boathouse to look for any of the broken pieces of the canoe. If he had some of the pieces, maybe just the glue would be good enough to adhere them together. But he dreaded getting into that water. The sea witch had come from the ocean, so the thought of hopping in for a few minutes made a shiver go down his spine.

Finn returned to the room full of bottled ships, sorting through a pile of old instruction booklets, long forgotten warranties for various appliances and gear, and dusty handbooks. He found a guide for birds, a guide for trees, even a guide for identifying fish. Damn, the shipbuilder sure had been a fan of nature. Of course, living out here on their own, they kind of had to be. A large, dusty pile of paperwork sat on a side table and continued into a second pile on the floor. The constant humidity of the lighthouse and sea spray had fused some pages together, making it nearly impossible to turn pages without damaging them.

Whiskers slept on the back of the brown desk chair, clearly one of his favorite places. With so many scratch marks and loose threads, it looked like it belonged to Whiskers more than it had the shipbuilder. Whiskers snored in his sleep, a high-pitched whining sound that made Finn smile.

He pursed his lips as he looked down at the chair, the shipbuilder's chair. It felt wrong to sit in a chair that didn't belong to him, but his back ached from washing those windows, and he really wanted to sit down for a bit. He pushed aside the feeling he was trespassing in someone else's personal space and sat down gingerly. It was very comfortable and worn in and the back tipped just a little, so that his back got some relief. Whiskers' snoring didn't even pause for an instant. Clearly, this was something he was very used to.

Leaning back in the chair, Finn looked around the room. The chair gave an excellent view of the space, especially when he leaned back and took it all in, from the ceiling down. So many ships surrounded him, all in their perfect bottled homes. Each one was a unique model, some military vessels, others commercial, and a few skiffs he had seen before. All of them were contemporary ships, too, nothing historical. No Clipper ships, or anything like that. Just modern day boats. It stood in such contrast with the rest of the lighthouse, which seemed stuck in a previous time.

Dad would know all the ship names. He may have only owned a simple skiff in his lifetime, but he had taken pride in knowing most of the models by heart. He would use a pair of binoculars and point out a ship in the distance and quiz Finn on what it was, not that Finn had a head for any of that. To him, a ship was a ship. But Dad had loved it. He would have loved this room, if he had made it here.

Tears misted his eyes, but Finn wiped them away quickly. He didn't want to go down that mental path, not yet anyway. Not with so much to do still. He couldn't break down and wallow in his father's memory until he knew they were safe. And right now, they were far from safe.

Keeping busy was better than facing the grief just beneath the surface. He could help maintain the lighthouse, help find a way off the island, and most importantly, he could keep Ash safe. These were all important. There was no saving his father any longer.

Finn sniffled and turned to go back to the stack of decrepit papers, looking for any scraps of knowledge to help him fix the canoe. Or even a map he could use to navigate to the mainland. Once again, it was a long shot, but with all these pamphlets of manuals and keepsakes, he had hoped to find a repair booklet for the canoe to give him some clue what to do. He dragged his fingers over the edge of the pages, looking for anything useful. Something caught his eye.

It was in one of the bottles on the lower shelves, standing on a ship. At first he thought it was a pile of fish or netting, maybe a bird added to help with the realism, but that wasn't it. The item was too tall for that, much taller than a net of fish or a flock of birds.

Finn got to his feet, then crouched down in front of the dusty bottle, furrowing his brow. He squinted, trying to make sense of what he saw. Using his thumb, he wiped away a thick layer of dust on the curvature of the cold glass bottle. The figure took shape. Once he figured out what it was, he let out a gasp.

Standing on the deck of the boat in a far corner stood the sea witch. Each of the hanging pieces of seaweed had been carefully crafted from clay. Each leaf was molded and printed by the shipbuilder's thumb print. He could even see the remnants of the swirls of their fingerprint on the tiny leaves.

His mouth dropped. Why was the sea witch here? Inside these tiny bottles? He looked at the other ships crowded on the shelves, dust so thick it was hard to see them. He dragged a finger over one, then another, and another. There were too many to count. Each time he wiped a finger to flick dust into the air, he spotted it. Standing on a corner of each ship stood a pile of black seaweed crudely formed into a human-like shape. Some had doll parts for the face, some had doll hands reaching out. It didn't matter how many bottles he wiped clean.

She was there in every single one. Always watching, always waiting, on every single ship.

The hair stood up on the back of Finn's neck as a pit formed in his stomach.

"Ash, you need to come look at this!"

Asʜ sᴀᴛ in the creaky brown chair as Finn paced back and forth in the narrow room, the wood creaking beneath his feet. Her eyes grew wider while he explained what he had discovered. Once he finished, she turned her gaze to the bottles. The tiny clay figurines of the sea witch surrounded them in the cramp little space just like she had them trapped here on the island.

"So that means the shipbuilder saw the sea witch, too," Ash said.

"Yeah, and then started obsessing over her. Isn't that bizarre? I think there's more to it than that, though. Look at the amount of detail they used in crafting each of them. This one has a hand coming out, a human-like hand. And this one has a face that's almost completely covered up. They must have seen her more than once to get that level of detail. And I don't think the shipbuilder was running away in terror like we were."

Ash narrowed her eyes, using one hand to scratch at her neck. "What are you getting at?"

"I don't know." He dragged a hand through his hair. "But this is important. Maybe it can help us figure out what happened to you, too. I just don't know how it all fits together. It's like a giant puzzle, and we don't have all the pieces yet." He sighed. "I wish I could figure out what this all means." He gestured to the dozens of bottled ships around them.

Ash was quiet as she stared at the first bottle Finn had found, peering in through the streak he had made in the dust to get a better view of the clay sea witch on the ship. Her forehead creased and her skin turned pink where she scratched. "It's hard for me to imagine, but... do you think they spoke together, the shipbuilder and the sea witch?"

The thought seemed impossible. Finn shook his head. "What do you mean?"

"The sea witch is always trying to chase me, but she does talk, like you heard. It's not all screams. One time, she told me she just wants to talk to me, but then she chased me. It has never made me interested in what she has to say, but maybe I should have been more curious, like you."

"Don't be ridiculous. The sea witch doesn't exactly strike me as a conversational type. She wants to kill us. You don't chase after people if you just want to chat." It was meant as a joke, but Finn felt little humor. "The sea witch is hellbent on getting her claws on you, and talking to her might just be a ruse to get you closer."

Ash sighed and dragged her hand away from the pink mark on her throat to pet Whiskers, who still slept soundly on the back of the chair. "I'm not sure about you, Finn, but she definitely seems like she wants to kill me. She could have killed you on the beach, but didn't."

He cocked his head to the side. "Or she wanted me to lead her to you, which I did. Doesn't mean she wouldn't kill me if given the chance."

Ash sighed. "We could spend all day asking questions about her motives and never know the answers. The shipbuilder is dead. They were the only person who could have told us anything and conveniently, they aren't around to do it. That leaves the sea witch herself." She gave a bitter laugh. "And that's not really an option."

"I know. I just feel like we're missing something. Like it's sitting right in front of our noses, and we just can't see it."

Ash took his hand, pulling him out of his thoughts. "You can't fix everything, Finn. I'm happy to never know the answer to this mystery—if it means we live through all this. I've been here way longer than you, and I'm doing okay. A few crying spells here and there, but that's pretty normal for me these days. We'll get through this. Even if you can't fix the canoe."

"Don't talk like that." He rubbed her arm. "I will fix it. I promised you, and I mean it." His voice didn't sound so certain.

She put a hand up to his cheek and her light touch made his head spin and his heart pounded faster. "We have plenty of food. We can last here as long as it takes."

"For now. When it runs out, what do we do then? Wait however many years it takes to get somebody to notice we're missing and send out a boat to rescue us?"

She leaned forward and kissed him. Her lips lighted on his only briefly, like the flap of a butterfly's wing, but it took the edge of panic out of his veins.

"What makes you think they would live long enough to save us, Finn? The sea witch could kill them before they ever stepped on shore."

He gaped at her. He hadn't considered that. It took him a moment to move past the salty, sweet taste of Ash on his lips to form a response. "The sea witch can't kill everyone, Ash."

"If there is no boat, there's no way off. And if that happens, we'll just have to make do with what we have here." She dragged her thumb along his cheek. "Don't get hurt trying to find a way off the island, Finn. We might just be better off staying."

Her gaze was sad when she turned and pulled away from his touch. All he wanted was to save them from this place. Why was that so difficult for her to understand? Ash was a good person. She didn't deserve this fate she seemed so desperate to keep. A fate that would ultimately lead to their doom. He had no intention of watching both of them starve to death. Why didn't she want him to save her?

Ash paused at the threshold to the stairwell, one hand on the creaky wooden door. She gazed at him over her shoulder, through her dark curls hanging into her eyes. "It's getting late. It'll be dark soon. We should have dinner first, then head upstairs." He could hear the sadness in her voice, the resignation of someone with no options left.

In that moment, he imagined exactly what their future would be like. Waking up to make sure the lighthouse was secure, prepare and eat food, enjoy the brief warmth of each other's arms, all before night descended again. Day after day, it would last. Until one day, there would be no food and their perfect little pattern would crumble to pieces.

Finn pushed away the dread. "I'll be down in a minute."

She gave him a brief nod, then left. Her footsteps echoed as she descended the metallic staircase. After a moment, Whiskers leaped off his sleeping perch and scampered after her, leaving Finn alone with his thoughts.

Paperwork spread out along the floor where he had been sitting. He had spent hours looking for pieces and parts, manuals, anything to help him do the impossible. He ought to continue the work, keep going before he ran out of daylight, but doubt whispered in the back of his mind.

What if they really didn't have a chance? What if this was it—this strange domestic simplicity he and Ash had fallen into. What if these were to be the last weeks or months of his life before famine showed its ugly face? He didn't want to spend the end of his days trying to solve an impossible puzzle. He ought to enjoy the time he had, regardless of how short it might be.

But Finn couldn't do it.

That doomed fate felt like a tidal wave, huge and all-encompassing, blocking out the sun, blocking out his future. He couldn't lose himself to their newfound love, knowing a giant tidal wave was getting closer to them every day, ready to crash down and destroy them both. He couldn't pretend to be happy like Ash was determined to do.

Regardless of what Ash wanted, he had to keep going. He had to keep trying, even if it was futile. Then maybe, just maybe, things might actually get better. What a shock that would be. They could really use a streak of good luck right now, but he had the feeling they would have to make their own luck.

Through the small grimy porthole window, long orange rays of sunlight struck out across the ocean, peeking out from behind clouds. Ash was right, night was coming. The days always seemed so short, even though he was always so busy.

With a heavy sigh, he organized the papers again and made his way out of the cramped space of the shipbuilder's room. He forced himself not to look at the tiny clay figurines of the sea witch, even though he felt their eyes upon him when he pulled the door closed.

Or perhaps it was just his imagination.

15

ASH REMAINS

DOWNSTAIRS, THE BEAT UP DOOR WAS hung on fresh hinges. Ash must have found the new hinges somewhere while he had been upstairs cleaning windows. She had also picked up all the broken bits of door from when the sea witch had entered the lighthouse. It was almost like she had never been there.

The door itself severely bent inward. The bolt on the door didn't latch properly, which meant they wouldn't be able to lock the sea witch out at night.

"I tried to fix it," she said as she spooned soup into bowls. "But I don't think we can get it to latch again."

"Yeah, I see," Finn said with an ounce of fear in his voice. They couldn't delay climbing to the top of the lighthouse each evening. The sea witch could now easily come inside and creep her way up the stairs. A pit of worry formed in his stomach, but there was little they could do about that.

"Sit down, please, so I can serve dinner," Ash said.

Finn did as he was told. The scent of the vegetable soup made his mouth water, and he dove in as soon as she place it in front of him. It reminded him of the soup Dad used to make for him when he was sick. It was like some kind of magic got put into it that always made him feel better.

"You're an absolute whiz in the kitchen, you know that?" Finn said as he slurped down another hot spoonful.

Ash smiled, chewing on some corn bread. With so much corn meal in storage, it was now a staple of all their evening meals.

"Thank you," she said. "I'm self-taught, so hearing that really makes me proud."

"Seriously?"

She nodded. "I found a bunch of recipe books and read them religiously. I saw all the ingredients in the storage room and knew I wanted to make something good to eat instead of chewing on jerky every day."

It was good to see Ash smile again. Finn had been afraid he might have chased it away with talk of his plans. Maybe it was best he simply didn't talk about it anymore with her. He didn't want to see her upset and fall into that pit of resigned sadness again.

"You would have hated the first meal I tried to cook." She laughed. "I tried to broil toast in the oven, and they burned to charcoal."

He gave a small smile and cocked an eyebrow. "Don't you mean burned to *ash*?"

She rolled her eyes, but didn't comment or even laugh. No, he would have to try harder than that to pull her out of her lingering depression.

"Ash is a lovely name, by the way. I don't think I've ever heard it before. Are you named after ash trees?"

She blinked and glanced away from him, turning to look toward the flickering flame of an oil lantern. "No, I was named after the ash left behind after a blaze."

His smile fell, and he reached across the table to take her hand. "Do you want to talk about it?"

She pursed her lips and her gaze slipped to the floor before she met his again. Taking his hand, she gave it a squeeze.

"Are you sure you want to hear it?" The breathy tremor in her voice almost made him say no. But Finn could tell this was important to her. This was something very close to her. Even though she would probably act like it was no big deal, if he said no, it would hurt her badly.

"I'm sure. Let's hear it," he said.

She let out a shaky breath and her shoulders dropped. For a moment, he wondered if he had been wrong and he shouldn't have pried. But then she spoke, still holding onto his hand. "I told you before that I only remembered the island. That my memories began and ended here. That's... not entirely true."

Finn raised his eyebrows and forced down his frustration. Once again, she was keeping information from him. No, he shouldn't think like that. She had needed the time to trust him. Telling him this was hard. He needed to be patient with her. "It's okay." He took a breath. "Go on."

"I remember something before the lighthouse and this island, but it honestly doesn't make much sense to me. That's why I didn't tell you about it before. You would have wanted to know more. I know how you are." She gave him a faint smile. "I remember a great fire." She reached a hand up and twisted a curl between her fingers. "The fire was so terrible it sent great plumes of black clouds into the sky. The smoke was so thick it blocked out the stars and the moon. I knew I needed to get out, but I was trapped. There were flames all around me, and the heat was burning my skin." She put her hand to her shoulder and rubbed, as though she was near the flames all over again. "I remember screaming and struggling, and everything hurt. But I knew I had to get away, or I was dead. The next thing I knew, I woke up here on the beach. I... think I must have fallen overboard and hit my head or something. I don't recall how I got here."

Finn rubbed her hand with his thumb. "I heard about a boat catching fire maybe six months back. Maybe that's the boat you were on. I don't remember much else about it. All they said was that they never figured out a cause for the fire and that there were no survivors."

"Except me," Ash said, her dark eyes piercing.

"Except you."

"I don't know if I had a name before. If I did, I don't

remember it. So I chose Ash. Because even though the fire was gone, I remained. The flames took everything from me: my mind, my family, my identity... but it couldn't kill me. In spite of the fury of those flames, I remain."

Tears streamed down her cheeks, but Ash didn't cry or weep. Rage drew those tears. Squeezing her hand, Finn urged her back to him, back to the present, and away from the horrors behind her eyes. For a moment, he was worried he had lost her to the memory, to whatever horrible event had dragged her here, but then she came to life again. With a huff, she wiped her cheeks and shook her head.

"Sorry, I guess it's a long, complicated explanation. I would have preferred to be named after ash trees. I've never seen one."

He gave her a kind smile. "No, it makes perfect sense. I'm glad you fought to remain here, Ash. Otherwise, we might never have met."

"I'm glad too, Finn. Love would have been something I read about in books, not something I knew myself."

He blushed.

"I never would have known what love felt like without you."

"I love you, too," he whispered.

Finn leaned in closer and his gaze drifted to her beautiful lips. Then he knocked a spoon onto the floor with a clatter, terrifying poor Whiskers who ran up a few stairs in a blur.

"Oops!" He chuckled, pulling back.

Ash laughed and Finn couldn't help but join in. He was grateful to see her smile again, her pure joy, even if it was because of his own clumsiness and Whisker's goofy antics.

After their laughing fit settled, she reached over to peck a kiss on his cheek. His stomach filled with butterflies.

"Your turn to do the dishes," she said in a throaty voice and a mischievous smile.

He chuckled. "Not a problem." He had to take a moment to catch his breath before getting started. The memory of her touch fueled him.

16

HURRY BACK HOME

THE BRILLIANT BEAM OF THE LIGHTHOUSE trailed across the rocky crags of the cliffside and spilled out over the open ocean. The beam screamed to anyone who came too close to beware. Danger lurked here. It screamed to be noticed in the pitch black night, but it couldn't scream for help. It couldn't ask for a boat to be sent for two lost, surviving teenagers.

After washing up, Finn took a moment to check the remaining rooms of the lighthouse, oil lantern in hand. The last few rays of sunlight streaked orange into the rooms, but he had to look for a way to call the mainland. He had to sate his own curiosity, to see if they could call for help of any kind. His father would have been irate with him if he didn't at least look. But his searched turned up nothing: no radio, not even a satellite dish. The closest he found was a sign posted for medical emergencies, giving a number to call, but there were no landline phones. The shipbuilder must have had a way to communicate with the outside world. But knowing their luck, it was probably a cell phone and currently at the bottom of the ocean with barnacles growing on it.

Ash was asleep, curled up against his chest. They had kissed and cuddled as the last rays of light disappeared over the horizon. Finn had almost dozed off at one point, but then his mind wandered and wouldn't stop. He thought about the sea witch and wondered if she would crawl back to the lighthouse again. Would the door downstairs creak open or the staircase rattle as she climbed, tendrils of seaweed hanging from her arms and legs? If she hunkered down at the door to their room, would he hear her raspy breaths? Or would she be as silent as a shadow, waiting for one of them to drop their guard and make a mistake?

Whiskers wasn't cuddled up in the blanket at their feet like normal. That had become his customary sleeping spot since he started sleeping indoors with them. Surely he hadn't slunk downstairs for a few bites of food before bed? He knew better than to do that with the sea witch lurking about at night, didn't he?

Then Finn wondered if maybe when he had gone through those extra rooms earlier if Whiskers had darted inside one of them. The cat was so fast he couldn't keep up with him. He had an uncanny ability of slipping by their legs and into rooms he wanted to check out for himself, especially ones normally blocked off.

A creaking sound came from behind him, and Finn gasped in surprise. That was disturbingly close. Above their heads, the beacon continued turning, shooting a beam of light that ought to keep the sea witch at bay, especially after he had scrubbed the glass clean. The unsettling image of the sea witch crouching on the top landing rose in his mind. Watching him with her disturbing yellow eyes.

Ash groaned in her sleep as she shifted positions. Should he wake her—just in case?

Whiskers jumped down onto the blanket beside him, all purrs and claws. Finn almost screamed, but closed his lips on the sound before it could escape, making it a muffled cry of alarm instead. Ash didn't even bat an eye. While Finn's heart still pounded in his chest, Whiskers came over for pets and scratches, clearly quite happy with himself for almost killing him in terror.

Finn smiled. "You almost gave me a heart attack, you silly boy."

Something creaked behind them. Whiskers froze and stopped purring. He turned to look toward the door, tail swishing in agitation.

Was it the sea witch? Finn strained his ears for anything to tell him either way, but it was silent. He swallowed down the dry spot in his throat. He reached out and patted Whiskers on the head, but the cat wouldn't calm down. It was like he was in protection mode.

"It's okay, buddy. If that's her, she can't get you in here. She's stuck outside, whether or not she likes it."

He was mostly certain that was true. If she could get them, she would have come inside already, right? Right. Truths weren't so certain in the dead of night.

He pulled Whiskers into his arms, mindful of Ash sleeping against his chest. The cat whined a little, then gave in and purred, burying his head against Finn's arm.

It didn't matter if the sea witch stared at them all night. Maybe she enjoyed watching them sleep, or was just seething over how she was so close, but couldn't get them. Either way, Finn couldn't stop her. But there was no point in letting her feed on his fear. He cuddled Whiskers in the crook of his arm. The cat's softness eased his anxieties. Whiskers purred and kneaded his paws on the blankets. Finn let the cat's purrs and softness lull him toward sleep. Fingers tangled in Ash's black curls, sleep finally found him.

Just before he fell into a deep slumber, he thought he heard the sea witch hiss from the door. Her annoyance made him smile.

THE SUN WAS TOO high in the sky when Finn cracked open his eyes. Both Ash and Whiskers had left him and the howling wind outside found all the cracks and seams between the glass, making the room icy. He was grateful he had washed those windows the day before because there was no way he would have been able to tackle the job now. Just the thought of it made him bundle deeper under the blankets.

Outside, the waves were higher than normal, though the water was just as blue. Occasional spray from the rocks below splattered against his freshly washed windows. He smiled a little and mumbled into the blankets, "A lighthouse keeper's job is never done."

With a yawn, he crawled to his feet and over to the little pile of clothes he and Ash had left beside their makeshift bed. Sorting through, he found a sweater and pulled it on, happy for any kind of warmth. Like almost all of his clothes he wore each day, he was sure this had once belonged to the shipbuilder. Something about the patterns on the shoulders and around the arms made him think this had to be good quality, especially since he already felt warmer. Something about knowing the sweater had belonged to the shipbuilder made the fabric crawl on his skin instead of sitting against it. But the air was so cold and the sweater instantly brought relief, so he pushed away the strange feeling. He didn't have time to ponder. Today, he had work to do.

He stopped at the top landing of the stairs and looked for any signs the sea witch had been there the night before, but saw nothing. He wondered if it had been his imagination last night, but then remembered Whisker's reaction. No, if the sea witch was getting brazen enough to climb up here and sit outside their room, that was a very bad sign. Eventually, they would make a mistake and fall right into her clutches. Finn couldn't let that happen.

Taking the stairs down, he glanced around for Ash, but didn't see her. Some freshly made biscuits sat on the counter in the kitchen and that relieved the slight panic that always came to his chest when he didn't see Ash immediately in the mornings. He scarfed down two biscuits and drank a big glass of water. In the back of his mind, he knew these were the same buttermilk biscuits she had made a few days before. He wondered how many ingredients they had left to make these. Another question made him more worried: how long would those ingredients last them? Even these tasted a little more stale than they had the first time she had made them, which wasn't a good sign. Baking required ingredients that needed to be kept fresh or else they could get food poisoning. Getting sick out here would be terrible. He would need to talk with Ash about it later, but not right now. She had struggled to tell him so much last night. It wasn't a good time to push. But later, he would have to.

Outside, the sun was blinding despite the chilly wind. It had been late summer when he and his dad had gone out crabbing. Apparently, fall was coming in quickly this year, and he wasn't a fan. That meant school would be starting, what would be his senior year. A bittersweet hurt swept through him at the thought he would be missing it. Not that he loved school or anything, but people would notice he was gone. And he felt a little guilty about that, even though he had no control over any of this.

It was also clear he had been here several days, maybe even a week now, but there was still so much to do. The weather was turning against them. Finn took a deep breath of the cool air and let it fill his lungs, grateful for the sweater that kept him warm. It reminded him of early mornings out on the water with Dad. Those brisk days in late summer and early fall when the work kept his muscles from getting too cold. He spotted Whiskers stretched out on some stone pavers, soaking up the little sunlight and heat.

"Are you heading out?" Ash stood along the side of the lighthouse, a plank of wood in one hand and a hammer sticking out of the pocket of her pale yellow cotton dress. Even carrying all that, she had still sneaked up on him.

"Yeah, I'm heading down to the beach." He couldn't meet her piercing gaze. There really was no reason not to tell her he was heading down to the boathouse. She probably guessed as much anyway, since he was being so cagey. But he couldn't stand to see the disappointment in her eyes. She wouldn't approve of him chasing impossible hopes instead of helping keep the lighthouse running.

"Ah." Her face betrayed no emotion. It was sometimes maddening how she could keep such a good poker face, especially when he was anxious about how she would react. He wished he didn't wear his emotions on his sleeve.

He gestured to the plank of wood she carried. "Was there some damage?"

She shrugged. "Nothing I can't fix. You get down to the beach, and let me know if you find anything useful."

He blinked. "Really? You're okay with me going? I could stay and help with keeping the lighthouse going, if you want."

She shifted the wooden board to her other hand and came over to peck a kiss on his cheek. "I love you. Just be safe for once, okay?"

"Okay." Warmth spread to his cheeks, and he deftly put a hand to the spot. It was amazing how just a kiss from Ash could take his breath away every time. He loved it.

"I want off this island, too. I just want you to come back home to me more." She pushed a strand of his hair behind his ear. "Don't stay too late. Keep an eye on the sky. Those dark clouds could bring a thunderstorm, and I don't want you getting caught in it. Not with the sea witch out there."

A great weight lifted off of his shoulders. He hadn't realized how much he had yearned for her approval until she gave it. He leaned forward and pecked a kiss on her cheek, earning a smile from her that brightened her eyes and swept away the worry always on her face lately.

"I'll be careful, I promise."

"Hurry back home to me, Finn."

"I will." He turned to walk down the path toward the boathouse. As the wind whipped around his face, Finn felt more alive than he had since washing ashore on this accursed island.

They weren't going to be trapped here forever. He

would find a way for them to escape, then they could finally leave the lighthouse for good. Maybe then, he could keep that sadness out of Ash's gaze and give her a real chance to feel hope.

Part VI:

Too Many Secrets

17

AN UNLIKELY ARRANGEMENT

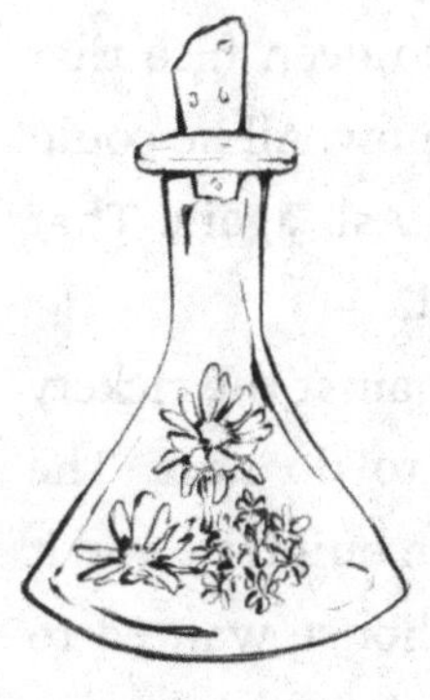

THE HOPE THAT SPED FINN DOWN THE path to the boathouse didn't last very long. After shoving open the creaky wooden door that whined on its hinges, he found the canoe had fallen down from where he had propped it. The excitement he had felt upon leaving the lighthouse deflated in his chest. He hurried over to get a better look. When it fell, it landed on an old toolbox, leaving a nasty hole right in the middle.

"I never knew these things could be so fragile," he muttered as he hauled the canoe out of the cold water. There was a small hole on the inside of the canoe, but the much larger one on the bottom would easily let in sea water, making the odds of it floating again very slim. All the glue and hope in the world wasn't going to make it buoyant again.

"Damn it!" he cried and tossed the canoe aside. He gripped the back of his head with both hands and paced around the room. He kept seeing Ash's excitement, the light sparkling in her eyes, falling into disappointment, despair, and resignation again. No matter what he did, he just kept disappointing her. He had finally gotten her to hope, to believe in him, to trust in his promises. Now he had dashed it all to pieces being careless with where he placed the canoe.

No, wait. The body of the shipbuilder in the water had distracted him. He hadn't been thinking straight. In fact, he had spent who knew how long pacing the beach as he disassociated before being able to even face that horror. But that didn't seem important now. All he could think about was how he had let down Ash again. That guilt ravaged him like nothing else could.

Breathing hard, Finn leaned back against the rickety boathouse, trying to figure out what to do next. The ocean waves crashed against the wooden building, and it creaked from the strain. Even the boathouse wanted to collapse.

"Why not?" he spat. "Everything else here is busted. Why not this place, too?"

Another wave sent a new series of creaks throughout the building, and it almost felt like the wall shifted. Finn pushed away from the wall and looked around, a bit alarmed. Had the water been this high the last time he was here? He hadn't realized the ocean waves came so close to the boathouse. Was it safe to be here?

A roar of thunder made him jump. Now that he

looked around, his eyes accustomed to the gloom that surrounded him, it was pretty dark inside the small, cramped building. The little broken boat he had discarded last time thumped into the wall, moved by the waves and hitting the wooden boards of the boathouse. It was eerily similar to the sounds the shipbuilder's body had made under the waves. The boat was still afloat, though; it hadn't sunk like he expected. Despite the extensive damage it had taken, it was still floating on the water. That had to be a good sign. He couldn't let Ash down. He had to find another way to save them.

With the canoe no longer an option, the boat was the only chance they had left. He would have to repair it somehow. He hung his head and grunted in frustration.

"I guess it's better than nothing," he muttered. "But I definitely need some light first." He felt a little silly talking to himself, but hearing his own voice made him feel a little better as he bumped around in the dark.

Cautiously, he moved around the boathouse, looking for anything that could provide light. Surely, the shipbuilder had left something in here. He found a very dusty oil lantern and a small lighter. He had to rub the lighter on his pants a few times to get the dust off enough to actually flick it to life. The tiny flame threw shadows around the small room, giving the illusion of movement. Finn swallowed down a lump in his throat.

Cupping his hand around the lighter to keep the wind off, he lit the wick of the oil lantern and put the glass casing over it. Then he turned the squeaky knob to make the flame bigger. The acrid smell of burning dust overwhelmed him, making him cough. A moment later, the more pleasant smell of burning oil took over.

Light made everything better. The shadows didn't feel so close and the cramped space didn't feel so small. Finn also got a better look at what he was dealing with. The boat was lodged under the deck of the boathouse, caught on something. That's what made it so difficult to look at before. To free it, he would need to drop down into the water.

"Great. Exactly what I wanted to do today." He sighed. "It just couldn't be easy, could it?" Outside, thunder rumbled and the rain roared. He let out a long groan. "Watch the skies, Ash said. Oh well. So much for getting back quick."

He looked around at the water. The waves were coming regularly, faster than normal with the oncoming storm, increasing the strength of the waves outside. But it didn't look too bad. He could probably manage it.

Part of him was horrified at the thought of crawling back into the ocean. Wasn't he grateful he got out last time? Did he have to tempt the fates by getting into the ocean again? But this wasn't a shipwreck, and he was only a few feet from dry land. This wasn't anything like that night. At least, that's what he told himself.

He had spent so much of his life out on the ocean, he refused to let the shipwreck take away his joy of the sea. Despite the terror that took hold of his heart, he wanted to keep something he loved from his life before. And the ocean had always brought him so much calm and joy.

Then there was the shipbuilder. His bloated body

had bobbed right outside this building for who knew how long. What if he hadn't just slipped and hit his head? What if something had gotten him?

That, of course, led to the most terrifying danger: the sea witch. These were her waters. She could easily pull him down into that dark abyss and drown him. But despite the storm darkening the sky outside, this was technically still daytime. She was only powerful at night, right? At least, that's what Ash had told him.

Ultimately, what gave him determination was Ash's disappointment. He wouldn't be able to return to the lighthouse and hold her in his arms, if he wasn't brave enough to climb into the waters to salvage their only hope of escape. Ash might fall into complete despair and hopelessness, resigned to their doomed fates, and Finn would never forgive himself for giving up.

With a heavy sigh, he pulled off his boots. He pulled off his socks and rolled up the cuffs of the oversized pant legs. Then he pulled off the nice warm sweater. He would want its dry warmth once he came back.

The water was icy as he put his feet in first. He had known it was going to be bad, but this was much colder than during his own shipwreck. Finn sucked in a breath through his teeth, then dropped into the water to his waist—then his shoulders. He was breathing fast to keep his body warm as he felt around the stuck boat, looking for a way to get it loose. Hopefully, it would be something he could manage quickly and easily. He didn't want to stay in the chilly waters any longer than he had to.

Waves beneath the surface of the water felt off. Something moved near him. Was it a school of fish? No, this was too big for that. Surely not a shark. This was too close to the shoreline. They wouldn't risk beaching themselves. Then again, the storms often threw wildlife onto beaches with the sheer force of the waves. He thought of the wave that had taken the Wishful and dread seeped into his veins.

No, he had to focus on the task at hand, not let his own fears hold him back. He felt along the edge of the boat to where it was stuck beneath the dock. He might be able to get it loose if he could get some leverage.

The hairs on the back of his neck stood up, and he turned around in time to see a shadowy form floating in the water.

"You love the girl, don't you?" The high-pitched creaky voice was too familiar.

Panic weighted Finn's gut. That, mixed with his existing terror of being in the water, was too much. He splashed and flailed. His heartbeat thudded too fast as he stared at what floated before him.

The seaweed wrapped face of the sea witch stared at him. Seaweed splayed out around her like hair floating in the murky water. Beyond the wrappings, he could make out gray white skin exposed around the mouth and nose. A dead woman's pale skin. Her gray lips were upturned in a grotesque smile. Her yellow eyes gleamed in the shadows with predatory glee. He would have honestly rather seen a shark.

"You love her." She pressed again, her gray lips barely moving. "You can't lie to me. I can see it."

Finn was aware he was shoulder deep in the water, dog paddling in place. She could easily get her claws into him here, drag him down, and drown him. Kill him like she had clearly wanted to before. So why wasn't she?

"Why do you care so much?" he asked with what he hoped sounded like anger, even though his heart wanted to beat out of his chest in terror.

She widely grinned, exposing a set of sharp canine teeth that resembled a shark. The sight sent an icy shiver down his spine.

"You didn't answer me, child."

"Okay." He swallowed down the tremor in his voice. "I do. I love her. Is that what you wanted to hear?" He blinked, surprised how saying it aloud to the sea witch made it even more real. He hadn't realized how much he loved Ash until the damn sea witch made him tell her. That was something he definitely would not tell Ash about later.

As the sea witch cackled, her laughter bounced across the creaky walls. The sound was too loud for the silent space, and it hurt his ears. "I knew it! You wouldn't have had the nerve to crawl into the water if you didn't."

Finn backed away from her, moving along the edge of the boat until his back hit the deck. He put a hand behind him to hold on to the edge and to keep from having to swim. Also to give him some leverage in case she attacked him.

"What do you want with her anyway?" he asked.

She laughed again, giving him that creepy smile. Then she floated toward him. Not swimming, or even looking like her feet moved underwater, but she floated like a grotesque mockery of a flower atop ocean waves. He didn't even feel the movement of water beneath the ocean surface. What the hell was she?

"There's more to her than you know."

Finn licked his cracked lips, tasting briny salt water. "What do you mean?" Part of him chided himself for listening to the sea witch, but another part of him felt a truth in her words. A truth he couldn't deny.

"I'm saying that you should take her words with a grain of salt, child." She gave her shark-toothed smile again and Finn shivered. She had already cleared half the distance to him, but Finn didn't climb out of the water. He could, but the thought of clumsily getting to dry land with his back turned to her seemed like a bad idea. Not only that, but he wanted to know. Finn had been searching for answers ever since he washed ashore, and he kept thinking back to what Ash said, that the sea witch was the only one with answers now. He needed to understand this shadowy, confused mess. Every day, he had more questions than answers, and the lack of knowing was driving him mad. Even though he loved her, Ash had no answers. She didn't know anything that could ease his confusion. That meant his only source of knowledge, if she was to be trusted, was the sea witch.

And here he was talking to her, much like the shipbuilder probably had. He swallowed down his worry at that thought. Look what happened to them.

"Ash is a good person," Finn said with a shaky voice. "She wouldn't lie to me."

"Ash..." The sea witch's smile dropped away to a more serious and menacing expression. "So that is what she calls herself now."

Finn gripped the boards of the deck, ready to pull himself out of the water. He didn't like that look on her face, especially when he was at her mercy here. He knew the sea witch's speed. She could still catch him if she really wanted to. Ever since he had climbed into the water, she had complete advantage over him. But Finn didn't climb out. He wanted to know. He had to ask questions, even if it meant risking his life.

"You knew Ash before she lost her memories."

The sea witch's eyes narrowed. "Yes, I did."

Finn took a deep breath, digging his fingernails into the old splintered wooden deck. The sea witch was so close he could smell the pieces of old seaweed on her. Her breath smelled like raw fish.

"Look, I don't know how she wronged you in the past, but you can't blame her for that anymore. She doesn't have any memories of her time before. Wouldn't it be easier if you just let this whole thing go?"

The sea witch froze and her yellow eyes bored into him as though something was wrong. A powerful grip took hold of his shoulder. Her seaweed-clad hand gripped him hard, her gray skin poking through the wrappings, revealing her powerful muscles beneath. She was beside him, crying out in her horrible high-pitched voice.

"You know nothing about me or Ash," she snarled through her sharp teeth. "You came to our island meddling in matters you can't possibly understand!"

She pulled at his arm and Finn struggled to hold on to the dock with his other hand. If he let go, she would pull him down into those dark waters, down into the ocean. Down to a fate that he almost hadn't escaped last time. He could feel the draw of it, waters that had business to finish with him. Panic flooded his veins. He clutched desperately at the old wooden boards, his fingers hurting.

"Do you fear the waters?" she hissed, her breath smelling like the piles of fish brought ashore by his fellow anglers.

"Yes!" he cried, with tears in his eyes.

She laughed a hoarse, sadistic sound. She released him, and Finn yanked himself back up onto the dock, breathing hard against the old planks of wood. His shoulder throbbed with pain and his entire body shook, but he had to get away from her. He crawled on all fours to the wall of the boathouse, knocking off the old hammers and a rusty saw that hung there.

The sea witch floated in the water, her long, black seaweed hair stretching out like a spider's legs. She watched him with large, bulbous eyes, her expression unreadable.

"If I wanted you dead, don't you think I would have

killed you when you drifted unconscious to my shores? Don't you think I would have dashed your brains onto the rocks before I let you come here?"

Finn gaped, his breaths less ragged now. It took him a moment to realize what she was saying.

"You wanted me to come here—to meet Ash."

She gave a wide, toothy smile. "Clever boy. I knew you would figure it out eventually."

"But why?" He shook his head, his hands shaking at his sides. "Why did you want me here?"

"Ash is lonely. I saw you float up after the storm, and I realized you would be more helpful alive than dead. You should be grateful to me for sparing you."

Finn licked at his lips, tasting salt and giving himself time to think. "You expect me to help you kill her, is that it?"

"No." Her furious snarl reverberated in the small space and Finn winced as his ears ached. "Why must humans make everything so damn dramatic? I want you to help her escape this cursed island. She needs to remember her past." She put a hand up on the dock, her five gray fingers wrapped in the long trails of seaweed. "I want you to help her."

Finn climbed to his feet, keeping one hand on the wall of the boathouse to steady himself. This wasn't at all what he had expected. If the sea witch wanted to truly help Ash, why did she chase her up the lighthouse and scream at her? This didn't feel right. Something about all of this was wrong.

The sea witch pointed a finger at him, slapping

seaweed down on the wooden dock. "Or I could just kill you now, if you're going to make this difficult."

Finn held his hands up. "No, no, I'll help! It sounds like we both want Ash to leave the island. But there's a problem with that."

She drummed her wet fingers on the wood. "And what is that?"

"Well, uh, we don't have a boat. The big boat is flooded, as you can see there." He nodded to the boat in the water.

The sea witch didn't turn to look at the damaged boat behind her or even seemed to care.

Finn swallowed down the lump in his throat. "And the canoe got cracked in the last storm."

She barked a laugh. "A canoe? That was your plan?"

He winced. "I mean, we don't exactly have many options."

She shook her head, wet seaweed slapping against the edge of the dock. "A canoe ... all the way to shore. I guess you have grit, child, I'll give you that. Not always smarts, but definitely determination."

Finn swallowed down the retort on his lips, thinking better of it. It wasn't a good idea to talk back to the sea witch, who now had admitted to nearly killing him multiple times.

"So... you'll help us fix the boat?" he asked.

"No, but I will get a boat for you. One that's a little more reliable to get you to shore."

Finn blinked. "Really?"

"Stop questioning me. I might be tempted to change

my mind. I have a requirement, though, if you want my help with this." A gruesome smile spread across her lips. "You must not tell Ash a word about this arrangement. This must be our little secret."

He blinked. It made sense, of course, since Ash was so scared of leaving to begin with. But having the sea witch explicitly request it be kept a secret made this whole deal more suspicious. Why would she not want Ash to know about this alliance, unless there was more to their strange relationship? But Finn knew if he said no, they would never get the chance to leave again. This was the sacrifice to escape. He had to trust the sea witch.

"Okay, I won't tell her," he said with a sorrowful pain in his heart.

"Good. And if you break your word, I'll know. I always know."

The hairs stood up on the back of his neck as the sea witch turned back to the water.

"Wait!" he cried, taking a few shaky steps closer. "I agree not to tell Ash, but only if you promise not to hurt her. You better not harm a single hair on her head, do you hear me? I'll help her leave this island, but only if you promise not to harm her."

The sea witch glanced back at him, her face in profile. A strange sadness weighed on her, but Finn wasn't sure why.

"I will promise you that easily, child. I will harm not a hair on her head." She gave a slow, respectful nod before sinking down beneath the murky waters.

Finn waited, half expecting her to pop back up. But

the waters only moved for the sheets of rain that fell outside and battered the small wooden boathouse. The oil lantern hanging on the wall swung on its squeaky ring, casting shadows throughout the room.

It took several minutes for his heart to stop beating so ferociously in his chest. After several more minutes, Whiskers appeared, coming out of his hiding place in the corner of the room. His white fur was damp and muddy from the rain.

"Whiskers!" Finn cried. "I didn't know you came with me, buddy. You crazy cat. In this weather?"

The cat mewed insistently, weaving around his legs until Finn bent down to pick him up. Finn scratched his neck and cheeks, realizing the cat would need some kind of bath. He had gotten very muddy on his trek over. Had he come down here in the pouring rain to find Finn? Was he worried something bad had happened to him? The thought made Finn's heart ache. Whiskers purred so loudly he could feel the vibration up and down his arms.

"I can't believe I made an agreement with the sea witch," he whispered. "If Ash finds out, she'll be furious. I must be losing my mind on this island, buddy."

Even as he pulled on his shoes, socks, and sweater, blew out the oil lantern, and clutched Whiskers to his chest to brave the heavy rain, he knew there was no other option. With the shipbuilder dead and the two other boats damaged beyond repair, this was it. Sure, they could try to wait until rescuers finally visited the island or someone came to check the lighthouse, but that could take years. He refused to sit by and let that happen.

They had both survived too much for such a pathetic death.

It wasn't night yet, but the storm said otherwise. The gray clouds had closed out the sunshine and the beach was ghostly in the dim light. Rain came down steady, but not in sheets anymore. Finn knew where to go because not only did his feet know the way along the mushy shore, but the lighthouse gleamed in the distance. Ash had lit all the floors, making the entire tower sparkle like a giant beacon in the darkness, driving away the storm and shadows.

Whiskers whined as soon as they stepped out into the downpour. It didn't help that Finn slipped more than once in the mud. Whiskers trusted him, but still had his claws dug into the sweater to hold on.

Finn's mind whirled. He couldn't tell Ash about any of this, which was hard because he shared everything with her. She was like another part of him at this point. But he couldn't let the truth slip out, no matter how much he wanted it to. He was already creating a new story to tell her instead of the truth as guilt bloomed in his chest.

Finn hoped he had made the right decision in making a pact with the sea witch. Hopefully, he wouldn't end up regretting it.

18

THE WICK BURNS

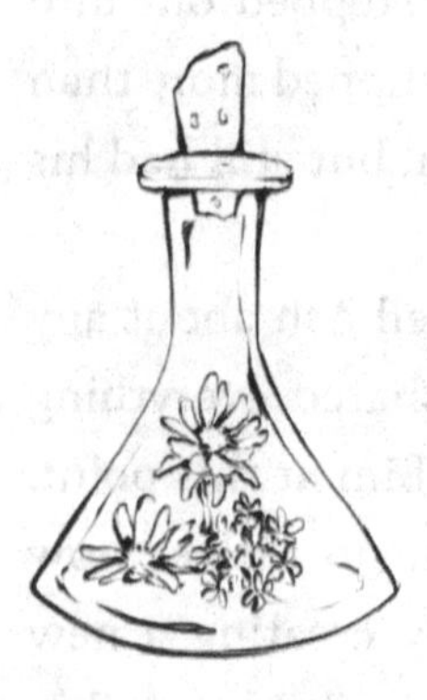

ASH WAS AT HIS SIDE THE MOMENT HE stepped foot in the lighthouse, Whiskers whined in his arms and both of them were drenched to the bone.

"Finn, are you okay? I've been so worried!"

She held an oil lantern in her hand, her knuckles white against the metal handle. Lightning flashed, followed by a roar of thunder that made Whiskers squirm in his arms.

"Yeah, I lost track of time out there. The storm came in so quick. And Whiskers followed me. He's covered in mud." He stroked the nervous cat's fur, trying to calm him down.

"You both are." She looked him over with a worried expression.

Looking down, Finn found his shoes covered in mud.

He had tracked in a mud pile around his feet, ruining the floor Ash had worked so hard to clean up earlier. The guilt in his chest grew. One more way he was letting her down.

"Hang on, let me help." She put aside the oil lantern and helped him take off his shoes, so he wouldn't track mud throughout the kitchen. Finn focused on keeping Whiskers calm while Ash removed his shoes and socks.

"You're wet all over!" she cried.

"Yeah, it was bad out there." It wasn't a complete lie. It had been pouring rain outside. She didn't need to know he had jumped into the ocean to salvage the boat. And she certainly didn't need to know about his encounter with the sea witch. He tensed up just thinking about that.

"We're going to need to get you out of these clothes. You'll get sick." She piled his things in the corner.

"But first, I've got to take care of this little guy. Can I use the sink?"

She nodded.

Finn brought Whiskers over to the sink and turned on the water. The poor cat meowed sadly. "It's going to be okay, buddy. Just stay calm, okay?"

Putting him in the sink, Finn grabbed him by the scruff of his neck to keep him still. Whiskers didn't struggle when the warm water flowed over his back and tail. Finn had expected him to try to jump out, but Whiskers only licked his lips while Finn soaped up his fur. His feet were the worst. Mud had caked between

Whiskers' toes and up almost to his belly. Eventually, Finn had to use both hands to work on each leg.

"He might jump. Can you keep an eye on him?" he asked.

"Sure." Ash leaned in and started petting him.

Instead of jumping out while Finn washed his tiny feet, Whiskers leaned over to drink from the faucet.

"He likes it!" Ash laughed.

Finn arched his eyebrows. "So what was with all the complaints outside, little guy?" He asked with a smile. When the back paws were done, he moved to the front. Whiskers contentedly drank from the faucet and let Ash pet his face like he was some kind of royalty.

"Such a good little baby," Ash whispered. "Finn is going to get you all clean, and you'll feel so much better."

Finn grinned as he finished up with the last leg. Then he lifted each one to the water to rinse. As long as Whiskers had his water from the faucet and Ash's kindness, he seemed happy. Finn couldn't stop smiling.

"I think he's good!" Finn cried as he checked the cat was free of suds. "Is there a towel we can use?"

"Sure!" Ash disappeared, coming back a moment later with a big fluffy towel. She picked Whiskers up out of the sink while Finn turned off the water. The cat was only halfway out before he shook himself. Water went everywhere, including on Ash and Finn.

"Oh, buddy!" Finn laughed.

"What a messy baby!" Ash said, but she had a wide smile as she bundled Whiskers into the blanket.

Finn was now even more soaking wet, and even

though the water was warm, he shivered. Ash took Whiskers over to the couch to dry him off. The poor cat looked so sad with his tail drenched and his fur flat. He looked like a completely different cat now, but at least he was clean.

"You're going to need some new clothes," Ash called to him.

"Yeah, definitely." He took off the sweater that had done its best to repel the water and added it to the pile by the door. "Do you mind if I use the sink to clean up?"

"Sure," she said.

When Ash released him, Whiskers jumped down and shook off again. She had gotten almost all the water off and Finn wished they had a brush to clean him up the rest of the way. But at least the little guy didn't have mud caked into his feet anymore.

"You look cold," Ash said as she came close to him again. "You've got goosebumps."

Finn gave a sheepish grin, trying not to shiver. "I need to get these off. Can you see if there are any more clothes I can use?"

She smiled. "Of course. And you probably want some privacy, too?"

He nodded and his cheeks heated at the thought of her watching him clean up.

"Hold on for a moment. I'll be right back." She turned and hurried up the stairs.

Finn rubbed his hands together, trying to stay warm. Jumping in the water at the boathouse had not been a smart idea. Of course, if he hadn't, he wouldn't have encountered the sea witch or given them a chance to escape. But feeling as cold as he did right now, he felt like an idiot.

Ash was back much sooner than he expected. She carried a pile of clean clothes and put them on the table. "Clean up, get dressed, and come upstairs to warm up, okay?"

He nodded, afraid if he spoke, his teeth would chatter.

"I'll be waiting for you." She gave him a smirk, then hurried up the stairs. Whiskers followed her up, shaking out his back legs as he climbed, leaving Finn alone at the bottom of the lighthouse.

He peeled off his pants, rolling them to get them off his legs. Next came the undershirt and the underwear. The belt he put aside, fully expecting to use it to keep the new set of clothes on. He had to peel everything off, but as he did, he shivered harder. He used the bathing sponge to wash off, getting the sea salt off his skin and scraping mud off his legs that he hadn't known was even there. When he dunked his head into the sink to wash his hair, he heard a creaking sound that sounded off.

In a rush, he turned off the water and listened. His hair dripped into the sink, droplets clinking against the metal. The rain came down in sheets outside, slamming into the windows. Thunder rumbled, vibrating everything in the building. He strained his ears and his mind, trying to decipher the sound. But other than the storm, everything was still.

Nervously, he resumed washing his hair, this time

working faster. He rinsed it out beneath the faucet, unable to resist the calm that came over him from the warmth.

When the creaking sound came this time, he recognized it. It was the front door.

He flung back his head, splashing water, and turned to look at the front door. He half expected the sea witch standing there. But she wasn't. The door was partly open, and he stared at it, waiting for those seaweed clad fingers to come around the edge. But the creaking sound came again and this time he saw what it was.

The door hadn't been closed completely, and wavered in the breeze. That's all it was. Not the sea witch, just the storm and the wind.

He let out a sigh and chuckled. Now he truly was jumping at shadows. Whether he wanted to admit it, the sea witch had gotten under his skin.

He toweled off using a fresh towel and pulled on the dry clothes, reveling in their coziness. Then he pushed the front door closed and made sure it latched this time. They couldn't lock it, but at least it could close properly with a little extra push. He shook his head, ashamed for being so on edge. Then again, everything about this place put him on edge.

He piled his dirty laundry and wiped up the mess in the kitchen, mindful to wash out the sink, so Ash could cook in there later. He really wasn't trying to be a burden, but everything he did seemed like it.

Still shivering, he climbed the staircase to join Ash and Whiskers at the top. If this storm lasted all day, they would probably have to stay up there together. With how dark it was outside, he knew he would probably be safe from the sea witch, but Ash wouldn't be. Making this even more complicated, he couldn't explain anything.

A whole day of maintaining the lighthouse had been wasted, but it wasn't all in vain. At least he had a plan now, even if his new collaborator terrified him.

THE NEXT MORNING, Finn awoke with a warm, fluffy cat asleep on his chest. Whiskers had done a pretty good job of cleaning himself after the bath yesterday. His fur definitely looked better than even before he had gotten mud all over. When Finn lifted his fingers, Whiskers sleepily rubbed his cheeks over his fingertips and purred. At least he wasn't angry about the bath. The cat rolled over and stretched his paws out with an enormous yawn.

Finn chuckled. He could relate. He had been utterly exhausted after his encounter with the sea witch and walking through the mud in pouring rain. And his muscles were still sore from cleaning those windows the day before.

The storm had passed while they dozed around the beacon, leaving clear skies and a brilliant sun in its wake. The waves bobbed on the ocean, and Finn resisted the urge to fall back to sleep again.

Downstairs, the clanging of metal forced him awake

again. He blinked. It sounded like dozens of metallic objects colliding in a rhythmic pattern.

"What is Ash up to today, buddy? She's always up to something." It sounded like a complaint, but he actually loved that about her.

Whiskers licked at his lip and rolled over, kneading Finn's shoulder. He petted the cat's warm stomach until the sound came again. He let out a sigh.

"Guess I need to figure out what's going on, don't I?" Worry tugged at him. His anxieties took little to trigger these days. He gently pushed off a disgruntled Whiskers, threw on some shoes and his belt, and hurried downstairs.

"Ash? What are you doing down here?" Finn couldn't repress the smile on his lips. He could get used to getting woken up by Ash causing a ruckus every other day. It was cute.

He hadn't quite reached the bottom of the staircase when he found her. Ash walked down the stairs, dragging what looked like a canvas bag full of cans. He paused and shook his head.

She turned back to him with chagrin. "Did I wake you? I'm sorry. I just wanted to get these out of here." Her cheeks were flushed, but an unhealthy sallowness had settled around her eyes. The discoloration looked a little off, like she was coming down with something.

"What are these?" he asked, gesturing to the canvas bag.

She took a moment to stretch her back and catch her breath before answering. "Apples. Well, they were a little after their expiration date about a month ago. But now, they don't smell very good. I wanted to get them out of here before they went completely bad or I accidentally use them." She gave a nervous laugh, not meeting his gaze.

Finn blinked. If the apples smelled that bad, then they had already gone completely bad. But Ash was already working hard and he didn't want to bother her. It wasn't a good sign to have canned goods going bad. Fruit, too, which Finn knew they needed to stave off scurvy, and similar nutrient deficiencies. That was something they absolutely couldn't scavenge up around the island. He had read about that when he dove into learning about pirates as a kid. Never in a million years did he think it would be something he would have to worry about.

Carefully, Finn stepped around the canvas bag that was overfilled.

"What are you doing?" Ash asked.

"Let me do this. You do enough around here. I can at least help where I can." He took the end of the canvas bag from her.

She sighed. "Okay, if you're sure. It is a little heavy. I think I put too much in."

He twisted the end of the bag around his hand before getting a closer look at her. "Hey, can I feel your forehead?" he asked.

She blinked. "Sure. Why? Did I get flour on me or something?"

"Hmm." Finn put a hand to her forehead. He thought

back to how his father had done this so many times for him over the years when he felt bad. He missed having an adult around, so he didn't feel like he had to pretend to be one all the time. "You don't feel warm. If anything, you feel a little cool. How do you feel today?"

"Fine," she said. "Like I guess I could have put a few less cans in that bag." She gave a nervous smile.

"No stuffy nose or cough or anything?"

She sniffed dramatically and tried a dry cough before shaking her head. "No, I feel okay. Why?"

"Your color looks a little off." He dragged a thumb over the skin beneath her eyes and her upper cheeks. Nothing rubbed off on his hand. "Maybe take it a little easier for a few days. Let me help some around here. I don't want either of us getting sick."

She put a hand to her own forehead. "I don't remember being sick before. It doesn't feel like anything."

He smirked. "Everybody gets sick, even you." He pulled on the canvas bag and got it down one more step. It was a lot heavier than he expected. "Do you have a place you're taking these?"

"I'll lead you there." Ash hopped down the rest of the steps to hold open the front door.

Outside, the birds were chirping and a pleasant breeze came off the ocean. Big puffy clouds floated over-head against a stark blue sky. It was beautiful. Too bad he had so many things to worry about here. This place could be a paradise at times.

Ash led him around to the side of the lighthouse to a

cellar. She pulled open the faded white doors and Finn saw several more piles of cans inside. Together, they dumped the canvas bag and Ash closed the doors again.

"Glad that's done." Finn huffed down big gulps of air, leaning one hand on the whitewashed wall of the lighthouse.

"Oh, there's still more cans to get rid of up in the pantry. Do you feel like helping me some more?"

He didn't, but damn, did he love her. And he knew if he didn't help, she would try to do it all and make herself sick. "It's probably best if we do it together. I want to take a closer look at what we have, anyway."

Still catching his breath, he followed Ash back inside and up the stairs to the pantry.

"I hadn't realized how much had expired until I started digging," she said. "When I got a whiff of those apples, I got scared I might use some of the expired food and get us hurt. So I started cleaning things out."

She had indeed been busy. Every single can in the room had been sorted. The expired foods were piled close to the door. The pile of good food was much larger, thankfully. That made him feel better.

"This is great." He stepped further into the room. Something on the wall caught his eye. A paper calendar with rip-away months. Something was off about it, and it took several moments of staring to realize why.

"Ash...?"

But she wasn't paying attention. Ash was explaining her organization and how the stacks of cans were sorted by vegetables, fruits, and meats. She had gigantic bags of flour and sugar lined up against the wall. She came over to join him.

"Oh, you found the calendar! I was so grateful to find that because it really helps to figure out what needs to be thrown out. It's hard to keep track of time here."

Finn took her hand and gave it a squeeze. She trailed off.

"Finn, what's wrong?"

He pointed to the calendar. "That's not today. Not even close. That's about two years old."

Her eyes went wide and she put a hand to her mouth. She glanced at the large pile of cans she had set aside to keep. "Oh...oh no..."

AFTER FINN FIGURED out the actual date, it took them hours to sort out the rest of the cans. It was almost September, when some of the worst storms would come through. Admittedly, he might be off by a few days, since he had spent so much time at sea, but it was nowhere near as off as the calendar Ash had been using. They worked quietly, and Finn's heart sank as the discard pile grew larger and larger.

By the time they finished, only a tiny pile of good cans remained in the corner. Thankfully, it included some oranges, so they at least wouldn't have to deal with the very real potential of scurvy right away, but it wasn't months or even years away like he had thought. It was maybe three or four weeks, if they stretched it.

"We're lucky," he said as he arched his back and felt his spine pop. "We could have gotten food poisoning if we had eaten any of this stuff. See those bloated cans in there? That means bacteria is growing, and those are definitely not ones we want to keep."

Ash shook her head. "I didn't know that."

"Yeah, it's not a good sign when you see that."

She stared silently between the large discard pile and the tiny pile of good food.

He went over and put a hand on her shoulder. "This isn't great, but it could have been so much worse. Who knows what would have happened to us, if you weren't already careful about this."

She twisted her curls in her trembling fingers, not looking at him. "I am so sorry about all of this. You trusted me with the food and everything. I let you down. I could have killed all three of us."

He pulled her into an embrace. She buried her face against his shoulder. No tears came, but she did whimper as he squeezed her tight.

"Don't worry," he said. "You didn't know any better. The fact that you've learned so much and cook so well is already amazing. You can't be perfect all the time, and that's okay."

"I'm a fool." Her voice was muffled into his flannel shirt.

"No, you didn't know what year it was. That's not your fault. You don't have any memory of your time before this. That isn't your fault. You were trying to keep us safe."

She sniffled. "I would never have forgiven myself if I got us all sick."

"But you didn't, and that's all that matters. You listened to your instincts, and you kept us safe. I still love you." He kissed her black hair with its salty, sweet smell and gave her another tight squeeze before she pulled back.

"I'll need to make some stew for tonight. This time with ingredients that I know for sure are good."

"Do you want me to cook instead? Let you rest for a bit?"

She quickly shook her head. "No. You helped me realize the danger I was putting us in. Thank you." She pecked a kiss on his cheek and headed for the door. "If you want to help, you can get these old cans out of here. But just be careful. I don't want you getting hurt going down the stairs."

"I'll take care of them." Lifting one hand to his cheek, he reveled in the memory of her kiss. He turned to the large pile of cans that needed to be removed. This was going to be an all day task.

Another day lost. He gave a heavy sigh. Maybe this was their fate, stretching a small pile of canned food as far as they could as they struggled to survive. He had to hope the agreement with the sea witch would play out in their favor. They were running out of options.

His shoulders ached and his lower back complained,

but he filled up the canvas bag to drag more of these cans downstairs.

Time was working against them, even with food.

FINN WAS on his tenth load from the pantry. He had stopped twice for food and to rest his poor back, but it still took forever. He didn't load up the canvas bag as much as Ash had, which was easier on him, but it was still exhausting work. It also was upsetting seeing all the food they couldn't eat now. Canned pumpkin, canned peas, canned carrots, and tons of canned fruit.

He stepped out of the front door and closed it behind him, then stopped and stared down the path that led back to the boathouse. The sun was dipping in the distance, making long shadows from the tall pine trees that loomed over the thin dirt path. It would be darker down there now with the sun setting. His heart pounded, but not from just the physical exertion. Was the sea witch down there now, waiting for him to show up? Maybe she had gotten the boat already and was annoyed at him for his tardiness. What if she changed her mind about the whole thing?

He gripped the canvas bag tighter, wishing he could go down there and find out. But it was dusk. They were losing daylight by the second. It was too dangerous to go down there now. Ash would suspect something. She was clever, and he already felt like a heel for having to lie to her about this at all.

As he had bagged and dragged cans all day, he imagined what would happen if he told her, then wondered how the sea witch might respond. But he pushed away those impulses. If Ash pressed him, it wouldn't take much for him to admit everything. He loved her too much. But for both of their sakes, he hoped she wouldn't find out. He didn't want to anger the sea witch and lose this strange alliance. It was their only chance to escape now; dealing with the cans had reminded him. He couldn't screw this up.

Inside, Whiskers whined for his dinner. Ash's voice was muffled through the concrete walls as she responded to the cat. Despite his negative thoughts and constant worries, Finn couldn't hold back a smile as he listening to them.

"Easy now, Mister! You'll get your food, just be patient. You're lucky the cans of cat food we found are still good."

Whiskers responded with more urgent whines, and Finn chuckled. He dragged the canvas bag around the side of the lighthouse. The white doors were eerie in the dwindling light and he fumbled with the handles to open it. Even his hands were tired. He dropped the cans in, the cacophony overwhelming everything else. Finally, the bag was empty, the last bag of cans to discard was done, and he let out a relieved sigh as he closed the white cellar doors and latched them.

"Finn! Come back inside. It's too dark to be out there!"

It was Ash. She shouldn't be leaning out in the dark to tell him this. It was too dangerous for her! Of course, he had made her do it, coming out when it was getting so late. He balled up the canvas bag and headed back. If she only knew who he had made a deal with, maybe she wouldn't be so worried about him. Hell, she might not talk to him ever again, either. Not that he would blame her. He was lying to her every day about this.

The thought dropped a weight into his gut.

Ash practically yanked him through the doorway, then closed the door quickly behind him. Finn had already lit the oil lanterns up the stairs and in the pantry as he worked. The lighthouse always got darker first. Ash had lit the rest of the oil lanterns in the kitchen and living room.

"I wish you wouldn't cut it so close all the time," she whispered as she picked up the oil lamp she liked to carry with her and turned up the wick so the flame cast more light.

"Sorry," he muttered, tossing the canvas bag aside. "I just wanted to get it done. That was almost the last load."

"Well, it could have been your last." She glanced around the room, as if the sea witch was lurking in the shadows, ready to pounce them. Then she turned the wick up some to make the room even brighter.

"Hey, you'll burn the wick out faster if you do that." He gestured to the oil lamp.

Ash arched an eyebrow at him. The light from the flame flickered in her dark eyes, casting strange shadows on her face. He felt drawn to her, protective of her in that space that seemed made only for the two of them, where the shadows and light danced together between them. He put a hand on her arm, and her skin felt cool beneath his touch.

"You saw our stock of food up there," she said. "Candle wicks are the least of our worries."

He sighed. She was right, but damn, it hurt to hear the worry in her voice. It was painful to even think about. Finn took the oil lantern, so Ash could hold her skirt as they hiked up the long stairwell.

When they had first gone up to stay near the beacon overnight, it had felt like a safe, protective space. Now it felt like they were going up to their prison. As darkness shut out the world every night, they shunned the world at the top of the lighthouse. Only able to look out and see the world around them, but not really getting to live in it. The more Finn fell into the familiar habits of the lighthouse, the more suffocating they felt. Whiskers trotted up past them, smelling of his fishy dinner.

Halfway up, Finn turned back, expecting to see the doorknob turn or to spot the lumbering figure of the sea witch in the doorway. But the first floor was motionless. Of course, the sea witch wouldn't come any longer to haunt the shadowy corners of the lighthouse. She had no need to. Finn was going to bring Ash right to her in a boat she provided. Right out on the ocean water where she wanted her to be.

Finn shivered. No, the sea witch had promised not to hurt her. This was their only way to escape, especially now with their food stores so low.

"Come on!" Ash hissed from farther up.

He turned and continued climbing the stairs, wondering for probably the hundredth time that day whether he was doing the right thing. The higher he climbed, the more his guilt weighed on him until he imagined it crushing him right into the metal stairs beneath his feet.

Ash was waiting for him at the top of the lighthouse, her expression earnest and trusting. She pressed a kiss to his cheek, then she closed the door behind him. Somehow, she gave him the strength to push the guilt away. Even if it was just for a little while.

19
SEEKING DARKNESS

 Sunny weather turned the island into a paradise over the next week. Every day Finn woke up to see it, his heart sank a bit more. The weather was more beautiful than he had seen on the seas in a long time, especially for late August, going into early September. This time of the year was supposed to be building up to storms, yet it was the exact opposite day after day. Not that he hated seeing the sunlight reflect off the ocean waves, or he didn't want to help with cleaning and maintaining the lighthouse. It was because he knew he wouldn't get to meet with the sea witch any time soon.

Since their strange agreement, he hadn't heard or seen anything from her. There were no signs she was coming into the lighthouse late at night. He didn't spot her skulking near the building when the sun sank beneath the horizon, though each night he tried to look. She simply hadn't come by. It was like she had stopped caring. Frustration built each day they had no boat and their food supply continued to dwindle. He couldn't just resign himself to this fate, though. He couldn't give in like Ash did. So his annoyance rose each day. He was careful not to lash out at Ash or Whiskers, but it didn't help, keeping those feelings locked up inside. He was too rough with cleaning, too loud closing doors behind him. But he couldn't help it. He felt like a fool.

The sea witch needed the rain. She needed it to be overcast to visit him down at the boathouse, and until that happened, he and Ash were slowly going through their limited food supply. He checked on it every day and watched with a sinking heart, as the cans got fewer and fewer. Even Whiskers was getting low on food, and though the cat could hunt on his own, that wasn't good for him. He could get all sorts of parasites and diseases since they couldn't get him to a vet anytime soon. It all felt overwhelming.

Ash was in fairly good spirits. She didn't comment on how they were out of cornmeal now, or that she was cutting down on the yeast in the bread, which made them sink more than rise. The sea witch had finally left her alone, so she was happy, oddly content in this dire situation. But Finn knew they wouldn't survive without a boat off the island. He had no fishing gear, no way to go out farther into the ocean, and without their canned goods, they would have no access to fruits. The path they were on couldn't end well.

Finn went down to the boathouse almost every day under the pretense he was working to fix the boat or the canoe. Really, he was hoping to get the sea witch to come see him, but she never did. He dropped his feet into the water inside the boathouse and splashed around. He called out to her, walking around the building. But the sea witch didn't come.

Ash thought he was determined to find a way home for them, using whatever tools he could find to fix the boat. But Finn was not a woodworker. He couldn't craft boats out of trees. He had searched the boathouse top to bottom, looking for anything he could use. All he found were some nails and some basic tools. No saw or even an axe to cut down trees. If Ash knew the truth, she would probably be terrified. Finn certainly was.

In the distance, he had seen storm clouds form, dump their downpours far away from the island, then float off, leaving behind only the humidity. It was maddening. Every day tested his ability to keep a secret he didn't want. And every day he lost more of his patience with the sea witch and her ridiculous games.

Finn went to the shipbuilder's study and closed the door behind him. Whiskers opened his eyes and yawned from where he lay on the back of the brown chair. Finn paced on the threadbare rug, grumbling his woes to the cat, the only companion he could confide in. He came back in this room often lately, staring at the tiny ships and their dusty bottles, staring at the piles of forgotten paperwork, and looking out through the foggy porthole window.

It was near dawn, and Ash was still asleep. Finn was jealous. Sleep had been finicky for him the last couple of nights as the prospect of escape slipped further and further away. He felt like a failure. Watching the love of his life and his new furry friend starve to death had him in a panic. His brain got stuck in a loop of worst-case scenarios, and nothing could break him out of it.

The only place that gave him any respite was here, the shipbuilder's room, surrounded by the miniatures and the comforts of his life. They weren't Finn's preferred comforts, but they made him feel better all the same. He questioned all week why that was the case. It was only after he rummaged around the drawers of the desks and found a reference book for boats that he realized the room made him think of his father.

The space reflected patience, something he didn't have much of these days. It also made him feel more in control, more logical, and less panicked than he did when he tried to sleep or when he saw the dwindling supplies in the pantry. The room was a place of sound advice and careful planning, which was a boon to his nerves while the walls of the lighthouse kept closing in.

Finn picked up a groggy Whiskers, buried his face in the kitty's flurry fur, and plopped down in the chair. Hot tears sprang from his eyes as he cuddled the cat.

"I just don't know what to do anymore. If the weather never turns, how is the sea witch supposed to get us our boat? Do we just all die here?" He sniffled, stroking the sleepy cat's head. "I'm a fisherman with no tools, buddy. I've looked everywhere for fishing poles, fishing lines, nets, hooks, anything. But there's nothing. The shipbuilder was definitely not interested in catching his own food. Even if I could fish for us, that won't last forever. You might be fine eating fish every day, buddy, but Ash and I couldn't."

Whiskers flicked his tail, clearly not happy with such an emotional way to wake up, but Finn was desperate for any kind of comfort, so he held him closer.

"What are we going to do?"

When he gave a final squeeze, it was too much for the tired cat. Whiskers turned around in his arms and used the base of his neck for a springboard to scramble onto the back of the chair again.

"Ow!" Finn leaned his head back to rub at his neck. "Was that really necessary?"

Whiskers fastidiously cleaned his side where Finn had been crying.

Finn wiped at his cheeks. "Sorry for messing up your perfect fur, buddy," he grumbled, still rubbing at his neck.

Up on one of the top shelves above his head, his gaze caught on a bottle that didn't look quite right. There were rocks inside of it where all the others had sand or water. Something black sat on top of the rocks, but he couldn't make it out. He needed a closer look.

He climbed to his feet, and then to his toes to reach it. The shipbuilder had definitely been taller than him. His fingers barely touched the surface when the bottle rolled to the edge, a hair away from toppling to the floor.

"Don't you dare." He stretched a little further,

leaning one hand on the chair for stability. He wrapped his fingers around the neck of the bottle, though the thick dust made it hard to get a proper grip. It was way heavier than he expected and Finn grit his teeth to pick up the bottle with one hand while keeping it horizontal.

Finally, he pulled it down and settled back in the chair. Whiskers readjusted himself on the back of the chair, wrapping his tail around his feet. Finn leaned over to the window to get a better look inside the grimy glass.

A small fishing boat sat on some sand. Pieces of it had been broken off or damaged. It was hard to tell if the broken ship was intentional. Not too far away were the rocks that had been glued down on one end. A small creature stood inside the rocks made of sticks and cloth with flecks of seaweed glued on. It was clearly the sea witch, but it didn't make any sense.

Why was she standing on rocks? She was on the end of the boats in most of the dioramas. Or she stood on a beach, near the waves and the water. This was the first time he had seen her near rocks, and he had spent a lot of time staring at all the bottled ships.

"Rocks," he said to Whiskers. "Where have I seen rocks like these before?"

Whiskers didn't seem to care, moving on to a full body bath.

Finn turned his gaze out to the ocean, out to the bobbing waves and glaring sun. He remembered floating out there somewhere between life and death. Salt water had filled his mouth if he nodded off wrong. The smell of sun-soaked plastic stained his nostrils. He shook himself, pulling back to the present, but the old smell of plastic still lingered in the back of his nose.

This morning, it had been a foggy dawn, and the humidity had him coughing awake, even though his body only wanted sleep. The splashing sounds of the waves up against the glass windows where they slept had sounded like rain in his sleep. He had hoped for a rainy day, but dawn appeared with just a thick fog. Then he remembered the rocks that sat right behind the light-house, dropping to the ocean. His mouth hung open as realization dawned on him.

"The cliffs!" Finn sprang to his feet, making Whiskers cling to the back of the chair with all of his claws out to hang on.

Looking at the bottle again, Finn committed the layout to memory as well as he could. It wasn't a map exactly, but it was the closest thing he had to one. "There must be a cave somewhere in there. That's what the shipbuilder was trying to create with the rocks. Maybe that's where she lives, Whiskers!"

Finn slid the bottle onto a lower, safer shelf, just in case he needed to come back and study it again. Then he hurried off to grab a raincoat and some sturdy boots. They might not have much more food, but they had plenty of clothes to ward off bad weather.

Where he was going, he would definitely need it.

Part VII:

Fears and Superstitions

20
ALL THE RAGE IN THE WORLD

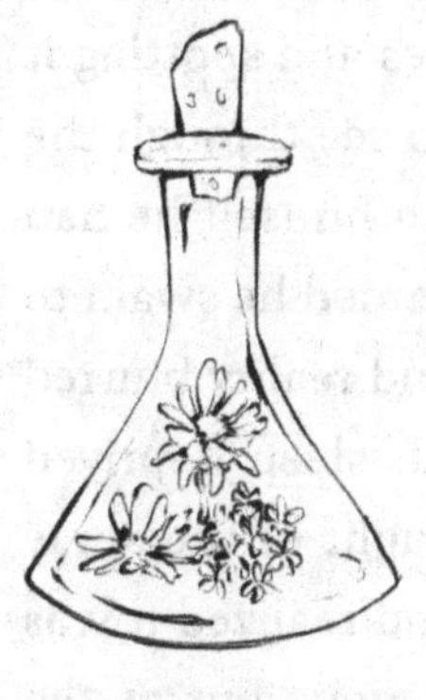

EVEN THOUGH FINN WORE SOME HEAVY duty boots, rubber pants, a rain slicker, and a hat, the cliffs beneath the lighthouse were far more treacherous than he had expected.

Having spent so much of his life on a fishing skiff, Finn had a pretty good sense of balance in slippery places. Or at least, he thought he did. The waters tossed spray so high up the cliffs, even on a sunny day that no matter where he stepped, every place was wet, slippery, and dangerous.

He couldn't imagine the shipbuilder coming out this way on their own, considering how they had slipped and fallen to their death at the boathouse. But if they had climbed these slippery crags and still fell to a watery grave, Finn had to be extra careful. If he got too cocky, he might meet a similar fate. The ocean had already taken two people. He didn't want to give it a third. So he took his time, pausing each time salty spray covered his face, his hands, and found a way into his mouth. He also rested after so many steps. His body ached from all the physical work he had been doing over the past few days, so he didn't want to push himself so hard he got hurt. That would be incredibly easy to do out here.

Normally, he would have considered the cave in the shipbuilder's diorama to be pure fantasy. Something they had put in just to vary up the bottles. But Finn remembered seeing the cave the morning he washed ashore. It had also been foggy early that morning. He had a vague memory of opening his sore eyes and spotting it in the distance, but it had been hard to see through the fog. At the time, he remembered telling himself he had imagined it. A mirage. He had even dreamed he swam to it and made a fire. Of course, dreams and reality blurred together, especially in the dehydrated, sleep deprived state he had been in. But then he thought of the spray against the windows he had washed and realized it was the same place. It seemed so obvious now, but at the time, he hadn't even considered it.

Finn inched his way cautiously across the black stones and wondered if the cave could have been in his imagination, too. Maybe the reason the shipbuilder put that bottle so high on the shelf was because it was their own creation, not a reflection of the real world. Maybe Finn had been so desperate for a refuge when he had been floating on the waves that he imagined the cave as a comfort. Much like he imagined the shipbuilder to be a sort of a surrogate parent for him now that he wore their clothes, had their cat, found their body, and spent so much time in their study. A therapist probably would have a lot to say about that. But it had been a strange comfort for him ever since Dad had died.

Damn, it still hurt every time he thought about it.

Another fierce spray of salt water shot up from below. Finn turned toward the rock wall, clutching the crags as he tried to minimize how much spray slipped into his eyes and wishing he had found some goggles to wear.

A gap appeared in the rocks. A small triangular shape, it was not big, only just large enough for him to duck down and step inside. Water sprayed in behind him, splashing into the cavern and against his rain slicker.

Darkness met him. It took a moment for his eyes to adjust and for them to stop burning from the sea water. While the opening was small, the cave itself was massive. A trickle now came through the entrance from the cave out to the ocean, but Finn could imagine during a downpour how it would turn into a drain spout, shooting water out the tiny gap when it gained enough pressure.

During the bright days, the dry days perhaps, this would serve as a perfect place for the sea witch to avoid sunlight. He thought back to the damaged ship in the bottle. Possibly this was a good place to prey on sailors and castaways, too. He shivered at the thought.

Finn took off his hat and raincoat, grateful to air out

his body. The clothes kept most of the salt water off of him, but it was super humid inside the cave. It felt good to let his skin breathe. He walked further into the cavern. Above his head, stalactites hung down, ranging in colors from red to white. It was beautiful. Finn had seen photos of things online like this, but it was so fascinating to see it in person. Water dripped throughout the cavern, growing the already numerous stalactites slowly over time.

He leaned his head back and spotted movement way up in the shadowy crevices of the cave roof. Behind him, the ocean continued spraying water through the gap in the rock. Only after several minutes did he identify what he was looking at.

"Bats..." he whispered.

"My roommates." The sea witch's high-pitched voice echoed off the walls. "They lived here first, after all, so I guess that makes me the interloper."

She was here! Finn was both elated at finding her and terrified at being in this cave with her. He pushed his fear aside and stepped further in, looking around, still not sure where the sea witch was hiding.

"You promised to get us a boat," he said, voice echoing throughout the cavern. "But every time I go down to the boathouse, all that's there are the broken ones. It's been over a week."

"So pushy. You were reluctant to even make an agreement with me in the first place, child. Now you want me to rush? Why the hurry? Getting tired of spending time with the girl?" Menace sounded in that last question and the hairs on the back of his neck stood up.

Finn pursed his lips. He didn't want to tell the sea witch about their food shortage, but she said she wanted to keep Ash safe. He had already risked his life coming out here to find her, and he wasn't sure he could make it back over those slippery rocks safely a second time if she continued to stall. They were desperate. To the point to where they would soon have to ration Whiskers' cat food.

"The lighthouse..." His tongue felt too thick in his mouth as he tried to find the right words. "Our food stock is much lower than we realized." The fear was clear in his voice, but he couldn't help it. He was terrified of losing Ash and Whiskers. He was scared of starving to death. If it meant saving the ones he loved, he didn't care if the sea witch knew or not. They were the only family he had, and he would beg for their lives if he had to.

Something tugged on his flannel sleeve, and Finn nearly jumped out of his skin. The sea witch stood beside him. She hadn't made a single sound to indicate she was near him.

Her arms, legs, and feet were bare, exposing her gray-blue skin and black clawed nails. Most of her body was still wrapped in thick shiny seaweed clumps up to her neck. But he could see her face now. It was creepy to see how normal and otherworldly she looked at the same time. Her yellow eyes bulged like a lantern and her mouth was full of razor-sharp teeth. Her fingers and toes were webbed, but she would almost pass as a human in the right light. Behind her streamed down more seaweed, but it wasn't really that. It was her hair. It grew from her head, looking so much like the seaweed she clothed herself in.

"The...seaweed..." Finn said.

"A covering to block out light, child. It protects me from your garish sun. But you came to my home. I don't need so much protection here."

"What exactly are you?" Finn asked, wishing his curiosity would be quiet for once, so it didn't get him killed.

"My kind are from the deep places of the world. The child of a superstitious angler would prefer to catch us in a net before talking to us." She poked him in the chest with a shiny clawed finger.

A flare of outrage shot through him and he spoke again without meaning to. "My father was not supersti- tious! He was kind and smart and knew more about the world than most!"

His fists trembled at his sides and hot tears filled his eyes. A part of him knew this anger had been building for a while, but it was foolish to unleash it on the most dangerous creature on the island. But the words spilled from his mouth like fire.

"You're a sea witch from the deep places. You could have saved his life, but you didn't. Our ship didn't just sink. You made it sink. You wanted me here to lure Ash to you so you could kill her!"

A sob broke through and tears came. The week of

terror and stress broke out of him in one violent eruption. His words couldn't possibly be true, but his emotions had more control over him than reason did. Hot tears spilled down his cheeks and Finn dropped to his knees in the cave.

Eventually, the tears faded. A weight had settled on his shoulder. The sea witch's webbed hand patted him.

"I wish I could tell you I plotted all that out. Take your father and everything. It would give you something to unleash all your anger at. But the truth is, child, that isn't how the world works. Sometimes there is no one to be angry at. Horrible things happen to good people every day. All the rage in the world won't stop that."

He sniffled. "I've kept your secret, and it's tearing me apart," he said. "You only want to help us get a boat, so you have Ash at your mercy. And now that we're so close to being out of food, there's no other option but you and your sick games."

The sea witch shook her head and pulled away. "I made a promise to you that I would not hurt her. Have I broken that promise?"

He shook his head. "No..."

"But you doubt my word."

He was silent. He wasn't sure how to respond.

The sea witch crept toward the opening of the cavern, careful to avoid the streaks of daylight. "You might expect that with a lighthouse here that we might have fewer shipwrecks. There are fewer, yes, but a surprising number of boats still meet their end here."

"Despite the beacon? It shines even when it's cloudy."

"There is no perfect system, child. People get lost, technology breaks down. And if someone is stubborn enough, not even a sea witch aboard their ship will deter them."

Finn blinked. "You... try to warn them." A memory returned to him, something he hadn't thought about in ages. "You tried to warn us. I didn't think that was real."

"The night before the storm. I knew it would be a vicious one. Yours was one of the few small ships out there still. You came out of the little cabin and saw me as I stood on the bow. I assumed you understood my warning."

The memory felt distant and foggy. A creature towered over him, glistening in the darkness. He had only gotten up to check the rigging like Dad had wanted. The next day, when they discussed it, Dad had said it was only a dream. He'd thought maybe Finn was sleep-walking.

"You tried," Finn said, wiping away the remnants of his tears. "Thank you for trying."

The sea witch clasped her hands and turned back to him. "Now. As for your boat, I believe I found one, but it's going to take a bit of work to get it. How much food do you have left?"

Finn climbed to his feet. "A week, maybe two at the most, before we have to start really cutting back." They had already lost a week.

"That doesn't give us much time. Once I find a boat, you'll find it on the shoreline near the boathouse. Look for it tonight or tomorrow night. That should give me enough time."

Finn stared at the sea witch. The creature both terrified and amazed him at the same time. One minute, she was chasing them up the lighthouse stairs, and the next she was standing on the bow of the ship in warning. He wasn't sure entirely what to make of her, whether or not she was really trustworthy. But she had tried to save him, and he felt bad for doubting her when she had kept her word, at least so far.

"Thank you," he said. "I don't know what we would do without your help."

The sea witch sprinted forward, grabbed him by the collar of his flannel and lifted him off the ground. A few threads and buttons popped as Finn's feet dangled beneath him.

"Do not confuse my helpfulness for kindness, child. I much prefer your fear to your thanks. If you tell the girl, this arrangement and negotiating ends. I will not give a second chance."

"Yep, I am definitely afraid!" he squeaked.

When the sea witch put him down on the ground, Finn stumbled. His entire body shook as he struggled to keep himself together.

"I will know when you leave the island. It will be up to you to steer the girl to safety."

Finn gulped. "Understood."

"And you must never tell her about any of this. She must never know. Am I clear, child?"

"Absolutely. I won't say a word."

The sea witch was silent. Finn looked up to see he was once again alone in the cave. Or at least the sea witch wanted him to feel alone. Likely, she was in a pool in the cavern somewhere, hiding in the shadows, watching him. He dragged a hand over his face and climbed onto shaky legs.

It took him way too long to pull his raincoat and hat back on. The sea witch probably didn't care how long he took, but he was eager to leave the cavern and put as much distance between himself and the sea witch as possible. As much as he appreciated her help, she was absolutely terrifying.

When he stepped back out onto the slippery stones and started the tedious and dangerous process of inching his way back along the rocky scrags, he couldn't shake the image of the sea witch standing on the bow of the Wishful. He'd seen no malice on her face that night, only pity and concern. Maybe if he and his father had been more superstitious, they would have turned back. Maybe if they had listened to their gut instincts, Dad would be alive today.

Regardless how the sea witch wanted him to see her, there was a kindness in her he couldn't ignore. When he first came out here, he wasn't sure if he should still trust the sea witch would keep her word. Now, despite her threats, he was oddly reassured she would. She had kindness in her, and she didn't want Ash to be hurt. That seemed at odds with chasing her up the lighthouse and scaring the daylights out of her, but the sea witch didn't seem to think in normal ways.

Despite her bizarre behavior, the sea witch was still their only hope of getting off the island alive.

21

FLEETING MOMENTS

FINN MADE IT BACK TO THE LIGHTHOUSE by midday. He hadn't expected it to take so long to find the cave along the rocky cliffside, but he should have. On one hand, he was annoyed about taking so long on the cliffs, but on the other, he was grateful he made it and had some kind of reassurance this plan was going to work.

If the sea witch had wanted him dead, she'd had many opportunities to kill him. But if she wanted Ash dead, all she had to do was wait. The only proof he had she was telling him the truth was if she really got them a boat, and that remained to be seen. He hoped he wasn't playing a fool seeking the sea witch's help, but they had no other options.

Ash was outside tending her garden, humming. She

would see him as soon as he rounded the bushes on the side of the building.

Shit. If she saw him like this with all the rain gear on, she would be suspicious. She would start asking questions. Especially if she noticed him coming from the back of the lighthouse and not from the boathouse, where he said he was going every day. If Whiskers was with her, he would notice him first and possibly draw attention to him, too. He had to think of a plan.

Finn hurried behind some bushes and yanked off the hat and slid out of the raincoat. The rubber pants were harder to pull off. They had plastered to his skin, so he had to peel them down. It was a slow, tedious process, and any second, he expected Whiskers to come running around to see him and meow, getting Ash's attention. But the little guy never showed. As Finn dropped the pants to the ground, he was relieved to feel the breeze again on his damp skin.

Sure, he was only in his briefs and a flannel shirt looking absolutely ridiculous, but at least she wouldn't suspect anything was wrong. Or—at least he hoped not.

He stepped out of the bushes, frowning when the leaves and branches clung to his bare legs. Thankfully, everything looked hidden, which was better than how he felt, half naked and exposed. He wiped off the evidence of the bushes, turning around in circles to make sure nothing would give anything away. Only once he was satisfied did he move around the corner. Maybe he could sneak behind Ash while she was busy and she wouldn't see him like this.

He had only gone a few steps when Ash cleared her throat.

"Finn?" she asked.

His face heated.

"Hi, Ash. Good morning."

She looked him up and down, her eyebrows rising on her forehead. For a few long, painful moments, she was silent. The heat moved down to his neck and shoulders.

"Could you not find any clean pants today?" A smile tugged at her lips.

"Yeah, I found some, but I—" Shit, he was completely messing this up! Why was he so bad at lying on the spot? "I just felt like no pants for a bit today. That's all."

She blinked. "Is that... normal for you?"

He waved her off. "Oh, yeah. I go without pants all the time when I'm home. Especially around girls I like." Sometimes he wished he could turn his mouth off for a while.

Ash's smile spread wide, and she pulled off her apron, carefully placing it near the door to the light-house. "Is that right?"

"Mm-hmm." He nodded, feeling like he was bright red from head to toe now.

She strode over to him, stretching her arms up to his shoulders. "Around a bunch of cute girls, huh?"

"Uh, sure." He swallowed down the lump in his throat.

She dragged a hand across the stubble on his cheek. "I like it. Do you think I'm one of those cute girls you have to impress by taking your pants off?"

He gave a nervous laugh and wrapped his arms around her waist. "I don't know. Is it working?"

She nodded and her dark eyes bored into him. Sliding a hand behind his neck, she pulled him down into a kiss. She tasted sweet, like lavender and hibiscus, her favorite morning tea brew. He had grown accustomed to the taste on her lips. Her taste always left him feeling drunk.

She pulled away to hug him tight. "I love you even when you do really weird things."

He smiled and kissed the top of her head. "Hey, I'm pretty normal most of the time."

She hugged him again and they leaned together in silence for several minutes. The ocean crashed on the rocks in the distance. Birdsong filled the trees. The wind swept through the branches.

Finn breathed in her scent. No matter what happened, he never wanted to forget this moment. Amid all the terror and panic he had struggled with for days, weeks, maybe even months, he didn't want to forget these simple, happy moments when they just could exist without all the fear.

He couldn't imagine a life without Ash now. Every time he thought about the future, she was a part of it. Even after everything was finished and the truth came out, if Ash never wanted to speak to him again or even see him again, he would understand. He would beg for her forgiveness for the rest of his life if he had to. But at least she would be alive.

Life was fleeting. He had heard that growing up, but until now, he hadn't really understood it. He had never really lost anyone before. His mother was a distant person, not someone he had met and loved and knew, like his dad.

Holding Ash in his arms, he felt her breath against his flannel shirt and thought how fleeting all of this was. It could be so easily snuffed out like a candle. After all, if the winds had blown a little differently, he might have met the same fate as his father. But that wasn't how this had gone. He and Ash had a life together, a future, even if they had to be separated somehow along the way. He wanted at least to know Ash was well. Even if it meant without him.

Gently, he pulled back from Ash, who wiped at her eyes.

"I'm sorry," she muttered. "I can't even hug you without thinking of everything. The food, the sea witch... I just want the world to leave us alone so we can love each other. Is that too much to ask?" She huffed a laugh and wiped at her cheeks. "I try to stay busy. Keep myself occupied because every time I slow down, I think. And thinking always leads to crying. I only go to bed when I'm physically exhausted and can't keep my eyes open because I'm afraid to dream."

"Hey, it's okay." He rubbed her arm.

Ash shook her head. "No, it's not. Every day, we get closer to starvation."

"Listen to me, please."

She turned her bloodshot eyes to meet his gaze.

"We are going to get out of here. That won't be our fates, I promise." Damn, he hoped he could keep that promise. Of all the promises he had made in his entire life, please let that one be true. "You and I are going to get to the mainland and I'm going to show you the apartment my dad and I share... er, shared." He pushed away the brief pang of sadness. "It won't be easy. It'll be tough the whole way. And I don't know what I'm even going to tell the landlord about all of this." He barked a laugh. That was going to be a whole process he didn't even want to think about now.

Ash's gaze softened as she took his hand. "You really think so?"

"I know so," he said. Just saying the words aloud made them feel more true.

"So the boat is nearly fixed. Is that what you're saying?" Her eyes were so loving, so trusting. Sweat beaded on the back of his neck.

"Yeah, it sure is," he lied. "Do you want to go see it?" Jesus, why did he say that? As soon as the words left his lips, a tightness formed in his gut. "Once it's farther along, of course," he added quickly.

"It's that far along?"

"Sure. If you feel like hiking out there. The boathouse is right on the water, so it's a little slippery getting in and out." His mind whirled, as he tried to figure out how he might show her anything that could give her hope and not be furious with him.

Ash's eyes went wide, then sallowness came across her cheeks and eyes again, giving her that strange sickly complexion.

"Are you okay?" he asked.

"Yeah, I just... I don't know if I want to go to the edge of the water just yet. I will once it's done. I promise. It's just... it makes me feel anxious."

"You're afraid of the sea witch?"

"Yes... I don't know. The idea of going to the beach. I think I have some terrible memory of it, but I can't remember what."

He leaned over and pecked a kiss on her cheek. "We'll have to eventually. The beach is the only way off this island."

"I know." She laughed. It was a nervous sound that didn't match the white-knuckled grip she had on his arm. "I just have a horrible feeling something bad is going to happen."

"On the beach?"

She shook her head. "No, on the water. I'm so scared to be out on the water, Finn. I'm scared to set foot into it. And it makes no sense, really. I know it sounds ridiculous."

A chill went down his spine at her words. That was probably part of the sea witch's plan all along. But Finn was so deep in his scheme now, there didn't seem to be any other way out than to go through with it.

Even if his instincts disagreed.

"No, that's not ridiculous at all," he said, and he meant it.

22

TORMENTED

Finn was an anxious wreck for the rest of the day. He was worried for Ash, worried the sea witch wouldn't fulfill her end of the bargain. But mostly, he wanted this all done. He was tired of keeping the secret that would take Ash away from him forever. He felt horrible every time he had to hide the truth from her. Every little lie he told felt like it took a bit of him with it.

Dusk had arrived when Finn decided to head to the boathouse. It was probably too soon to see if the sea witch had kept her word, but he needed to get rid of the anxious energy. A light jog to the boathouse would distract him.

He squinted when he reached the beach. The reds and oranges of the dwindling sunset were brighter than he expected. The beach was empty with no signs of washed up seaweed. More evidence the sea witch hadn't come yet. At one point in time, that would have comforted him, but now it was frustrating.

The boathouse was just as he had left it before. The pieces of the boat were shored up against one side of the building, along with the broken canoe. Looking at them brought back all those insidious feelings of failure again. He hated it. In the red light of the setting sun seeping into the dusty room through cracks beneath the boards of the walls, he saw the cat carrier. They would need that when they finally left.

He pulled it from the pile, remembering when he had first found it, the first night he came down here. Why hadn't he grabbed it then? He had come down here more days than he cared to count, but he left it behind every time. Clearly, he wasn't thinking properly. He was so focused on escaping he had almost forgotten their furry cat companion. The carrier would need cleaning, but he could do that at first light.

Rummaging through the shelves, he searched for anything else he might have missed. It was soon so dark he had to light the oil lantern and it cast shaky shadows throughout the room. It wasn't much, but it pushed back the darkness some.

A compass covered in cobwebs appeared to still work. He also found some flares. He had never had to use them before, but his dad had explained them once when he was a kid. He wished he had been given the time to use them when the Wishful sank, but it had gone down too quickly. Having flares onboard had done little for

Dad, but it would still be smart to have them. With a grimace, Finn dropped them and the compass into the cat carrier. He felt like a fool for overlooking all these things before. He had so much time to prepare to leave, but he just kept looking for the sea witch, like she would magically fix everything for him. He needed to focus on actually escaping, not communicating with the mainland, not repairing impossibly broken boats, or any other task. Only leaving and what they would need to get them home.

He found no food staples or emergency manuals. No radio, or anything he could use to call for help, but that wasn't a surprise. He hadn't found anything for that on his previous searches.

Finn gave a hefty sigh and looked once more around the room. Without the sea witch's help, their fate would be sealed. How horrible to rely on their tormentor for a chance at survival. And Ash was the most at risk.

He blew out the oil lantern then trudged back to the lighthouse. It was almost pitch dark now, but he didn't need to see the path. His feet knew the way already from the many times he had come out here.

The moon was a sliver of a smile as it rose into the night sky, almost a new moon. A new beginning. He felt like he had been on the island for years, but it had only been a few weeks.

Had anyone gone out to find their boat, or their bodies? The coast guard would have likely sent someone once they realized they were missing. Maybe they were lucky and found Dad. The thought was comforting. For the first time he truly allowed himself to think about the reality of the situation, to take in what would have happened to him if he hadn't washed up on the island. He had pushed it away every time the thought came floating around before, terrified it would beat him down and break him into pieces again. But it didn't. If anything, it helped to calm him now.

Dad's body could still be lost at sea, never to be seen again. That was a real possibility. But knowing someone went out there looking for him, that someone cared, that part oddly comforted him. Sure, there wouldn't be anyone coming for them on this island, but maybe someone had found Dad.

The ocean was a vast abyss able to consume thousands of lives in an instant. It was a truth he had been taught since childhood. But even if his father had died a silent, invisible death, someone out there cared. Some stranger might have gone out there looking for him and maybe had already found him. Maybe they were looking for Finn, too.

Finn picked up the pace, returning to the lighthouse. The cat carrier felt lighter in his hands. He pulled his gaze away from his feet as a small glimmer of hope filled his chest. Up ahead, the giant building emerged from the thick, shadowy trees and loomed above the entire island. Its beacon spun and sliced like a knife through the thick darkness.

Another light flickered at the base, moving like the flame of a hurricane lantern.

A horrible dread overtook him, and Finn started running.

Breaking through the trees, Finn spotted Ash. She was dressed in a long, flowing nightgown that billowed in the breeze coming up off the ocean. In her hand was a hurricane lantern. The flame flickered, struggling to stay lit despite the glass flute that enclosed it. He was still a couple of dozen yards away from her when she spotted him, and shadows flickered across her wide eyes.

"Finn!" she hissed through clenched teeth. "Why did you go out at night again? What were you thinking? She could be out here!"

He paused to catch his breath and to figure out what to say. He couldn't explain the deal he had with the sea witch, or why the night wasn't as frightening to him anymore. Nothing he thought of would sound plausible. She was risking everything coming out to search for him. Honestly, he should have thought about all of this before he ran off to the boathouse, but he hadn't even considered it.

"Look, I'm sorry. I just had to get a few things to prepare to leave. I just lost track of time, that's all." He lifted the cat carrier as proof. "See? For Whiskers."

She only briefly glanced at it. "I'm all for preparing. You know that. But not with that sea witch lurking about!"

Something moved behind Ash. Finn narrowed his eyes, trying to see it better against the glare of the lantern's flame.

"Never go out at night!" she said. "I didn't think we needed to talk about it again. I thought it was pretty damn obvious when she chased us up the stairs. But clearly I was wrong." She grabbed at his shirt and tried to pull him inside, but Finn only barely moved as he tried to make sense of what he was seeing.

When it lurched closer to Ash, suddenly Finn could see the shiny strips of seaweed on the gray skin exposed around the mouth. Yellow eyes gleamed in the candlelight like a nightmare brought to life. The sea witch looked so much different at night than she had in the cave. Less human and more monstrous than ever. Finn couldn't move. She kept coming toward them in the darkness, footsteps silent on the ground. The sight froze him to the spot. Strands of her seaweed blew out from her sides, like an unraveling mummy. The sea witch drew closer until she stood behind Ash, who was still tugging on Finn's shirt to get him to come inside.

Then the sea witch outstretched a clawed hand toward Ash's shoulder, only a few feet away.

Finn broke free of his stupor and shouted. "Ash, run!"

Ash only paused for a moment at his words. The sea witch lunged forward, but Ash darted off, sprinting into the lighthouse. Finn stayed close on her heels, both running as fast as they could.

He still held the cat carrier when he got inside the lighthouse and closed the door behind them. As he pushed the door closed, he got one last look at the sea witch for just a moment. She stood with a bemused smile on her lips.

What game was she playing now? Just that morning, she had promised to work with him, and now she was chasing them again. Terrifying Ash while making him promise she wouldn't be hurt. What the hell was going on? Why was she doing this?

He closed the door and reached to bolt it, only to remember that the warped door couldn't bolt any longer. Outside, the sea witch gave a horrifying screech and he jumped backward. Upstairs, Ash screamed in terror. He needed to get to her.

Tossing the cat carrier down beside the door, he took the stairs two at a time for as long as his thighs allowed. He finally reached the top, panting and shaky, and pulled the door open, only to be blinded by the beacon. It was like his first night all over again.

"Damn!" He blinked to shake the ghost of the light from his eyes. Ash sobbed not too far away from him. It was gut-wrenching.

He closed and bolted the door, then went around the beacon. Ash huddled amid their blanket bed, the hurricane lamp on the rickety side table beside her. Whiskers paced around her with worry, meowing. Once he saw Finn, he burrowed under the pile of blankets, leaving only his tail visible. Ash was bent over, crying into a pillow and curled into a ball around it.

Finn didn't know what to do. This all felt like his fault. The sea witch's smirk burned into his memory. He had made a deal with her and given her more power than she deserved. She still hadn't fulfilled her side of the bargain. He kept her secret while she tormented Ash. He was still waiting for a way to escape. Maybe he was a complete fool, and she was getting his guard down, so she could get to Ash. But if the sea witch wanted to kill Ash, she could have charged the door tonight and easily gotten her claws into her. So what was going on? What did she really want?

When he rubbed Ash's back, she jumped.

"It's okay," he said. "It's just me."

Her face was red and her eyes bloodshot. When she wrapped her arms around him, he wondered for a second if she might squeeze the air out of his lungs, then she let go.

"I can't keep living like this," she said on a sob. "It feels like she's waiting for me around every corner. Eventually, she'll find me."

"I'm sorry, it's my fault. I shouldn't have been out so late."

She shook her head against his chest. "No, I'm the one she wants. I shouldn't have gone outside to find you. She might have left you alone, but not me. Never me."

He rubbed her back. "This isn't forever. We're going to get out of here. Together."

The sea witch shrieked again, farther away this time, but Ash jumped in his arms and her whole body went rigid.

Why did the sea witch choose to terrify her tonight? Why did she decide to appear at all? Was this her way of backing out of their agreement, or was it the terrible whims of a creature that simply liked to hurt Ash?

Finn had never felt so helpless in his life. Even his promises of safety could be a lie, if the sea witch ignored their arrangement. Ash needed someone who could protect her, someone who was reliable and could keep her safe. He didn't have faith he could do any of that.

All he could do was hold her close, wait out the long night, and curse the sea witch for endlessly tormenting her. All he wanted was Ash to feel safe and be happy, but the sea witch wouldn't even let them have that small respite.

Whiskers emerged from the blankets, meowing sadly, and cuddled up next to him and Ash. Fluffy tail between his legs, he kept glancing in the direction the sea witch had last shrieked. Even the poor cat was terrified of her.

He reached out and rubbed Whiskers' back to calm him down. Finn didn't just have a team, he had a new family. One he loved with every fiber of his being. It certainly wasn't perfect, but it was his family. If the sea witch truly was the only way off the island, he would make sure she helped them escape.

Whether she wanted to or not.

HOURS PASSED. Finn slipped in and out of sleep, though he didn't want to. He wanted, no, needed to stay awake. He shifted his legs around to fend off exhaustion. His eyelids were heavy and Ash was so warm and cozy curled up against him. The rotating beacon of light continued its endless spinning. It was so soothing to him now, a giant nightlight fending off the darkness. Normally, he would have slept comfortably all night with Ash—happily surrounded by her and Whiskers. But not tonight.

Tonight, he was determined to face the sea witch and demand answers.

How? He wasn't sure. The sea witch was fast and dangerous. She held all the power here and possessed all the keys. He was just a kid in way over his head. Challenges like this shouldn't happen to people his age. They should be tackled by adults with far more years and experience, people who could keep themselves from panicking. He struggled with that. Looking back over the past few weeks, he was certain he had made more mistakes than progress. He wanted to set it right somehow. Even if the attempt was futile, he had to try.

In her sleep, Ash untangled from him and turned away. Her breathing fell back into its steady rhythm. She had spent most of the night curled tight in a ball against him, knowing even in her sleep he would protect her. He hoped he could.

"I love you," he whispered in the glass room. He didn't want to wake her, but he also wanted to say it before he did this. Finn wasn't sure what was going to happen or even what he would do, and even if Ash wasn't awake to hear it, he wanted to tell her. He didn't know what else he could do for her.

Quietly, Finn escaped their blanket bed and pulled on his clothes and shoes. He turned back to make sure Ash was asleep still. He didn't want her to know he was leaving. He didn't want to worry her anymore than he already had. She was still breathing deeply, covered in a mound of blankets.

With resolute patience, he descended the stairs, careful to make little sound on the metal steps. In the kitchen, he found a plate and silverware Ash had left out for him, for a meal he hadn't gotten to eat. She must have been so worried when he didn't come home. Guilt reared its head, but he pushed it back down. No, this wasn't his fault. The sea witch had caused this chaos, not him.

He pulled out a match from a nearby matchbox and lit the wick of one of the hurricane lamps, filling the room with light. The smell of lantern oil hit his nostrils as he carefully lowered the glass lid and tightened it down on the edges. He needed to make sure it would stay fastened tonight.

A little trill spun him around, heart thundering in his chest. But it was only Whiskers.

The cat sat a few steps up on the staircase and gave a big toothy yawn, looking at Finn with bleary eyes. His tail flickered back and forth with curiosity and probably a little bit of annoyance. Finn didn't even realize he had followed him down here. He must have sneaked behind him.

"Whiskers," he whispered, putting a hand to his chest. "You can't make me jump like that, buddy."

The cat trilled again, and turned his head to look up

the stairs before turning back to Finn. It was like he was urging Finn back upstairs to the safety of the beacon. Even the little cat was worried about him.

Finn gave a small smile. "Not tonight, buddy. I'm sorry." He shook his head. "I've got to sort this all out. One way or another. It's on me to fix this."

The cat cocked his head to the side as Finn opened the metal front door. With a heavy sigh, he stepped out into the cold, windy night.

"Keep an eye on Ash for me, okay, pal? Keep her warm while I'm gone."

Whiskers gave one last trill, and stood up as if to follow Finn, clearly alarmed by him leaving. But Finn pulled the door closed.

He didn't want Whiskers following him. The little guy could get hurt tonight otherwise. Especially where he was going.

Finn wasn't entirely sure what he intended to do, or even what he would say. All he knew was he couldn't let the sea witch torment Ash any longer. He couldn't stand by and watch her glee as Ash sobbed against his chest.

It had to stop.

Part VIII:

Determined Hearts

23

TOO MUCH

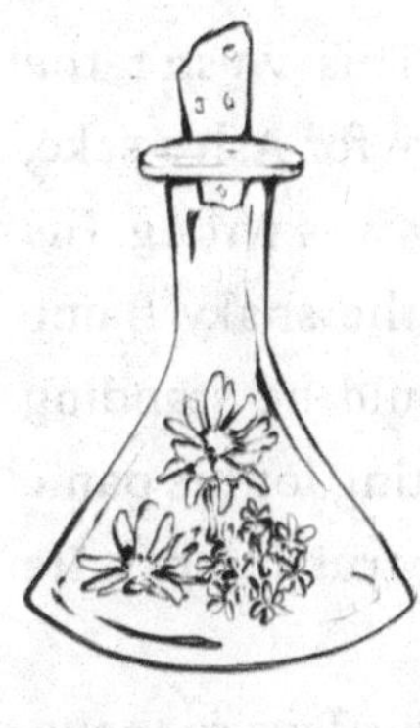

THE WIND WAS BITING COLD WHEN FINN walked to the boathouse. It was definitely close to fall because this was too cold for a normal summer night. He wished he had brought his jacket for more warmth or at least a raincoat to keep the wind off. At least, the shaky flame of the hurricane lamp fended off the shadows. It was so dark he would have gotten lost in the forest otherwise. It didn't help that his half awake state made him jump at shadows. The metal hanger of the hurricane lamp was icy in his hand.

In the distance, he spotted the shadowy mass of the boathouse, lurching out of the inky black waters like a monster from the sea. The tide roared to shore, and he had to walk along the craggy grasses to keep from stepping in the tide pools keen to yank each foot deeper into the sand.

The lack of moonlight, the high winds, and the roaring ocean made him think back to the shipwreck again. His mind just couldn't let go of that night, like it was forever burned into his memory, reliving it over and over again. One minute, he was back in the boat as it flipped upside-down with water up to his knees. Next, he was struggling to walk in the rapidly filling cabin. It made his stomach uneasy because the memory kept trying to take over. Finn paused on the beach to get his body and his mind under control.

He wasn't asleep; he was awake. This wasn't the ocean; he was on the beach. He was here for Ash's sake, not to have a panic attack when nothing was wrong. His hands shook, bouncing shadows from the shaky flame over the tall grasses. The sea witch could be standing right there in the weeds beside him, waiting for his panic to take hold, waiting to laugh at him for trusting her. He swallowed down his fears.

Grunting with the effort, he forced his legs to move, even though the sand tried to suck down his feet. The beach resembled the deck of the Wishful. The sand looked so much like the shiny wooden planks of the ship, glinting in the limited light. The wind howled like it had that night, like it was trying to sweep him away. His eyes watered and the taste of briny seawater filled his mouth. He wasn't stepping across sand, but the deck of the ship again. And just like before, he started running for the door. He had to make it to the cabin where it was dry.

Even though it wouldn't stay that way for long. He had to get to shelter to get out of the storm, but that shelter could quickly turn into an underwater coffin.

A wooden handle met his grip, not the cold metallic one his mind expected. The dissonance pulled him out of the horrid memory and back to the present. Finn stumbled into the boathouse, heaving air into his lungs like he would never get enough of it.

He shut the door with his foot and leaned his back against it. Slowly, he slid to the ground as his muscles loosened one by one. He kept his wits about him enough to put aside the hurricane lamp, but afterwards he curled in on himself. That hadn't been real. This was only the beach, that's all. He was safe; he needed to calm down.

Wrapping his arms around his legs, he dipped his head, pressing his forehead against his knees. He was still breathing hard, like his body just didn't want to let go of that horrible night. He pressed his eyes closed, focusing on the creaking wood of the boathouse and the waves hitting the shoreline. This wasn't the Wishful. He was practically on dry land here.

Slowly, his heart rate returned to normal. Eventually, his hands stopped shaking, though sweat covered him from head to toe. The tightness in his chest eased. The memory of the shipwreck was still in his mind, but it was merely a memory now, not something that could overtake him. Not something that could steal away his goal and determination here.

He opened his eyes and stared at the flame of the hurricane lamp. It didn't shake in here like it had outside.

It was a steady flame inside the boathouse, strong and resilient. His focus came back, his body his again. He had to remember why he came here. He had to think of Ash, not the shipwreck. Not about his father.

"Coming here was not easy for you, child." A familiar high-pitched voice said. "I wonder why you came?"

Finn swallowed down the dryness in his throat. Why did the sea witch only come to him when he was in this wretched state? She never came to him when he was on his feet and ready for her. In the shadowy waters, her head floated on the waves. The boathouse took away the height of the waves in here, but they were still strong. The sea witch floated on them as if she was one of them. Long tendrils of seaweed stretched out around her like the petals of a dead flower.

He took a shaky breath before climbing to his feet to face her fully. "You frightened Ash tonight!"

The timber of his voice echoed along the wooden walls, filled with the fury and outrage he intended. Part of him was scared to speak to her in such a way, but he knew he was the only one who could. And that gave him strength.

"I did," she said with a sort of wry humor. "I suppose you came here to thank me for that?"

He blinked, taken aback by her words. "What?"

The sea witch put her long fingers onto the edge of the boat deck, pulling herself up out of the water. She moved with such speed and grace it was alarming. One moment, she was a mere floating head in the water and the next, she towered over him, seaweed dripping around her bare feet. Gray skin showing through gaps in the seaweed like a suit that had burst at the seams.

He tried to back up. He had probably made a mistake. But his boot touched the door. There was no escaping now, no running away from her. He had to face her. So he stood firm.

"You ought to thank me for pushing away any suspicions she might have about you. I'm sure she had many. You have been quite careless in your behavior. Don't think I didn't see you down here last night, strolling back to the lighthouse in the darkness like you had no cares in the world. That hardly shows you're still frightened of me, does it? We can't have that. We can't have her suspecting anything."

Finn gaped at her.

"Now that I terrified her silly, she'll have not the slightest notion you and I are working together to help you escape the island." She looked pleased with herself. "You're welcome."

Finn shook his head. That made sense in a weird, twisted way, but the sea witch always twisted things around so they put her in a good light. Even if she didn't deserve it.

"You didn't have to frighten her! I was right there. You tried to grab her and let out that horrible scream. It's too much!"

She laughed, the creepy sound slithering around the room. "Yes, I did. And it scared the daylights out of her, didn't it?" She cackled again.

Finn dragged a hand over his face. "Look, if you really

care about her like you say you do, you'll stop upsetting her. She was so scared, she cried for hours."

The sea witch's creepy smile faded. "Oh... well, that's not good."

"No, it isn't! You've run her ragged ever since she came to this island. You give her nightmares. All you seem to care about is terrifying her, yet you say you don't want her hurt. I can guarantee you frightening her like that is definitely hurting her! Now, I don't know what issues you have with Ash, and neither does she. But if you really want to help us, and this isn't some ploy to kill us and eat us or something, then you better act like an ally and not an enemy. Otherwise, I refuse to take the boat you promised and we'll just die here on this damn island together."

The sea witch fell silent.

Finn hadn't meant to tell her off like that, but the words and the outrage kept coming. All the pain and heartache of watching Ash suffer these many weeks came back in full force. Would he truly refuse a boat if the sea witch gave them one? He doubted it. They were desperate, maybe more than the sea witch realized. But his words had clearly shaken her, and maybe that was for the best. Maybe it took risking their lives for her to actually pay attention. Nothing else he had tried seemed to faze her, but his threat to not take her help seemed to get through. The sea witch didn't care about him, but she seemed to care about Ash.

The sea witch paced the small boathouse once, then again. Her bare feet slapped on the warped wooden floorboards, sounding like a fish on dry land. Finn panicked a moment. Maybe he had pushed her too far. Maybe she would refuse to help them, but he didn't think so. At least, he wouldn't listen to his anxious thoughts until he had reason to do so.

She finally stopped in front of him. "Alright, no more frightening the girl. Even if I am still annoyed with her and it is just a little bit of fun, clearly she's very sensitive now and it's upsetting her."

When she moved closer, Finn resisted the urge to curl in on himself.

"But you must promise me you will take the vessel I find and take her off this blasted island."

Finn swallowed hard, looking up into her golden, glowing eyes. "I promise."

Her hand shot, snatching the collar of his shirt and hoisting him off the ground. She held him up with a single hand, his feet dangling beneath him. She seemed untroubled by his weight. "And once on board, you had best not let a single hair on her head be damaged. Do you understand?"

Pain reverberated under his arms and on the back of his neck as he struggled against the sea witch's powerful grip. He thought about mentioning she had caused Ash more harm than he had, but this was not the time.

"Yes, ma'am," he said.

"Good," she said with a hiss.

He wrapped his hand around hers, around the slimy sea weed that wrapped around her fingers while she held him aloft. He stared directly into her golden eyes.

The sea witch cocked her head to the side.

"But if you scare her again on dry land or anywhere else, this arrangement is done. We're through with you," he warned.

When her eyes narrowed, Finn knew he made a mistake. She looked up at the ceiling and shrieked. The sound was so high-pitched and loud Finn immediately clasped his hands over his ears. Though she closed her mouth, his ears still rang with the sound. Finally, the ringing dimmed and he heard again the lapping of the waves against the boats in the boathouse, and the creaking wood all around him.

The sea witch leaned in close, showing him a strange smile. "I appreciate how protective you are of her, child. I chose well with you." Then she dropped him to the ground like he was nothing.

Finn fell to his feet, lost his balance, and tumbled to his hands and knees. He wasn't sure where his bravery had come from, to talk back to her like that. But he was grateful to still have his head attached to his shoulders. He looked up to see the sea witch lowering herself into the water with her unnatural grace.

"I should have a vessel for you tonight, and you should leave as soon as possible tomorrow morning. A storm is coming at nightfall and it will be strong. You won't get the chance to leave for several days otherwise, and I can't promise the boat I get will last long, either." She held up a clawed finger to him. "And if you allow this boat to be destroyed, I won't get another. This is the only one I'm fetching for you."

Finn struggled to speak. "Okay." He swallowed and coughed. "Understood. We'll leave at dawn."

Soon, the sea witch was just a head floating in the water again. "And remember, child. No harm is to come to her. And I won't frighten her again. That I can promise you."

She submerged. Other than a few tiny waves, there was no other sign she had been there. No bubbles emerged, no obvious kicking of her feet underwater. In a matter of seconds, he had been left alone in the empty boathouse. It was eerie.

Finn waited a moment, as if the sea witch might return with more demands or more threats. But she didn't. Only when he realized she was truly gone did he feel comfortable taking a deep breath. He dragged a hand through his hair, to calm down and loosen up his tense muscles.

Part of him felt like he should have stood up to her more, but he got her to promise to stop scaring Ash. And he'd even brought forward his own threats. The sea witch was more reliant on him in this arrangement than he thought. Maybe he had more power than he knew in this. He didn't care if he was humiliated or tossed around like a rag doll, as long as he got his family out of this place alive.

He picked up the hurricane lamp and braced himself for the walk back to the lighthouse. The night was still pitch dark outside of his small ring of candlelight. But the wind had died down some and the tide was coming back in. It was still treacherous walking back, but this time he didn't have the memories of the Wishful sinking or of going underwater like before. He wasn't sure how his mind made the connection between the shipwreck and the beach. But he was sure that experience would haunt him for years to come, and clearly the Wishful would come back to him again.

The trek back to the lighthouse was cold, but Finn found he had more determination in his steps. He had felt like he was powerless here on this island for so long, yet he really had more power than he'd expected. The sea witch needed him to help her and she really was going to get them a boat. He was sure of that now. For the first time since he washed ashore, Finn felt like he had more control over what was happening around him.

He stepped into the lighthouse to find Whiskers asleep by the door. The cat had to move aside as he came in. Squinting up at him, he gave a little, sleepy meow in greeting. Finn closed out the wind and darkness behind him while Whiskers stretched and gave a happy trill, making figure eight loops around his legs.

"Hey, buddy! You didn't have to wait up for me like that. You could have gone back upstairs to bed."

But Whiskers had waited on him and that made Finn feel so loved. The cat purred happily while Finn blew out the hurricane lantern. He stooped to give Whiskers some good pets and scratches, then padded his way back upstairs. Whiskers ran ahead of him, his tail bouncing and his fluffy paws barely making a sound on each metal step. It was no wonder the cat had slipped past him before. He was like a ghost here.

Though a little breathless, Finn made it to the top floor. He pushed open the door to find Ash still deep asleep. She had one arm reached out to where he usually slept, and a pang of affection and guilt rose. She had noticed he was missing despite his best efforts. Whiskers moved onto the blankets near her, kneading his paws happily, ready to go back to bed in their little pile.

Finn peeled off his outer clothes, noticing the buttons that had popped from around his collar from when the sea witch had manhandled him. There were tears in places, too. No wonder he was always bruised up in that area around his neck. His underarms still ached from where the sea witch had lifted him, and his body was exhausted from the mental and physical stress. With the weariness of the day weighing on him, he was so happy to climb under the blankets and curl up to Ash again.

Ash lifted a groggy eyelid, then reached out, putting an arm around his waist and pulling him closer. He cuddled around her.

"You're so cold," she said, words sleepy and slurred. "Where did you go?" There was a cute whine in her voice and a crease in her brow like she was really trying to solve a mystery even though she was exhausted. He smiled. Even deep in slumber, she worried so much about him, probably as much as he worried about her.

"I wanted a snack, that's all."

It took a moment for her to speak again. "Missed dinner."

"Yeah, sorry about that." He kissed her cheek. "Go back to sleep. It's okay, I'm here."

"You better be careful. The sea witch'll get you." With that, she fell back into light snores almost instantly.

"I know," he whispered. "Do I know…"

He closed his eyes, listening to the sounds of Ash's breathing. Whiskers purred as he made biscuits on his leg.

Maybe this really would all work out in the end. With that happy thought, sleep finally took him.

24

THE MOMENT THAT LASTED FOREVER

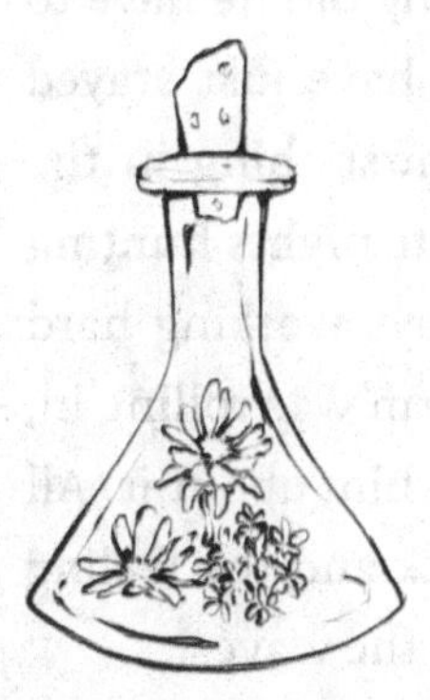

WHEN FINN NEXT OPENED HIS EYES, HE was met with a cloudy sky. He had no idea how late it was or even how much daylight they had left. His first thought was he had told the sea witch they would leave at dawn, but it was definitely much later than dawn.

"Shit!" He groaned into the pillow where he had left a pile of drool. He must have been sleeping hard last night, so hard he had slept in. Groggy and sore, he climbed to his feet, staggered over to his clothing pile, and pulled on the same shirt and pants from last night. He rubbed at his eyes to get rid of the sleep crust. Then he looked around the glass room and studied the cloudy sky, trying to determine the time of day like his father had shown him years ago.

The sun glinted through a thin patch before disap-

"

pearing again amid the fast-moving clouds. It was after midday by several hours, which meant probably three or four o'clock. Damn, he hadn't just slept in a little, he had slept through most of the day. That gave them only a few hours left before nightfall.

Finn yanked on his shoes, then hurried down the stairs. Each metal step echoed up and down the staircase since he was in such a rush. Everyone in the building would know he was coming, but he didn't care. They had to hurry.

Only a few hours of daylight, probably less with the cloudy sky and incoming storm. Oh, why did he have to sleep in today of all days? He should have just stayed awake overnight so they could leave first thing in the morning. But he had spent too many late nights hunting down the sea witch. And too many days working hard labor around the lighthouse. Now a storm was rolling in, bad enough the sea witch had warned him about it. All he could think about was the shipwreck and the feeling of his father brushing past him beneath the waves.

No, he wouldn't let that happen again. He couldn't.

Finn reached the ground floor and went for the cat carrier he left by the door the night before. A little water inside still and caked mud in some places, but he didn't have time to clean it out. Whiskers would hate it, but he would be okay.

"Finn, what's going on?" Ash sat on the couch by the windows reading a book. She looked so calm and peaceful there, Finn hated having to interrupt it with his problems. "What's wrong?"

"Nothing," he said breathlessly, but judging by the crease on her forehead, she didn't believe him. He pulled the compass out of the cat carrier and shoved it into his pocket. He pulled out the flares and put them on the counter. "We just have to go. Now."

She put the book aside and got to her feet. "What happened? Tell me what's going on?"

"I slept in, that's all," he said.

She shook her head in confusion. "What?"

"I promise, I'll explain everything soon." He rushed over and pecked a kiss on her cheek. "But we have to go before the storm hits."

Her gaze swept over him, and Finn hoped she saw nothing that would make her question his words. Nothing that would make her hesitate or question his sincerity. They were so close now to escaping. He just needed her to trust him a little more.

He put down the cat carrier and took her hands in his. "Trust me, please? I promise I have a good reason for all of this. I just can't tell you yet."

She nodded and gave a resigned sigh. "We're leaving the island."

"Yes, finally."

She leaned up to plant a kiss on his lips. "And you promise I will get answers eventually?"

He nodded. His head spun, and the world suddenly got a little brighter.

"I love you," she whispered. "But sometimes you're very bizarre."

He grinned. "I'll take that as a compliment."

A poor joke, but she was kind enough to give him a small smile. It didn't change the worry in her eyes.

"I'm sorry for all this," he said.

She put a hand to his cheek. Her skin was cool against his. "I love you and I trust you. You wouldn't do anything to hurt me."

"I love you, too." The taste of regret and betrayal sat in the back of his mouth when he stared into her beautiful dark eyes, but Finn pushed aside the feeling. Instead, he leaned and gave her a proper kiss. When their lips met, time slipped away. He wrapped his arms around her and she pulled him tight against her. When he finally pulled back, his face was hot and Ash was blushing, and as breathless as he was.

Staring into her eyes, he could lose himself there. She was like a vortex, pulling him in, yet he would be happy to drown in her presence, in her affection and love. Chamomile lingered on his lips. In another world, he wondered if they could have lived happily on this island, living out a wondrous love story together. If only the world could be kept out of their lives, maybe that could have been true.

Outside, the waves crashed on the rocks, salt spray flung against the windows, but with Ash he couldn't care less what happened around him. He suddenly wanted this moment with her to last forever, living in a bubble of safety and calm, away from anything that could ever harm them.

Their love was stronger than the sea, stronger than the wind that howled across the lighthouse. In that moment, Finn knew he would do anything to keep Ash safe.

Anything.

IT DIDN'T TAKE them long to gather their things. Ash had already prepared a bag with clothes, food, water, and even cat food. The hardest part was capturing Whiskers. Finn was able to pick him up without too much trouble, in fact he purred and settled in his arms, probably ready for another adventure. But getting him into the cat carrier was another story. The cat howled and scratched, fighting hard to keep from going in. He didn't bite them, but his claws did break the skin. It was like he turned into another cat.

Once the door to the cat carrier was closed and Whiskers was secured, Finn caught his breath and changed his shirt. Whiskers had clawed a long hole through the chest and another down the sleeve.

When Finn came back down with a fresh shirt, Ash was crouched down beside the carrier trying to calm Whiskers down.

"I don't think he likes his carrier at all," she said.

"Yeah, I didn't get a chance to clean it out. It's pretty gross inside."

She shook her head. "No, I think something bad happened to him in the carrier. He's very scared."

The shipbuilder. Had Whiskers seen his old owner

die from inside the carrier? Or maybe he associated it with his old owner dying, and now he was terrified of it. Finn tried to imagine someone resurrecting the Wishful and asking him to step on board again, or even getting locked inside of it. That would have him kicking and screaming, too.

Finn crouched down to the carrier and slipped his fingers through the metal grid. Whiskers whined, then leaned in to mark his fingers again and again, dragging his cheeks so hard Finn felt his little kitty teeth. Then he put out his pink tongue and licked at him in apology.

"I'm sorry, buddy. I hope this won't be for long."

Whiskers turned once, twice, then a third time in his cage, clearly agitated. Finn felt bad for him, but there was nothing he could do. It was either bring him or leave him alone on the island again, and he refused to do that to him.

"I guess we both have to face our fears sometimes, buddy," he said, then climbed to his feet.

Ash pushed one of the raincoats in his hands. "I grabbed the flares you found, too, and got them packed. I even put in some spare raincoats for us, just in case it got bad."

Finn pulled on the raincoat on with a smirk, and made sure it was secure. "You've thought of everything, haven't you?" he asked.

"No, I've missed something, I'm sure. But it doesn't matter. We have to leave." She pulled a large bag over one shoulder. It was so big and close to bursting it hung down to her knees. She gestured to the carrier. "Can you get Whiskers?"

"Sure." The carrier with Whiskers was heavier than he expected, especially with Whiskers agitated and making laps inside. But Finn would manage. He couldn't carry the bag Ash had.

Together, they stepped out into the cold, cloudy day. The wind whipped their hair around and they weren't even on the ocean yet. The smell of rain was strong.

He pulled the faded red metal door closed behind them, looking up at the massive lighthouse he had called home for so many weeks. Finn couldn't help but think back to the day he and his dad left home for their final crabbing trip, never expecting the fate that would meet them on the open waters. That was how it was going out on the ocean. Everything was unpredictable. Lives thrown to the whims and peculiarities of nature. Every time you left land, you could only hope you would come back in one piece.

He and Ash turned and headed down the path to the boathouse. The path Finn almost knew by heart. He braced for what was to come and couldn't quite shake the taste of regret and betrayal in the back of his mouth. The taste only grew stronger as they drew closer to escaping the island.

He hoped for the hundredth time he had made the right decisions.

25

INTO THE HEART

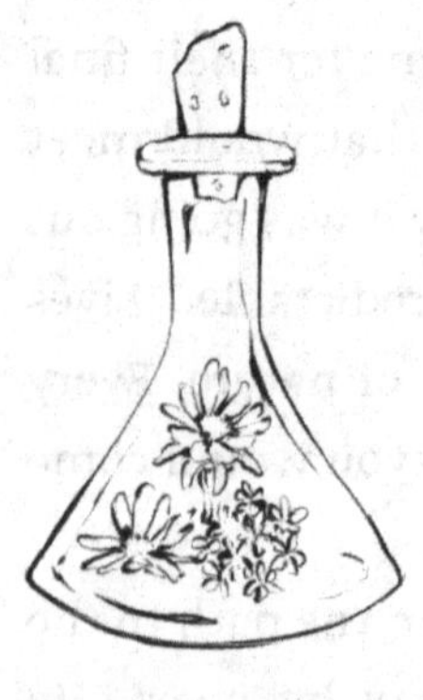

"THERE'S A BOAT!" ASH CRIED. SHE hurried ahead across the beach, her raincoat flapping in the intense wind and her black curls tossed mercilessly around her head.

Finn slowed down to a stop. He couldn't believe his eyes. An aluminum boat with a cabin, complete with a door to close out the brunt of the weather was docked just beyond the boathouse. Exactly where the sea witch had told him it would be. It was a much more expensive model than the one his dad had purchased preowned when Finn was a kid. It looked brand new, too. Where in the world had the sea witch gotten this? A shipyard, maybe? Or had she found someone on the ocean enjoying the waves, killed them, and taken their boat? A sinking feeling hit his gut because it took little to imagine her doing just that.

Ash stopped just on the edge of the waves, clutching her giant bag in front of her like a shield. She stared at the waves drawing up just to the toes of her boots. He caught up with her and put a hand around her waist. She didn't even acknowledge him as he slid up beside her.

"You'll be okay," he said, giving her a squeeze. "We're going to do this together."

She gazed at him with wide, fearful eyes. "I still have that bad feeling, Finn. Like something is going to happen to me if I step into the water. It's ridiculous." She stared out at the boat with fear in her eyes.

Finn admitted it seemed like the boat was farther out than it needed to be. To Ash, it probably looked like miles.

"Is there no way to get the boat any closer?" she asked.

He shook his head. "The boathouse is blocked from the broken boats inside. It had to be docked out there." He rubbed her back. "This is our only chance out of here, Ash. We have to take it. We can't give up now."

She gave a brief nod, breathing out slowly. "It looks nice. Do you think anyone is aboard?"

He had an image of the previous owners' bodies strewn about inside the cabin, but shook it from his mind. "No, I doubt it."

"Where did it come from?" she asked, turning her piercing gaze to him. Finn couldn't meet her gaze. His guilt was too strong.

"I'll tell you later."

"Finn..." she pressed, worry in her voice.

"Later. I promise. Come on, I'll help you in." He stepped one foot into the water, letting go of her waist. He held a hand out to her and gave a smile. "Do you trust me, Ash?"

She stared at his outstretched hand, then to the water, and breathed out slow. "I'm still scared. But I trust you. This may be the only chance we get, like you said. I can't stay on this island being afraid of the water forever. Eventually, I have to get my feet wet." She slid a chilly hand into his and followed him deeper into the ocean. The water was up to his knees when he could carefully put the cat carrier onto the boat. Whiskers cried out. Then he pulled himself up into the boat.

The sea witch had moored the boat with a rope to one of the wooden pillars on the boathouse. Even though it dipped and bobbed in the waves, it wasn't going anywhere. But she had been right to say the boat wouldn't last if a severe storm came in. The boat would be dashed against the boathouse or on those rocks easily with how much it was already moving in the waves.

He turned to Ash. The water was up to her thighs, and her eyes were as big as saucers. He bent down and helped her up the side of the boat until she could reach the railing and the steps formed in the gunwale.

Once on board the ship, Ash dropped her bag and gripped the handrail with pale hands, breathing hard. "That was terrifying, but I did it. I even waited for you to get on board without running away," she added with a shaky laugh. "Aren't you proud?"

He grinned. "I am proud. You did great!"

Ash crouched down to Whiskers meowing sadly in his carrier. "It's okay. We're going to make sure you're safe."

Finn pointed to the boathouse and the rope tying them in place. "I have to get the mooring line," he said. "But I'll be right back."

She nodded. "Don't get hurt."

He dropped back into the water, wading over to the boathouse keeping one hand on the rope. He wished he had his thick gloves from back on the Wishful. It would make this much easier. As it was, he had to be careful, slowing down to keep from hurting his hands with the rope. Each minute he took, the storm was getting closer. He had to hurry, but he also had to be cautious. The water was so deep here he had to swim. But he also had to hold on to the rope the whole time. If he let go, he would have to go back to the boat, find it again, and start all over.

Finn passed the rocks where the shipbuilder had fallen. He had a horrible image of the shipbuilder's body beneath the water, still drifting near the boathouse like they just didn't want to leave. The thought came to him of the bloated white corpse floating up and tangling in Finn's feet like some kind of gruesome dead weight. He swam a little faster, his hands shaking as he struggled to keep the rope with him. Finally, after what felt like forever, he reached the pole of the boathouse.

He had to take a moment to catch his breath as he held on. The mooring line was tied off at the top of the pole, so he had to climb out somewhat to untie it. Then he got back into the water and swam back toward the boat, holding onto the rope as he went and loosely rolling it up as he went. It was dangerous work. The rope could easily get tangled in his legs if he wasn't careful. If Finn hadn't spent so much of his life on a crabbing skiff, dealing with ropes and nets in the water when they got tangled, he probably wouldn't have been able to do it safely. But he took his time, even though that was the one resource they were quickly running out of.

The boat should have been moored much closer to the boathouse, but the sea witch was clearly not familiar with that. The rope she had used was far too long. But she had gotten a boat as promised, so he couldn't be too annoyed. He grabbed onto the handrail of the steps that led up the side of the aluminum boat, and pulled himself up out of the water, careful to wind up the rope at his side.

Ash stood there with a towel for him.

"Thanks." He secured the rope and used the towel to dry off his face, hair, and clothes as best as he could. The raincoat had been more of a hindrance than a help in the water, and his clothes were soaked through and clung to his body. But at least he hadn't lost a boot or anything. And the boat and mooring line were still in good condition. It could easily be worse.

"I got Whiskers into a seatbelt in the cabin." She pointed behind her. "He's not happy, but at least he's safe."

He followed Ash into the cabin, still toweling off as he went. Inside, it even smelled new. No bodies of previous owners lay about. In fact, it looked like it had just recently been manufactured. That made him feel better. The sea witch was vicious, but she wasn't that cruel, at least.

He saw the cat carrier secured to a hard plastic seat. Inside, Whiskers meowed urgently and Finn looked inside to see some water had puddled inside, probably from being carried out to the boat. Not much, but obviously enough to make poor Whiskers anxious.

"Hey, I'm sorry buddy. That's my fault." He pressed his fingers into the grate and let Whiskers mark him over and over again until he calmed. Once the cat was less panicked, Finn turned to the instrument panel.

Ash was looking over the buttons and levers. "This is nothing like what I read about in the old manuals I found. They didn't show anything like this."

"They were probably outdated." Finn used the towel to wipe off his hands as he settled into the captain's chair. When he was little, he used to dream of getting to sit in this seat, taking charge of the boat all on his own. He thought it would be under better circumstances than this, but the childlike part of him still lit up as he pulled on his seatbelt.

A few items Finn wasn't familiar with, but thankfully, a manual was still attached to the dash. He scoured it for all the details to fill in his mental gaps. He had almost figured it all out when Ash spoke.

"Finn, where did this boat come from? You said you would tell me."

He tried to keep his face blank as he stared at the

pages of the manual, no longer really reading it. "I don't know."

A pang of guilt hit, but it helped that it wasn't a complete lie. He really had no idea where the sea witch got the boat. That made him feel a little better.

"Could someone have come to the island?" she asked. "Maybe they came to look for us—or they came to look for the shipbuilder! Maybe they didn't check in after a certain time or something, and they finally sent someone out here to look for them."

Finn bit his tongue to keep from saying anything. But a mean question slipped out. "Are you scared of leaving the island?"

He wasn't sure where the question came from other than his need to distract her from her current line of thought. He hated himself for even asking about it.

"What?" she asked, deflating almost instantly.

He winced, but kept his gaze on the manual. "You've lived here longer than I have. Are you scared to leave the lighthouse?"

She was quiet for a moment. "I don't know. It's the only place I can remember. I worked hard to cook and clean it, to take care of the place. I guess it has been my home for a long time."

He put away the manual and turned on the engine. A roar came from the back of the boat.

"It's probably weird to think of the lighthouse as my home," Ash said, "but it really has been that for me."

She reached over and took Finn's hand, pulling him away from the instrument panel. Reluctantly, he looked up to meet her gaze. Her expression was of pure affection, vulnerability, and fear.

"What about you?" she asked. "Are you scared to leave?"

"The lighthouse has been good to me. It brought me to you. But I'm honestly happy to leave it behind. We wouldn't have lasted here forever, Ash."

She nodded and glanced away.

Of course, she was afraid to leave. He was, too, just for very different reasons. This whole arrangement made him feel like such a heel. Now it was making him be mean to the girl he loved more than anything in the world. It was so they could survive; he knew that, but damn, did it feel awful. He loved her and would do anything for her. But hurting her like this was painful.

He decided he would tell her everything. All about the arrangement with the sea witch, the late-night visits, who had found the boat for them, and how he wasn't worried about a visitor to the island. Let Ash decide if she wanted to risk going out on the open waters with him, or go back to the lighthouse instead. If the sea witch killed him over it, so be it. He would be dead soon, regardless of the choice he made. He just didn't want to die with this guilt weighing on him, with the trust in Ash's gaze pulling at his guilt with every glance. Damn the sea witch's threats. He couldn't hurt her anymore.

"Ash, I have something I need to tell you. Something that's been weighing on me for some time."

Her brow furrowed, and she clasped his hand with

both of hers. "You can tell me," she said, her gaze searching his.

He opened his mouth to speak and a giant peel of thunder cracked down from the sky, reverberating the entire boat. They both jumped in their seats. Whiskers went silent.

Ash's eyes went wide. Rain pattered on the windshield as the wind picked up, howling through the metal bars of the boat.

"It's a storm," she said with fear in her voice. "You've got to get us out of here before it gets worse."

Finn nodded. As the rain came down harder, he looked to assure himself everyone was buckled in securely. He turned on the windshield wipers and studied the map and compass, finally turning the boat in the direction of the dark clouds.

The storm had arrived. Worse yet, they were heading straight into the heart of it.

THE WAVES TOSSED the boat until Ash had to hold tight to the built-in handle on the wall. Finn struggled to keep seated as the boat bounced on the waves. At first, he could see the path before them, dark blue waters cresting with white foam against the windshield, battering the sides of the boat. But the sky quickly grew too dark, and the waves too high. Finn turned on the outside lights, but the rain was so thick it only helped a little. He relied almost solely on the tiny radar and his compass as he white-knuckled the steering wheel.

The island with the lighthouse was near several rocky islands he could see on the radar, and he knew to steer clear. But it was hard to keep the boat steady in the raging storm. Lightning streaked across the sky like rope unraveling, illuminating the dark waters that stretched out endlessly before them. He barely spotted a giant wave growing and tumbling toward them. Not again.

"Hold on!" he cried just as the lightning dissipated, leaving the small LED lights to struggle to fight off the suffocating darkness around them. Rain pelted the aluminum boat that had looked so big from the shore, but now seemed a small child's toy in the face of the ocean's intensity.

The wall of water hit the boat hard, obscuring all view through the windshield. The boat tilted to the side and he almost fell out of his seat.

"Ash?" he called.

"I'm okay!" she said, though panic filled her voice. "Whiskers, baby, you'll be okay!"

Finn glanced back to see poor Whiskers straddling the bottom and side of his carrier. The seatbelt was holding the carrier in place, though, so Finn focused back on the boat, trying with all his might to get them righted again before another wave hit. This was a newer boat, built for storms like these. But the panic that filled him said otherwise. He had to right the ship before they were pushed upside-down in the water. Just like last time.

The image came back to him: upside down in the

Wishful, waiting for it to fill with water enough until he could open the door and not get killed by the pressure. Swimming in the darkness, looking for the surface. All it would take was one more gigantic wave, one more act of nature to slap him aside and seal their fates.

"Finn, we'll turn over if we—"

"I know, Dad, I know! I've got this. Just hold on!"

Water spilled into the cabin, a few inches at first, then a foot. It sounded like a small waterfall. The water slid into his tall boots and soaked his socks, then rose to his calves.

"Finn!" Ash was begging him now.

He kept pulling the small aluminum boat to the side, begging the waters not to take them, begging the storm to let them pass. Don't kill them like it had Dad.

"Please..." he whispered to whatever would listen. "I don't want to lose them! I can't lose my family again!"

More waves thrashed the boat, but nothing as big as the first. Slowly, the ship reversed the tilt and landed hard on the water again. Whiskers meowed behind him, urgency in his tiny voice. He must have gotten water into his carrier, way more than just a puddle this time. But if he was meowing, he could breathe. Finn didn't look to be sure, though. He did not want to risk taking his eyes off the water, in case another giant wall of water came at them. He risked glancing at the gauges, to make sure they wouldn't crash into something.

The waves continued battering the boat. Every time the lightning flashed, he looked for another rogue wave, another beast of water that could mean their end. Like Dad. Like he'd nearly met that horrible night.

The sky grew brighter. The waves calmed, and the lightning and thunder grew more distant. A constant drizzle of rain obscured the windshield, but Finn could see the waves again. He could see the ocean ahead, illuminated by the stars peeking through the clouds.

Pressure fell on his shoulders, and he jumped. Ash stood beside him. He hadn't even heard her unbuckle her seat belt and come over to him. She leaned down to face him, her face pale and her hair damp. She rubbed his shoulders.

"You can let go now. We got through it."

He blinked at her, then realized how hard he was gripping the wheel. With effort, he unclenched his hands and let go. His fingers throbbed. Ash took one of his hands in hers and rubbed it. He hadn't realized he had been so tense.

"We did it," he whispered.

She grinned. "You did it. You were amazing."

He gave a sheepish grin, then unbuckled his seatbelt. He climbed to his feet, stretched out his legs, and hugged her tight. She laughed and wrapped her arms around him. She smelled like the ocean. When he pulled away, tears filled her eyes.

"Do you think it's very far to the mainland?" she asked.

"Not at all. If the waters stay calm and we don't have to slow down, we should be there by morning. Just like I said."

Ash leaned up and kissed him, her lips cool and soft against his. She pulled back, her dark eyes gazing into him.

"I love you," she whispered.

His head swam. "I love you, too." He pressed his forehead against hers, relishing the feel of her, the scent of her. Relishing the simple act of being alive together, surviving such a horrible storm, and coming out on the other side in one piece. Somehow, Finn had done it. He had gotten them through, and he hadn't let his panic take hold of him either. They made it.

"I didn't think we would ever get off the island," she said.

"For a moment there, I wasn't sure we would live through the storm either." He gave a nervous chuckle.

An unnervingly familiar voice filled the cabin, breaking their fragile joy. "Isn't this cute? If you had listened to my advice, all that nonsense with the storm could have been avoided."

The sea witch stood in the doorway of the cabin. His stomach dropped.

He never should have trusted her.

26

THE FINAL BREATH

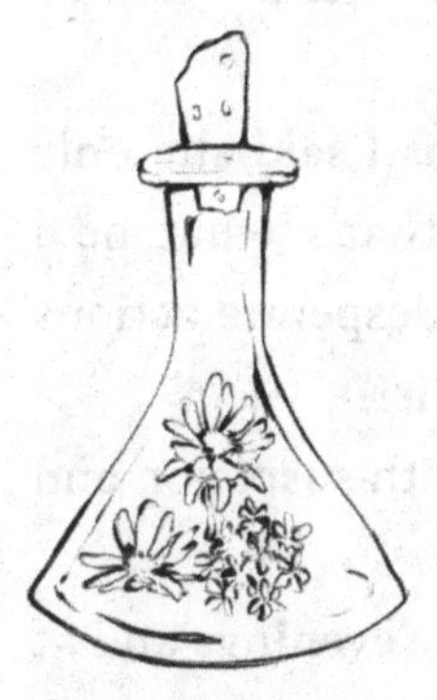

THE SEA WITCH STEPPED INTO THE CABIN, her seaweed clad feet slapped wet on the metal floor as she entered the flooded room. She placed her hands on the doorway, digging her nails into the metallic walls. She blocked any chance of escape and leered at them both.

"Young boys are always trying to prove themselves. Always trying to show off and be a hero. You don't have to nearly kill the girl just because you like her." She cackled, and the sound echoed in the tiny metallic room.

"Leave us alone!" Ash shouted, stepping forward with her hands balled into fists. "Your lies won't work here, sea witch. Stop tormenting us! Can't you see we barely survived that storm? Show us some pity for once!"

Ash's outrage pulled Finn out of his shocked stupor.

He didn't want Ash getting too close, knowing how strong the sea witch was. He grabbed the sleeve of Ash's raincoat, but she barely noticed and didn't budge from her stance.

The sea witch smiled. "Lies! You wound me with your accusations. Didn't he tell you that you would have died on that barren island without my help?" She splayed her fingers across her chest in a mockery of offense. "You should be thanking me, or you would both be still there starving and shivering on that pathetic little spit of land."

Finn leveled his gaze at the sea witch. "Don't... please."

This wasn't part of the deal. She had said she only wanted Ash to be safe. Or at least, that's what he'd thought. Now, she was using his own desperate actions against him. Like a fool, he had trusted her.

Ash turned to him, her eyes filled with suspicion and hurt. "Finn? You worked with her?"

"All those times he slipped out in the evenings and at night, he told you lies. He was coming to see me, to seek my counsel. Do you really think he could have fixed any of those boats and make them float again on his own? Ha! He came to me because he needed help. He practically groveled."

Ash didn't turn to the sea witch. She searched Finn's face. "Finn, is this true?"

He shook his head, not sure what he could possibly say to defend himself. The sea witch spoke the truth, but somehow it sounded so much worse coming from her.

He had been trying to save them. How could she twist this around so much that it sounded like he was the monster here? What really bothered him was that there was a kernel of truth to her words.

"In fact, I found the very boat that you stand in now. That's why he didn't worry about anyone else on the island. He knew I brought it to give you safe passage. He knew who had provided it."

"Damn it, Finn, say something!" Ash yanked the sleeve of her coat out of his grip.

He had never heard her so angry before. It was jarring. Finn dropped his arms to his sides, feeling numb. He couldn't lie to her anymore. He knew he should to avoid her wrath, but he had always known this moment would come. When Ash found out the truth and rejected him forever.

The words tumbled out of his mouth. "It's true. All of it. I lied to you because I knew you would hate me going to the sea witch for help. Everything about the boats and me fixing them. They were all lies. There was no way to fix them, Ash. I'm no woodworker, no mechanic. We were going to die there. I didn't want to watch you and Whiskers starve to death. Even if it meant working with her, I couldn't let you die, Ash." He reached out to put a hand on her shoulder, but Ash pulled away.

"I can't believe it," Ash whispered, wrapping her arms around herself. "All this time, you've been lying to me. I cried in your arms. You held me. But it was all a lie, wasn't it?" She sniffled and wiped at her nose.

"Please, I didn't want to hurt you. I would do

anything to save you. Even if it meant making a deal with the devil herself."

The sea witch scoffed. "So damn dramatic..."

Ash cut him with her gaze. "You said you loved me, Finn. Was that another of your lies?"

"I do love you, I swear! All of this"—he gestured to the boat, to the sea witch—"I did it all for you. All of this I did to keep you safe."

"I was safe! I was perfectly safe at the lighthouse until you showed up."

Finn winced. It felt like he had been lanced through the heart and he couldn't find the breath or the words to even respond.

The sea witch raised a clawed finger. "Another part of the bargain, my dear, is you."

"What?" Finn gasped.

"Me?" Ash's voice was small and fearful as she took a step back from the sea witch. "What do you want with me?"

"He kept you quite safe on your journey here, and for that, I am grateful to him. But now, I've come to collect what I'm owed."

"No!" Finn cried. "That wasn't part of the deal. You said nothing about that. You said you didn't want a hair hurt on her head. That meant you didn't want to hurt her!"

"Listen to all the assumptions you made!" The sea witch cackled, dragging her nails along the aluminum wall, gouging deep gashes as they went. "And you never asked what I wanted in payment, child. I will say you are a terrible negotiator."

Finn shook from head to toe. She had fooled him. All those demands, all those threats. He had gotten promises out of her, but those were just words. Now here they were alone in the middle of the ocean at the sea witch's whim. They were no longer trapped in the lighthouse, they were trapped with the sea witch. He shook his head. "That's not fair."

The sea witch turned to Ash. "So I suppose the decision falls to you. I will have you either way. There are no lighthouses here, nowhere for you to run. You are completely at my mercy, my dear. As for him, I care not if he lives or dies. If either of you struggles against me, I will kill him. And I promise, it won't take much." She held up her hand and curved her fingers like she was grabbing Finn's neck. "It would take so little pressure." She turned her hand to the side and made a cracking sound.

Ash gasped. Finn swallowed down the panic in his throat.

"If you come quietly, he can live, a survivor of two terrible storms finally making his way back to the mainland. I'm sure his friends would be proud of him. Or... his story ends here. You get to make the final decision, my dear. His fate lies with you."

Ash wiped at her eyes, turning her back to Finn.

"You don't have to do this," he said to Ash. "I don't care if I die, but you don't know what will happen if she takes you. She could kill you, or do something even worse."

Ash turned to him, eyes sad and brow furrowed. She pulled him into an embrace.

Giving a little gasp of shock, he wrapped his arms around her. Tears sprang to his eyes. "Ash…"

"I love you still, despite it all. I guess it makes me crazy or foolish. Not that it matters anymore. Whatever happens, Finn, just know that I still love you. I hate that you lied to me like this. I hate that I trusted you so completely."

He squeezed her tight. "I honestly did it all for you. I wanted to save you, Ash. That's all. Maybe it was stupid. Maybe I messed this all up. But I really did it because I love you. I wanted to keep you safe."

She sniffled and pulled back, her cheeks red and puffy. "I know. And you're right, I wouldn't have agreed with any of this if I had known." She gave a sad laugh. "I would have happily starved to death on that island. So maybe you were right about some of this, at least."

"I'm sorry. I had no idea she would do this. Any of this."

"I know, Finn. You always see the best in everyone. It's kind of a bad flaw sometimes." She sniffled. "You even see the best in a messed up girl like me."

"We can still fight her," he whispered, glancing at the sea witch in the doorway drumming her fingers on the metallic doorframe.

"Please don't. She will kill you. I don't want to see that."

He sighed and pursed his lips. "I won't. But I wish you would let me fight for you."

She planted a feather-light kiss on his lips. "You already have." Ash turned to face her tormentor. "I suppose I knew this day would come eventually."

"You couldn't outrun me forever, my dear." The sea witch stretched her seaweed clad hand out to Ash.

"I tried," Ash whispered.

"And failed. Now come, I have waited as long as I patiently can."

Ash turned once to look at him. She looked so small and delicate next to the grotesqueness of the sea witch. "Goodbye, Finn."

"Don't..." he muttered. But he knew full well she had no other choice and hated it.

Ash took the sea witch's outstretched hand. In a flash, the sea witch pulled her into her arms. Her scream made every fiber of Finn's body ache.

"Ash! Please—don't hurt her!" Finn rushed forward, but the sea witch held up a hand to stop him.

"Don't try a damn thing, child. She has made her decision." The sea witch gave a wicked grin before turning and bounding across the boat like something out of a nightmare. Ash didn't make another sound.

Finn sprinted after them out of the cabin. Icy rain pelted his face, but he barely noticed. "Ash!"

Ash stretched one arm out toward him, her eyes wide. In the next moment, in one fluid motion, the sea witch leaped into the water, dragging Ash down with her. To his horror, bubbles came up from the depths below.

Ash's final breath.

27

A MONSTROUS MEMORY

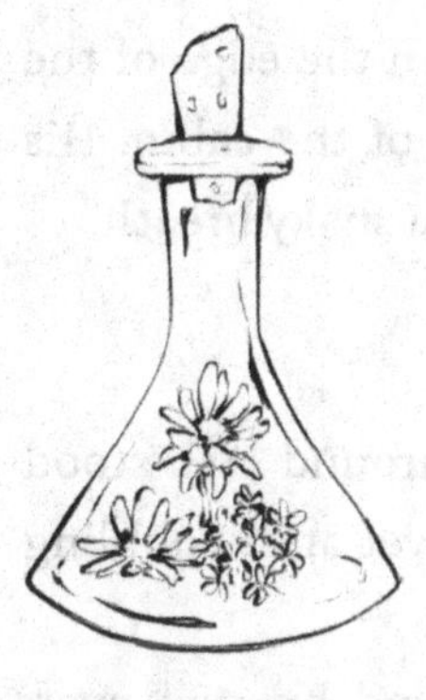

"ASH!" FINN CRIED AT THE ROLLING, dark water. The bubbles disappeared. In the distance, lightning flashed, revealing just how alone he was out on the endless ocean.

He had to dive in. He couldn't let Ash be drowned by that monster. The very thought of jumping back into the deep waters sent panic through him. This wasn't like wading or dog paddling over to the boathouse to get the mooring line. He had no way to anchor himself here and would be completely at the mercy of the ocean. Back into the dark water, back into the deadly storm eager to drag him down into its depths.

Just like Dad.

He cried out of frustration and sorrow. He couldn't do it. Not without something to help him make his way back. Every second counted, but he was too panicked to count each second as they rolled by. He searched the half dry storage boxes built into the sides of the boat until he found what he was looking for: a spool of nylon rope.

He tied one end on a metal hand railing on the side of the ship, pulling a few times to make sure it was solid. The other end he tied around his waist, pulling to make sure it was secure. Tight on his midsection, it hurt a little, but that didn't matter. Ash needed him. Even if jumping into the stormy waters terrified him, it was nowhere near the terror of losing Ash.

He kicked off his boots and stood on the edge of the boat, one hand holding onto the wall of the cabin. His heart thundered in his chest as he took a shaky breath.

"I'm coming, Ash! Just hold on!"

"Finn?"

His heart skipped a beat. He spun around. Ash stood on the other end of the boat, soaking wet and wobbling on her feet.

He jumped down from the edge and hurried over, wrapping his arms around her as she leaned into him. "It's okay, I'm here!" Tears sprang into his eyes, hot against the freezing cold of his skin. He pulled the nylon rope off his body as he held Ash upright. "I saw the sea witch take you under. I thought I lost you." His throat clamped up.

"I remember..." she whispered. "I stopped breathing."

Finn's eyes went wide. "What?" He looked closer at

her pale features. She looked a little blue, which was definitely not a good sign. "Let's get you inside."

He mostly carried her back into the cabin, where he laid her down with her back to one of the plastic seats. The flooring was no longer flooded and he got a better look at the design, clearly made to drain far more easily than the Wishful.

"Let me get some heat on. We need to get you warm." He fumbled with the controls on the dash for a moment before finding the heat. He put it on high, which wasn't as strong as he would have liked. Then he found the towel Ash had given him earlier and used it to cover her like a blanket. It wasn't as dry as he would have liked, but it was better than nothing. He searched the containers in the cabin for more towels, and found a pile of dry ones. He pulled them all out.

Ash put a hand to her head, wrapping her fingers in her wet, black curls. "It finally makes sense now, Finn. All of it."

He hurried back to her side, knelt next to her, and exchanged the wet towel for several dry ones. He gently pushed some of her wet curls away from her face. "Did you fight her to get away?" he asked.

"No," she muttered. Her voice was higher than usual, like she was about to cry. "No, I didn't fight her at all. What would be the point?" She squeezed her eyes shut like she was hurting. "No, she let me go."

He furrowed his brow. All that work to get hold of Ash only to let her go? Something didn't seem right about this. Something was wrong. "Are you in pain?"

Her skin faded to a sickly shade of gray. Her fingernails darkened to a deep purple, almost black. And her black curls twisted into long stretches of what looked like black seaweed.

Finn stared with his mouth gaping. "Ash..." he whispered, too shocked to move. "What did that monster do to you?"

"Nothing." She opened her eyes, but instead of the kind, dark eyes he knew and loved, awful golden glowing eyes stared back at him.

He gasped and backed away.

"Finn," she said in a hoarse, high-pitched voice that was eerily familiar, "the sea witch is my mother."

Finn froze.

On one hand, this was Ash, the girl he loved more than anything in the world. The girl he wanted to spend the rest of his life with. On the other hand, she looked so much like the sea witch it made a shiver go down his spine.

"How?" It was the only word that could escape his lips. Even though it didn't even come close to the millions of questions rattling around inside his brain.

Ash held up her hand, flexing her clawed fingers. "I had forgotten who I was on the island. There was a small boat. I climbed aboard to frighten the anglers away, so the storm wouldn't take them. But instead, they attacked me. They shot their firearms at me. Something beside me exploded. I remember fire all around." She clutched at the leaves of her hair, and twirled some of the seaweed strands around her fingers. "I was desperate. I ran through the fire and found a broken-off piece of the ship and clung to it for dear life. The ocean took me where it would. And it led me to the lighthouse. It led me to you."

Finn gave her a small, nervous smile. "But on the island, you weren't a monst—I mean, you weren't a sea witch. You were human." He blushed. "All of you... you were human."

She nodded. "My father was human. I have a foot in both worlds, Finn. Just like you'll always have one foot on land and one in the sea." She reached out and took his hands. Her skin was cool to the touch, always so much colder than his own. He let her draw him closer.

"Could you love me still if I look like this, Finn? Could you love a monster?"

"You're not—"

"Shh." She shook her head. "Don't start. You almost called me a monster just now. I know what I look like." Her golden glowing eyes searched him. "I'm still the girl you love under here somewhere. I promise." Her hands were clammy against his. Her skin was more like fish scales than human skin. "Tell me, could you love me like this?"

Finn searched deep inside his heart. Ash was absolutely terrifying when she looked like this. But it was still Ash, still the girl he loved more than anything in the world. She wasn't cursed. This was how she looked, that's all. He touched her seaweed hair. The strands crinkled together like paper.

"I wouldn't hurt you, you know that," she said. "I promise."

More promises. More tests of trust. But he had been the one to break her trust before, even if his intentions were good, and she still loved him despite it. This wasn't something she could control. And it was clearly still her. Now that he wasn't panicking, he could still see his lovely Ash beneath it all. She still had her voice, her mannerisms, and most importantly, her heart. Even though she made his skin crawl like this, Finn would still do anything for her.

"I love you regardless of what you look like." He squeezed her scaly hands.

She arched an eyebrow and cocked her head to the side. "I creep you out, don't I?"

He sighed. "Definitely."

She smiled.

"Sorry." Ash reached up to push some hair away from his face. He forced himself not to flinch. "Maybe eventually you'll get used to it."

"Yeah, eventually. But it's going to take a while."

She nodded. "That's fair. It took a long dip in the ocean to bring everything back. My mother was trying to get me to go in for ages, but she's not exactly the subtle sort. I couldn't just put a foot in, or a toe, or a leg or two. It had to be all of me, and for a while, too. I think that's what I have to do to transform. That's why my mother had to drag me under."

Finn huffed a sigh and shook his head. "She could have been less creepy about it. Heck, if she had told me about all this to begin with, it would have helped a lot."

The drumming of fingers on metal drew his attention to the doorway to find the sea witch standing there. He hadn't even heard her come out of the water or climb aboard the ship. She wasn't as menacing this time. Probably because she was no longer trying to loom over them, but her mere presence sent dread through his gut.

"I wasn't certain of your caliber, child. I don't trust humans easily, and those interested in my daughter, even less. She's the only one I have, after all, and I am very protective of her."

Finn squirmed under her piercing gaze. Then he pulled away from Ash, climbing to his feet. He looked between the two of them. "You aren't going to take her away now, are you?"

The sea witch smirked. "Well, that depends on her. Ash? That's the name you chose for yourself these days?"

Ash climbed to her feet. "I like it, even after getting my memories back. I think it suits me."

The sea witch shrugged. "It's a bit odd, but it fits you, I suppose. What happens next is up to you, my dear. Do you go with this flimsy boy and live out a human life in their boring, dry world? Or do you want to come with me and swim the seas around the globe, diving to impossible depths, and scaring superstitious sailors as we travel?" She grinned at her daughter, revealing rows of sharp teeth. "Surely you've grown tired of the dry world after that lighthouse business, my dear. What a bore that had to be!"

"I think my choice is obvious." Ash folded her arms.

Finn stared at his feet. He had already guessed at what she would choose, but he didn't want her to see the pain in his face.

"I want to go live with Finn."

He snapped his gaze up to her. "What? Really?"

She took his hand and gave it a squeeze. "I love you. Those aren't just words. I really mean it. And I rather liked our little simple life at the lighthouse." She smiled, showing her own sharp rows of shark teeth. Somehow it didn't make his blood run cold like when her mom did it.

Finn tried to find words, but his throat clamped closed again as tears sprang to his eyes. He loved her so much, but he had never really expected her to choose him. Not when she had the entire world to swim in instead. He never felt like he was worth choosing.

But she had. She chose him.

Unable to speak, he pulled her into a hug. He didn't care if he pinched his skin on her many tiny scales or if the sound of her breathing was eerie when she was so close. He loved her and she loved him. That was all that mattered.

When they pulled apart, the sea witch stepped toward him. "Now, Finn, my daughter will be in your care. Promise me you will keep her safe in the dry world. There are humans who would try to kill her for simply existing. You must let no one know what she is. I cannot stray from the ocean for long, so I am relying on the two of you to stay safe. Do you understand me?"

"Yes, ma'am," he said.

"And my kindhearted daughter." She pulled Ash into an embrace. "I will always love you and be looking out for you. If you need me, you know how to call me."

Ash chuckled. "I do now."

"Be safe. When you're ready to return to the warm waters that are your true home, call for me. I will always welcome you back."

"Even if I just want to chat?"

The sea witch gave a toothy smile that made Finn shiver involuntarily. "Of course."

She left the cabin and strolled out to the end of the boat. "Use your human devices to follow me, Finn. I will lead you back to the mainland. And Ash—be sure to change back, my dear. You'll give those fragile humans heart attacks otherwise." The sea witch dove into the water with barely a splash.

"She's right, I forgot." Ash closed her eyes. Her hair changed first, returning to the black curls Finn knew so well. Then her skin shifted to a bluish color before finally returning to the pale human skin he recognized. Her eyes opened and her dark gaze turned to him. She was back in the body that he knew so well.

Relief washed over him. He loved her either way, but he was grateful to see Ash as a human again.

"Did I get everything?" she asked.

He smiled, walking up to her. "Let's see. Cute curls, check. Beautiful eyes, check."

She shook her head with a laugh. "You're so weird."

"Oh, wait, I think you missed one."

She blinked. "What?"

"Hang on, I have to test just to be sure." He leaned in and kissed her, sliding a hand behind her neck as she slid her arms around his waist. It was a deep kiss, one that he hoped would help convey all the love and affection he struggled to say with words. When they pulled away, they were both breathless.

"Yep," he said, still catching his breath. "Lips check out."

She grinned, showing off her very normal human teeth.

"You're such a problem."

He chuckled. "I guess I better follow your mom before she loses her temper."

"Yeah, I've heard it can be pretty bad."

He grinned as he headed back into the cabin to start the engine again. "Hey, she'll be mad at me, not you!"

"I know," Ash said as she buckled in behind him. "Why do you think I'm helping to delay things?"

He grinned at her laughter. "Wow, so rude."

In front of the boat, they heard the sea witch call to them. "Are you coming or do I need to climb up there and drive it myself, child?"

"Coming!" Finn called back while he got the motor moving. He turned to Ash. "You're so bad!"

She smiled.

Behind them, the lightning continued to flash, but diminished more and more as Finn steered the boat in the sea witch's wake. He followed her blip on the radar, careful not to get too close.

So the strange girl on the island turned out not to be fully human. After the bizarre few weeks he had, that was probably the least unusual part.

The radar picked up the mainland before he could see it. But once he spotted the dim lights through the misty darkness, his body relaxed.

A couple of weeks ago, he never would have imagined coming back to shore without his dad, let alone with a new girlfriend. He thought about the other kids at school and wondered what they would say. But their opinions had never really mattered to him. Only Dad's did.

As the mainland lights grew brighter and the docks more visible, relief washed over him.

He was home.

28

BROKEN PEOPLE

THE MIDDAY SUN WAS SO BRIGHT ON THE calm ocean waves Finn had to put on sunglasses. The small, metallic fishing boat cut through the waves with ease, forming white crests in the dark blue water as they sailed deeper into the ocean.

It had been almost a year since the incident at the lighthouse. There were still a couple of weeks until summer, but Finn couldn't wait. As soon as the spring storms died down and the warm weather hit, he had to come out on the water. A visit was long overdue.

Everything had moved so quickly when he and Ash came ashore a year ago: the small media frenzy, the insurance disputes, and the volunteer divers who gathered proof of the wrecked Wishful. They had to have proof so Finn's story would be believed before the insurance companies would pay out any money. It was all so exhausting. Repeatedly reliving his father's death, first for the media, then the insurance companies, then even for his supposed friends at school. Everyone had wanted a piece of him despite the old wounds they opened up with their endless questions.

Giving Ash amnesia for the reporters seemed like it would help matters, but it only made her more mysterious and intriguing. She became a case to be solved by online sleuths rather than a person wanting to live her new life in peace. Finn had wanted to chew out every one of them, but Ash took it all in stride. She politely declined offers to help find lost relatives or to locate evidence about her fictional past. Finn wished he had an ounce of her patience and poise.

Once the insurance finally paid out, Finn was shocked. Dad had taken out a large policy in case of his death, leaving it all to Finn.

Ash helped him go through everything from his old life. They found a tiny house on the outskirts of town where nobody would give them trouble. It was close enough to the ocean and far away enough from the neighbors. In short, it was perfect.

Finn glanced down at the coordinates. "I think this is it." He slowed the boat to a stop, letting the vessel bob on the soft waves.

Ash moved to stand beside him, her black flowing dress billowing in the breeze. She held up a single white lily.

"It kept wanting to fly even here in the cabin, so I had to hold on to it pretty tight. Hope I didn't crush it."

The stem was a little mashed on the bottom, but the petals looked fine.

"It looks great. Thank you."

They walked out onto the deck of the boat. Finn pulled out a folded up piece of paper from his wallet. He carefully unfolded it and walked to the edge of the ship. Sunlight glinted on the water and a light breeze cut through the heat from the sun. It was such a beautiful day, so different from the last time he had been here.

"It's hard to believe this is where it happened. Everything is so peaceful," he said.

"Never underestimate the ocean. It's amazing how quickly she can turn dangerous." Ash took his hand and gave it a squeeze. "Do you want to say anything?"

Finn pursed his lips. "That's the trouble. I want to say so much. I never got to say everything I needed to tell him. We... we fought before the wreck. I feel bad."

Ash thought for a moment. "Why not talk to him as if he's right here with you?"

He winced. "That seems so awkward."

Ash put an arm around his shoulders and hugged him. "There's nothing awkward about any of this. It's called grieving, and it's very normal. Besides, it's just the two of us here." She pulled away but held his hand still, giving him quiet strength.

He huffed. She was right, but this was hard. He didn't even know where to begin.

Finn tried to imagine Dad there with him, listening

just out of sight. Suddenly, the words came, slow and clumsy at first, then smoothing out.

"Hey, Dad. I really miss you. If you were here, you would be so mad about how they're treating us. It's definitely been an uphill battle." He chuckled weakly, then swallowed because he felt bad about it. "Um. This is Ash. She's my girlfriend and she's amazing. You would love her. I wish you could have met her because I know you would have welcomed her with open arms."

When Ash gave his hand a squeeze, he continued.

"I start college in the fall. Yeah, you said I should, and I enrolled. I'm going into oceanography. Can you believe that? It wouldn't have been possible without the money you left." Tears stung his eyes and his throat clamped up, but he pushed through it. "I know I won't be able to come out here easily all the time to visit. I don't even know if you can hear me now wherever you are."

Ash dropped her hand to his waist and leaned her head against his arm.

He held up the unfolded paper. It was a picture of him and his dad. He'd probably been only ten years old at the time and Dad had fewer wrinkles and gray hairs back then. They stood in front of the old fishing schooner with fresh black paint on the side that spelled Wishful. The boat had two owners prior to them, but based on their toothy grins, it had felt brand new.

"I miss you, Dad. All the time. I wish you were here. I'm sorry for fighting with you... for everything, really. You were right and I should have listened. I love you, Dad."

He took the white lily from Ash and spun the flower between his thumb and middle finger. In his other hand he held up the photograph with its white fold lines along the worn creases. He swallowed down the lump in his throat before he could say the words he knew he had to say, the words that were some of the hardest to say.

"Goodbye, Dad."

With that, he dropped the flower and photograph. The lily floated on top of the waves, but the photograph darkened quickly in the sea water. In a matter of moments, it sank; the picture becoming more difficult to see as the waves churned over it. Finn stared at it in silence until even the glimmer of white paper was lost completely to the waves.

Just like Dad.

This send-off felt fitting, more than a stuffy funeral parlor. That had been great for friends and distant family to come pay their respects, but Dad needed more than that. Finn had needed more than that. Dad died in the place he loved—on the sea. He had deserved some kind of funeral here, too.

Finn realized Ash was rubbing his back, but he wasn't sure how long she had been doing it. He leaned against her.

"Thank you for being here. This was tough."

She gently pulled him around to face her. "Do you feel better?"

He gave a heavy sigh. "Yes, and no. There's a part of me that will never feel better. But I am satisfied. We did all we could for him."

Ash put a hand to his cheek, dragging a thumb down his stubble. "You did all you could for him. Especially that night."

He slowly lifted his shoulders and let them fall again. "I don't think so. I could have done more. Who knows what, but I should have done something."

"You have to let it go, Finn. You can't keep beating yourself up for something you couldn't control. Please be kinder to yourself. You got me out of the lighthouse, didn't you?"

He smiled. "With help. I couldn't have done anything without your mom."

She shook her head, leaning toward him. "You're impossible, you know that? You're always beating yourself up for things you can't control." Before he could respond, she pointed a finger at him. "Do you know what you need? Some major cuddle time with Whiskers tonight. That will put you in a good mood."

"Yeah, and he'll probably be annoyed with us for being gone for so long. You know how lonely he gets. We should probably head back."

"Only if you're really ready to move on. We can stay here for hours if we need to. Whiskers can wait. This is important."

Moving on. He knew he had to do it, even if his heart ached to even try. Dad was gone. It didn't matter how many flowers he left or how many funerals he planned, nothing would bring Dad back.

Finn blinked when he realized it wasn't the media or the insurance company, or even his friends opening the wounds of his grief again and again. They hadn't bothered him with questions for months now.

He was keeping the pain alive. Or rather, his guilt. Ash had been kind enough to put it gently, but she clearly worried about him. He had basically allowed his grief to take over for almost a year. It was more than the storm, more than the shipwreck, or his ordeal at the lighthouse. He blamed himself and beat himself up for it all—all the time. He was letting his dad's death hurt him and keep him distant from his family. The family he had worked hard to save.

Yet here Ash was, standing at his side, turning her back on adventures around the world with her mom because she loved him. Because she wanted to see him happy.

Finn pulled her into his arms and hugged her tight.

"Oh." She gasped, then curled against him. "Finn, are you okay?"

"Yeah, I am. Now I am. Thank you for supporting me through all this."

She chuckled, breath warm against his neck. "You did the same for me, you know. You stood beside me at the lighthouse when I fell apart, when I was lost and couldn't figure myself out. I can't count the nights you held me until I fell asleep. Or the number of times you hugged me until I stopped crying." She pulled away. "We're both broken people, Finn. And that's okay. With you at my side, I know we'll get through it."

Her cheeks flushed pink from the wind and her dark

gaze bored into him. When she leaned in close, they kissed deeply, wrapping their arms around each other.

Despite everything they had been through, they had survived. They were each other's anchors amid the storms. They kept no secrets between them. The world had shattered them, broken them into tiny pieces. But together, they put themselves back together, formed a family, and chose love over fear.

A pair of broken people who had come to fit perfectly together.

And that was all that mattered.

ACKNOWLEDGMENTS

This story came to me unexpectedly.

I was on a ship on the Atlantic Ocean and I looked down off the coast of New England to see a little spit of land with a lighthouse on it. The island looked so small from where I sat, and I couldn't help but wonder what life would be like there, and how lonely it had to be.

Months later, one of my favorite cover artists, JV Arts, revealed this cover on their site, and I thought about that lighthouse on the island so far from the mainland. I suddenly had the urge to write a story around it. I wanted a place where light meant safety and where monsters lurked in the shadows. There was a love story, too, that demanded to be told.

This novel took me about a year to write, mostly because of personal life changes. But every time I picked this book up, I could almost smell the salt in the air, feel the thunder rolling in, and catch flashes of lightning in the distance.

There is simply something romantic about light-houses. History is full of tales of people living in them alone, working day to day, sometimes widowed and taking the job up out of necessity[1]. Deaths have happened at many lighthouses as well, some from sickness, others from shipwrecks, and a few with no reasonable cause.[2]

These stories clung to me as I wrote this book. I couldn't help but add my own supernatural flair, but I kept harkening back to those tales, to the rough labor, the minimal meals, and the ever chaotic ocean all around.

A big thank you to my editor, Lara Zielinsky, who is absolutely amazing to work with every time. She never balks at my wild tales. Without her, this story would never be polished. Also, thank you to JV Arts, whose talented team is always creating amazing fantasy covers.

I have to give thanks to Candace Robinson, an amazing author and friend, whose romantic dark fantasy books have inspired me so much. This book in particular made me think of her work a lot over the year it took to write it.

Thank you to my sister, Kelley, for all her support with my writing when I inevitably hit that road block that makes me feel like everything is awful. She's always

1. Yang, John. Interview with Nancy McDowell. "The women lighthouse keepers who saved countless lives from coast to coast." *PBS News*, 29 Mar. 2025, https://www.pbs.org/newshour/show/the-women-lighthouse-keepers-who-saved-countless-lives-from-coast-to-coast. Accessed 28 Jun. 2025.

2. Johnson, Ben. "The mysterious disappearance of the Eileen More lighthouse keepers." *Historic UK*, 26 Aug. 2016, https://www.historic-uk.com/HistoryUK/HistoryofScotland/The-Eilean-Mor-Lighthouse-Mystery/. Accessed 28 Jun. 2025.

there to remind me it's not and help me onto my feet again. Thank you to my parents, John and Connie, for their understanding and support over this past year and a half. I've been so grateful for their help and their support through these tumultuous times.

A big thank you to my Ko-Fi monthly supporters, Donna and Connie, who are my biggest cheerleaders in the background. They keep me motivated to continue even when the words don't flow and the ideas seem silly. You two are amazing and I'm so grateful to you both!

And thank you, dear reader, for being here. I hope you enjoyed this novel and that you'll check out more of my books. This story has been a joy to write, and hopefully an entertaining read.

If you have a moment, please be sure to leave a review. As an indie author, these help me so much. Even a few words can put a big smile on my face for entire week. Thank you!

ALSO BY MARLENA FRANK

Monstrous Creatures Series

Stand-alones, Young adult, Teens vs. monsters

The Seeking

The Sea Witch Follows

Ominous Hour Series

Horror, short stories, standalone

A Beautiful Specimen

Undertow

The Collectors

Weird western, werewolves, vampires, short story

Night Feeders

The Man Who Dealt in Death

The Stolen Series

Young adult, portal fantasy, faeries

Stolen

Broken

Chosen

The Wolves of Kanta Series

Young adult, dark fantasy, steampunk, werewolves

The She-Wolf of Kanta

The Blood of Kanta

The Hunters of Kanta

The Fury of Kanta

The Howl of Kanta

Anthologies

Short stories, horror, dark fantasy

The Impostor and Other Dark Tales

Mystery, film noir, humor, short story

The Mysterious Disappearance of Charlene Kerringer

 **Join the Mailing List** 

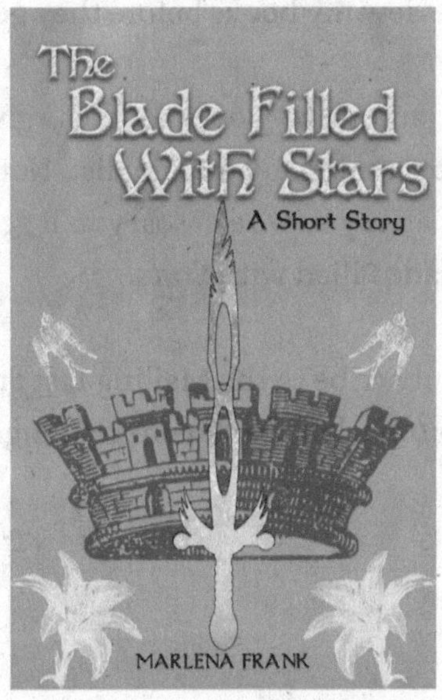

The Blade Filled with Stars

A kingdom is under siege from a familiar enemy. Families and friends are pitted against each other without reason. Slaughter is imminent while the winged Queen Khafil soars overhead. Desperate and terrified, Anna works with her sister, Lilah, to summon aid from their mother's ancient spell book.

Determined to save their people, the sisters summon Death to help them, but Death is not easily swayed. Neither of the sisters are prepared for the consequences.

Want a peek behind the scenes?
Want to preview my books before they get released?

Get exclusive access to book goodies, giveaways, and cover reveals by joining my mailing list. Not only will you get notified of all my new releases, you'll get an exclusive copy of The Blade Filled with Stars.

Subscribe to the Mailing List at:
http://marlenafrank.com/mailinglist/

Support Me On

Ko-fi

Follow me on Ko-Fi for regular updates on my writing progress.

Monthly subscribers get access to sneak peeks at stories way before anyone else. They also get access to cover reveals, monthly shout-outs on social media, and thanked by name in the acknowledgements in my books.

http://ko-fi.com/MarlenaFrank

ABOUT THE AUTHOR

Marlena Frank is the author of young adult fantasy and horror novels, short stories, novellas, and book series. Many of her books have hit the bestseller charts, including her debut novel, Stolen. Readers' Favorite has praised several of her books with 5-star reviews. The Reader's House featured her work in March 2024, and De Mode of Literature Magazine in November 2021. Her stories have appeared in anthologies such as The Darkest Lullaby, Emporium of Superstition, Heroic Fantasy Quarterly, Georgia Gothic, and The Librarian Reshelved.

Although born in Tennessee, Marlena has spent most of her life in Georgia. She has various professional memberships, including the Atlanta chapter of the Horror Writers Association and the Science Fiction and Fantasy Writers Association. She enjoys cosplaying, gaming, and spoiling her adopted cats. Her drink of choice is a dairy-free chai latte. As a wildlife enthusiast, she can share a plethora of weird animal facts and talk about her favorite cryptids.

Follow her at: MarlenaFrank.com

www.ingramcontent.com/pod-product-compliance
Lightning Source LLC
Chambersburg PA
CBHW011128190726
48289CB00012B/2951